Lallie dropped her gaze to the floor.

She was afraid suddenly that she would see pity in his eyes, where once there had been love.

'Good afternoon, Major Haldane.' The words came out of her mouth like stones, cold and hard.

'Good afternoon—is that all you have to say after—?'

'After five years?'

'Lallie, I cannot blame you if you have come to hate me.'

'Hate you?' she said brittlely, her brows lifting. 'I feel nothing towards you, Major, except what I should feel for any old acquaintance.'

Marie-Louise Hall studied history at the University of London, where she met her husband. Now living in rural Aberdeenshire, her ambition since marriage has been to find time to write. Domestically incompetent, she was thrilled when her husband took over the housework so that she could write. She also works for her husband's oil industry consultancy, looks after her young son, three cats, and three delinquent donkeys.

Recent titles by the same author:

SWEET TREASON
THE CAPTAIN'S ANGEL

MAJOR'S MUSLIN

Marie-Louise Hall

MILLS & BOON

First published in Great Britain 1996
Harlequin Mills & Boon Limited,
Eton House, 18–24 Paradise Road, Richmond, Surrey TW9 1SR

© Marie-Louise Hall 1996

ISBN 0 263 80008 3

Set in 10 on 12 pt Linotron Times
04-9701-82702

Printed and bound in Great Britain
by BPC Paperbacks Limited, Aylesbury

CHAPTER ONE

LALLIE leant on the sill of the small casement window in her attic room and looked out over the sea of grey slate roofs shimmering in the heat, to the distant dome of St Paul's.

She sighed, wishing for the bright blustery moors and the cool clear burns of Scotland where she had spent her childhood, wishing she was anywhere but here in London on this stifling late May morning of 1810.

Amid the clatter of hooves and rumble of iron-rimmed wheels and the cries of the street-sellers and hawkers at the nearby market she heard the nearest church clock strike the hour and knew she could not put off her departure any longer.

Dragging in a breath of the humid air, she turned away from the window and picked up her faded blue silk shawl and straw bonnet and the brief letter from Lady Carteret, acknowledging her application for the post of governess and inviting her to attend for an interview. It was stupid to feel so sickly nervous about the prospect of going to this particular house, she told herself sternly. It was not as if she had ever met Alex's sister and was likely to be recognised. And there was no danger of Alex being there.

Alex was dead, lying in some Spanish grave. She had known that for more than a month and yet she still could not really believe it, no more than she had been able to when she had opened a purchase from the market that had been wrapped in a tattered copy of the gazette and his name had leapt out at her from among the death notices.

Her grey eyes darkened, as memories she had tried so hard to bury came tumbling back into her mind. Alex, riding down her godmother's drive at the head of his troop of Hussars, his blue and silver uniform glistening in the sunshine. Alex, laughing, his dark head thrown back as he had spun her around the ballroom until she had been giddy. Alex with his blue, blue eyes that had darkened to the colour of cornflowers when he bent his head to kiss her. Alex, who had left her—

Her fingers clenched upon the brim of her bonnet. She would not cry. She had done with crying for him five years ago! Angry with herself she crammed her bonnet upon her head and tied up the strings so tight they pinched. Then, snatching up her reticule from the battered blanket box which served as wardrobe and table in the tiny attic room, she stuffed Lady Carteret's letter into it and opened the door. For a moment she stood motionless, listening to the noises in the house below. She could hear her landlady's raucous laughter drifting up from the kitchen. Good. Mrs Crouch had company and a jug of gin by the sound of it, she thought, as she quietly shut the door of her room and began to move quietly down the uncarpeted stairs, skipping the treads that creaked. Her rent was more than a week overdue, and she had no desire to discuss the matter with Mrs Crouch at this particular moment.

She tiptoed through the dark and dingy hall, and slipped out of the door into the blinding sunshine and hot, humid air, which engulfed her like the blast from a furnace. Nevertheless, she walked briskly, not slowing until she was around the corner and out of sight of her lodgings.

Only then did she stop and untie the ribbons upon her bonnet and let her shawl slip off her shoulders to her elbows. The heat was furnace-like, almost tangible, she could even feel it burning up from the paving stones through the paper-thin soles of her shoes. And there were already wisps of her hair clinging to her forehead. She sighed. At least her overwashed and tissue-thin muslin had one advantage left it, she thought wryly as she began the long walk to Mayfair. It was cool.

Please, please, let me get this position, she prayed silently, a little while later, to any deity who might be listening as she stood in the wonderfully cool shade of the trees that formed the centrepiece of the square of elegant white houses and retied the strings of her bonnet and straightened her shawl. Please—

In the six months since her father's death she had applied for post after post as governess or companion and been turned down more times than she could count. With a surfeit of respectable ladies and their daughters, left without a breadwinner by the war against Bonaparte, there was no shortage of governesses or companions.

She touched her fingers to her reticule, feeling for the carefully forged references and character. She hated to deceive anyone, but she no longer had the luxury of choice. She had to get this position. It was that or starve or worse—her mouth thinned and she felt the churning sense of revulsion and fear that she had had since the moment Mathias Robson had shown her the debt against her that he had purchased and had suggested exactly how she might pay it. Lifting her chin, she exhaled slowly and touched the references again. Surely they were good enough to persuade Alexander Haldane's sister to give her a trial.

It was a hope which was already dying an hour or so later, as the last chord of the sonatina she had played ebbed away into a silence broken only by the first flurries of rain against the windows of Lady Carteret's drawing-room as the oppressive heat gave way to a thunderstorm. She replaced the lid of the pianoforte and then folded her shaking hands in her lap. She had tried so hard to impress, but felt she had played badly — a fear which turned to certainty as the silence stretched. It was several seconds before she had the courage to look up and meet the cool, green gaze of the woman seated upon the sofa.

'I am a little out of practice, the pianoforte in my rooms is in need of repair.' She dropped her eyes as she uttered the lie — she doubted there had ever been such a luxury as a pianoforte in Mrs Crouch's lodging house.

'Yes,' Lady Carteret said coolly. 'But there is scarce need for apology, you play Mozart a deal better without practice than I ever did with it, Miss Smith.'

'I am sure that cannot be true.' Lallie's hands clenched in her lap as she made the polite protest. Please let her have imagined that faint ironical emphasis upon her name, she prayed silently. If Isabelle Carteret knew she was lying, lying about everything, then there was no hope.

Lady Carteret shook her auburn head and gave a

half-laugh. 'I am afraid it is, I always preferred to hunt and fish with my brothers, and was far too lazy to acquire many of the accomplishments. Not that I can say I have ever really felt the lack of them,' she added unashamedly.

No, thought Lallie wryly as she glanced at Isabelle Carteret's heart-shaped face, taking in the perfect features and blemishless creamy complexion, I don't suppose you have. Isabelle Carteret did not look as if she had ever had to work at anything in her life, except the repelling of the Prince of Wales's advances, if what Alex had told her once was correct.

'You, however, would seem to have them all,' the redhead said drily, as she glanced down at the letters of recommendation lying upon her lap.

A faint flush of colour rose in Lallie's face. For all her indolence, there was a keen intelligence in the redhead's gaze. Her heart sank. Isabelle Carteret had not been fooled by her invented employment history or her forged references for a moment.

'Come—sit down here, Miss Smith.' There was the faintest hint of amusement in the older woman's voice as she gestured to a well-cushioned chair beside the fire. 'You are beginning to look uncomfortable there.'

'Thank you.' Lallie got up gracefully, determined not to appear as disconcerted as she felt. Always, always remain calm was a rule she had imbibed at her father's side in the gaming hells during the last five years. All was never lost until the last card was turned. But this was her last card, and she no longer had any hope of it being a winning one.

A glimpse of her reflection in a large gilt-framed mirror upon the opposite wall did nothing to raise her spirits. She had long since sold her cheval glass, and her hand mirror had not revealed the shabbiness of her muslin, or that by scraping her silvery-fair hair into a severe knot she had made herself look younger than her twenty-three years, not older as she had hoped. How had she ever thought that Alexander Haldane's sister would consider employing her?

'With so much lightning I suppose I should have had the maid cover that,' Isabelle Carteret said as she followed Lallie's gaze to the mirror. 'But I dare say we shall survive. I have never heard yet of a house struck because of an uncovered mirror.'

'No,' Lallie agreed absently as she dragged her gaze from the depressing image in the glass. She sat down in the chair Lady Carteret had indicated, outwardly perfectly poised, but inwardly wincing at the contrast between her own appearance and the expensive simplicity of Isabelle Carteret's lavender muslin as the green gaze flicked over her from top to toe. Involuntarily she tucked the mended toes of her shoes beneath the hem of her gown.

The corners of Isabelle Carteret's coral lips quirked as she noticed the surreptitious movement. Then she turned her head away to the window.

'Listen! Can you hear above the thunder? They are ringing the bells again. We must have had another victory against the French, though heaven knows where, General Bonaparte seems to occupy half the globe these days.'

'Yes,' Lallie answered flatly. Poverty, she had discovered, left one little time to worry about the progress of the war. And what interest she had taken had vanished the day she had read of Alex's death.

It was all such a waste, she thought as her eyes flicked upwards for the hundredth time to the portrait of Alex at seventeen, looking absurdly young in his pristine new lieutenant's uniform. An Alex she had never known. He had been twenty-five when she had met him, and he would have been thirty now—

'That's my younger brother. He was very handsome, wasn't he?' There was the faintest of catches in Isabelle's smooth voice as she, too, looked up. 'That was done when he purchased his first commission, he is a Major now—or was—he was killed in Spain at the beginning of the year.' Her voice grew lower. 'He always was quite irresistible to women, even at seventeen.'

'Yes, I know—' Lallie began absently, lost for a second in the past.

'You knew my brother?' Isabelle stared at her.

'No. I meant I had heard he had been killed—I'm very sorry.' She stumbled over the words, horrified by the admission she had so nearly made. Had she fallen in love with him at first sight? At first glance she had been prepared to dislike Lord Alexander Haldane. With his blue eyes and aristocratic indolence he had been almost too handsome, too confident as he had ridden up with his men to take charge of the French spy her godmother was convinced she had apprehended and imprisoned in the pigeon loft.

But he had been kind. He had not mocked or laughed when the new and very irate minister of the local church had been released bedecked with feathers and other unmentionable substances. He had not laughed until her godmother was safely indoors. It was only as he had turned from watching the minister depart in a flurry of feathers and injured dignity, with a pigeon flapping persistently about his head, and his eyes had met hers, that he had dissolved into helpless laughter. Laughter she had shared—

'Well, Miss Smith, shall we begin again?'

'What do you mean?' She started. For a heart-stopping moment she thought Isabelle Carteret somehow knew her real identity, knew that she had lied about not knowing Alex.

The cool green eyes met her gaze assessingly. 'I suggest that you explain to me why you have invented references and why you are using an assumed name that you do not answer to half the time?'

'Invented! Assumed! How dare you! If you would but refer to Lady MacCleod—' Lallie began furiously, her outrage so instant, so genuine, she almost believed herself.

'She would tell me what? That she employed you as a seamstress?' The redhead's brows lifted a fraction as she looked pointedly at Lallie's hands, marked and rubbed from the endless hours of backbreaking sewing she had done over the last few months in exchange for a wage that did not even pay the rent.

It was hopeless, she thought, as Isabelle Carteret stared at her coldly. It had always been hopeless. She rose to her feet, hating herself.

'I apologise for trying to mislead you,' she said stiltedly. 'Perhaps you would be so kind as to have your maid show me out.'

'Yes,' Isabelle Carteret answered vaguely as she moved gracefully to the embroidered bell-pull. Then as she glanced at Lallie's thin, upright form, her pale face, she let the hand she had lifted fall back to her side.

'You were obviously raised a lady. Could you not get better than sewing?'

'No. It seems I am too young, too inexperienced, I have no character—and the agencies I approached said I had not the right looks for a companion.' And I have a dependent child, she added silently.

'I can only agree with them,' Isabelle Carteret said. 'Even scraped back hair and that ugly gown will not disguise your looks, Miss Smith. Passably pretty governesses or companions cause problems enough, but a beautiful one—' She shook her head and gave a low laugh. 'Even if your references were honest, I doubt any sensible woman would employ you for fear her older sons would make fools of themselves and her husband an even greater one, not to mention making her daughters look plain into the bargain. If I were you, I should go back to the husband or family you have run away from, Miss Smith, and beg their forgiveness, or failing that—' she gave a silvery laugh '—find a wealthy protector, my dear. With your looks it really shouldn't be too difficult.'

Before Lallie could even begin to stammer a reply, the door to the drawing-room was flung open by breathless, beaming woman.

'M'lady! M'lady!' the woman gasped. 'You must come at once, m'lady!'

'Really, Meg, have you not learnt to knock yet?' Lady Carteret sighed. 'Whatever is it?'

'Major Haldane, madam, he's here, downstairs. I heard the doorbell, opened it and there he was—'

'Don't be a fool, Meg!' Isabelle snapped. 'Have you been at the brandy or has this storm turned your wits?

Major Haldane was killed in January, you know
that—'

'No, madam,' the maid said, 'the reports were wrong,
he was wounded and he's been a prisoner of the French
all this time, he's alive, madam, come and see for
yourself!'

'Alive.' Isabelle Carteret repeated the word blankly.
Then Lallie saw the same joyous disbelief and dizzying
shock that she was feeling mirrored upon the other
woman's face. Then Isabelle was running for the door,
her aristocratic languor gone as she bunched her skirt
carelessly in her hands like a girl. 'Alex, Alex! Is it
really you? Tell me you are not a ghost!'

Her joyous voice floated back, and then was joined
by another. A rich laughing, masculine voice, cut off
suddenly by the sound of a shutting door.

The last vestige of colour left Lallie's face. Alexander
Haldane was not dead. He was not dead! He was here,
in this house. She put out a hand to the mantle to
steady herself. Since the moment she had read of his
death there had been a sort of frozen blackness in her
mind, a blackness that was now dissolving and whirling
about her as her heart pounded crazily against her ribs.

Alex. She dragged in a breath. It should make no
difference to her if he were alive or dead. Had she
learnt nothing? It was five years since she had last seen
him, five years since he had walked away from her. So
how could she long to do as Isabelle Carteret had done
and run to him—and beg him to hold her just once
more—so that she might feel the remembered warmth
and strength of his long lean body and know beyond
all doubt that it was true? He was alive. But she had
no right, had never had that right. Her hands clenched

upon the mantle until the knuckles of her slender fingers were white as she took another juddering breath. Had she no pride? she asked herself furiously as hot tears burned behind her eyelids. She had not let herself weep for him when she had thought him dead. So why weep now—?

'Miss? Are you all right, miss? You're shaking like a leaf in a gale—' Meg touched her arm, making her jolt at the same moment as there was a roll of thunder overhead.

'No. I need some air,' she blurted, knowing suddenly she could not bear to see him. She had dreamed of it so often at first. Dreamed that he would come and tell her it was all some dreadful misunderstanding and tell her that he would never desert her, not even for some Earl's daughter—but in those dreams she had not been a liar in an ugly gown, begging for a position in his sister's household.

'Please, show me out, quickly,' she pleaded, turning to Meg.

'Of course, miss. The storm is it?' Meg smiled at her sympathetically as she led the way out of the room. 'They always take my sister like this, she can't bear to be upstairs when it's thundering and lightning.'

'Yes, the storm,' she agreed mechanically as she followed Meg. Storm was not such an inappropriate word for what had happened between her and Alexander Haldane. The attraction had been immediate and overwhelming for them both—at least that was what she had believed at eighteen.

The storm reached its zenith with a deafening crash of thunder as they reached the galleried landing that joined with the great horseshoe-shaped flights of stairs leading down into the pillared entrance hall. The sky above the glass-dome roof, two storeys above, was black, making it almost as dark as it would be at night.

'Watch your step, miss,' Meg said. 'If this keeps up we'll have to light the chandeliers early. You'd think it winter, not May. Still, it'll soon be over.'

Yes, she thought, as she began the descent of the long curving flight of stairs. It would soon be over. Another minute or so and she would be safely out of the great double doors. Out of sight and sound of Alexander Haldane.

And then when she was halfway down the flight, a door opened below. She halted, knowing it was him from the sudden skidding beat of her heart even before he stepped into the pale marble-lined hall with Isabelle Carteret clinging to his arm.

Instinctively, she shrank back into the dense black shadow of an alcove containing a pedestal and bust of Admiral Nelson. She stared helplessly as they began to climb the opposite flight, so deep in conversation they had not noticed her or Meg. All she had to do was continue quietly and he would not even see her, but she could not. Her legs would not obey her any more than her eyes, which followed him as he moved up the stairs with the careless, easy grace she remembered so well. His face, turned down and away towards Isabelle Carteret, was in shadow. Not that it mattered. The curl of dark hair at the nape of his neck, the slanting line of jaw and cheekbone was enough to trigger her memory into producing every detail, from the lines at the corner of his mouth and eyes when he smiled, to the sweep of his black lashes upon his cheeks when he had bent his head to hers. She slumped against the cool marble wall feeling as if she were falling apart inside. Where was the anger, the contempt she should feel towards him, why was there only this sickening sense of loss, longing? She stared helplessly across the stairwell as he came level, half hoping, half dreading he would turn his head. He did, just as there was a dazzling flash of lightning overhead.

'Lallie!' In the sudden lurid white light, she saw his lips frame her name disbelievingly. He looked older; his features were sharper, more defined, there was no trace of the laughter which she remembered as ever-present in his face and voice. She saw that in the space of one stopped heartbeat, and something else in his brilliant blue gaze that held her transfixed. Something that twisted and tore at her insides. And then all was dark again. Suddenly she was running, almost tumbling down the marble steps because in her panic she forgot to pick up her skirts.

'Oh, dear, I had quite forgotten about her. Miss Smith—wait!'

Isabelle Carteret's voice rang out after her as she reached the hall and pushed past a bemused Meg. She fumbled with the ring handles for what seemed like eternity before one of the great white panelled doors swung open and she was outside, running into the driving rain.

'How very odd of her,' Isabelle Carteret said as another flash of lightning illuminated the square and the slight figure framed by the open doors. 'A little weak in the head, I suppose, and to think I almost considered giving her a trial—'

She broke off abruptly. Alexander Haldane was

standing stock still, his face ashen, his hand clenched upon the balustrade.

'Alex?' Isabelle frowned at him. 'What is it? Your wound? Are you feverish—?'

She broke off as she found herself addressing empty space. Her brother was already down the stairs and halfway across the hall, running as if his life depended upon it.

CHAPTER TWO

'ALEX! Come in at once!' Isabelle called to him crossly a minute later from the portico as he stood staring across the deserted cobbled square, apparently oblivious to the driving rain. 'If she wants to catch her death, it is no concern of ours.'

'I suppose not,' he said heavily, his eyes narrowing as he tried to discern a figure amidst the slanting sheets of rain. But there was no clue as to which way she had gone. How the devil had she vanished so quickly? He put a hand to his unshaven face and rubbed it, wondering if fever and tiredness had made him imagine the resemblance.

A few feet away, Lallie held her breath and pressed herself more tightly against one of the great columns of the portico that hid her from their sight.

'Oh, do hurry, Alex. You must be exhausted,' Isabelle said impatiently, shivering in her thin gown. 'And I am getting chilled to the bone—'

'Sorry, Izzy,' he said, as he followed her back into the house. 'It's just I thought I recognised her—'

'Really? I cannot think from where unless it was Vauxhall Gardens or the Haymarket,' Isabelle replied derisively. 'Miss Smith, if that was her name, which I seriously doubt, was certainly not from respectable society.'

Lallie exhaled as the doors shut behind them. She did not know what had made her run away or why she

had hidden. She only knew that just seeing him again
and knowing she had no place in his life and never
would, hurt—hurt so much she could scarcely breathe
or think. Slowly, head bowed against the stinging rain,
she made her way across the square, too shaken even
to notice as the rain soaked her gown in seconds and
made her hair so heavy it pulled free of its pins and
tumbled down her back. And she was almost a mile
away before she realised she had left her shawl and
bonnet behind.

'You haven't heard a word I have been saying,'
Isabelle Carteret said to her brother at the same
moment as she watched him staring into the flickering
flames of the drawing-room fire. 'You're thinking about
that creature who came to apply as a governess aren't
you?' She laughed and shook her head. 'You really are
incorrigible, Alex. You've not been back in England a
day—not that I can blame you, give her a decent gown
and she could match any incomparable of the last six
seasons.'

'A governess?' He gave a half-laugh. 'Then she
cannot be the person I mistook her for. *She* was an
heiress to a considerable fortune.'

Isabelle laughed lightly. 'I should say the only thing
Miss Smith is heir to is misfortune. Judging by the
marks upon her hands, she has already been reduced
to sewing shirts. . .' She paused and frowned as she
watched his face with sudden attention. 'Just who did
you think she was?'

'The girl I met when I was in Banffshire for the
summer, just before I took the despatches to India.'

'Not Miss Ross, the one who let you think she was
her widowed cousin!' Isabelle laughed. 'Oh, Alex, I

always wondered how you could have been so duped by some provincial miss scarcely out of the schoolroom, but if she looked like Miss Smith—'

'You have never come across her, then? She must be out by now.' He gave a slightly forced laugh. 'Wed, with a brat or two, no doubt.'

'Can't say that I've ever come across her,' Isabelle said, 'but then I don't suppose she would have had vouchers for Almack's if her father's fortune was from trade.'

'No,' he agreed drily as he regarded his sister. 'Letting Miss Lalage Ross into Almack's so she might be insulted by her betters, if she were not bored to death first, would never do, would it? The nation would surely crumble to its foundations.'

'Don't be sarcastic, Alex,' Isabelle said, giving him a sudden incredulous look. 'You were not actually in love with her, were you?'

'In love?' He snorted and leant against the arm of the green silk sofa, dislodging the neatly folded silk shawl which Lallie had placed there when she had got up to play the pianoforte. 'A Haldane in love with someone who has connections with trade?' His dark brows lifted. 'Come, Izzy, you know me better than that!'

'I know you better than you think,' his sister said tartly. 'Now I begin to see why you took yourself off abroad, and have kept Cressida waiting unpardonably long for her wedding— Oh!' she gave a sudden gasp as he bent forward to pick up the shawl. 'Cressida, you will not know about Cressida!'

'Cressida?' he repeated the name absently as he straightened, the shawl still in his hands.

'Lady Cressida Penwyrth! Your betrothed! You have not forgotten her entirely, I presume?' Isabelle said exasperatedly. 'Though given your lack of correspondence and refusal to take leave these last five years, she might be forgiven for thinking you had!'

'I could not take leave, Lord Wellington needs every exploring officer he has,' he said, toying with the folds of soft silk and then frowning at the shawl. 'And what of Cressida?'

'Oh, fiddlesticks! There is no easy way to say this. You can hardly blame her, Alex, not when you volunteered to take those despatches to India before the ink was even dry upon the announcement, and no sooner back from there and you left for Spain without even calling upon her—'

'Get to the point, Izzy,' he said wearily, as his blue eyes lifted momentarily to her agitated face.

'She became betrothed to Harry Rutherstone last week. She thought you were dead, as we all did.'

'Betrothed?' he said impassively, his eyes dropping back to the shawl. 'Then I must write and thank my French hosts for timing my resurrection so well. To think, a week earlier and I'd have been facing a lifetime of Cressida's babble at the breakfast table.'

'Is that all you have to say?' Isabelle exploded. 'Alex, the girl was distraught when she heard of your death—her friends feared she was so out of her mind with grief that she might take her own life!'

'I'm sure they did, until she became bored with playing the heartbroken heroine and realised that black does nothing for her complexion.'

'Oh, don't be so horrid!' Isabelle snapped crossly. Then as she saw that he had suddenly gone very pale beneath his weather tan, her expression softened. 'They're not married yet, Alex, and you do have the prior claim and Harry Rutherstone is a gentleman—'

'This shawl.' He cut her off in mid-sentence as he held up the garment. 'Who does it belong to?'

'Does it matter?' Isabelle said, giving the faded silk a disdainful glance. 'It's certainly not mine. Miss Smith must have left it behind.'

'Did she?' He exhaled slowly as he ran the pad of his thumb over a neatly mended three-cornered tear near its fringed hem, knowing suddenly that it had been Lallie. How could he have doubted it for a moment, he wondered, thinking of her face, so white in the glare of the lightning. Thinner, more fragile than he remembered, but still as breathtakingly beautiful.

Involuntarily his fingers tightened on the shawl. She had been wearing this the first time he had kissed her. They had been walking in the grounds of her godmother's house in Banffshire. It had been one of those bright blustery mornings and the breeze had come buffeting in from the North Sea, sending the ends of the rich blue shawl fluttering against a wind-scorched rosebush.

She had been laughing as he leant across her to free it. Laughter which had died abruptly as his hand had brushed her shoulder. Her great grey eyes had come flashing up to meet his gaze, part startled, part afraid— but not knowing, as he had expected of a young widow.

That was the moment at which he should have made his excuses and left. But somehow, inevitably almost, his arms had closed around her, and her mouth, softer than the silken shawl which had slithered unnoticed to the ground, had opened to his, and all his good intentions and resolutions about having no more than the lightest of flirtations with Mrs Russell's god-daughter had been lost. When she had confessed that she was Lalage and not Letitia Ross a week later, it had been too late. He could not more have given her up than stopped breathing.

But that had been five years ago, and now, now she was begging for a post as a governess under an assumed name—

'I must see her. Where does she live?'

His sister started at his sudden barked question.

'At Penwyth House as she always has done,' Isabelle said, looking at him worriedly. 'Don't you think you should send word ahead, it will be a dreadful shock for poor Cressida to see you—?'

'I meant Lal—Miss Smith, where does she live?' Haldane snapped at the question.

'Miss Smith!' Isabelle looked at him incredulously. 'I have not the faintest idea. One glance at her references told me that they were false, so I did not take over much interest in her after that. She might have said something to Meg, I suppose—' She broke off as the slamming of the drawing-room door indicated that her brother was already out of earshot.

He had not even been certain it was you, Lallie told herself savagely as she trudged along the dreary street of shabby houses, stumbling now and then as her sodden skirt clung and tangled about her legs. He probably had not given her a thought since the day he had left Scotland five years before and yet... And yet, just for a moment in the glare of the lightning when he had first noticed her, there had been something in his face and eyes that had caught at her heart— Fool! Fool!

She yanked angrily at her hampering skirts. Would she never learn? He cared nothing for her, he never had—

'Didn't get the place, then?' An all-too-familiar sneering voice halted her in mid-stride and mid-thought as she reached the door of her lodgings and a burly man in a shiny black frock coat and greasy moleskin waistcoat stepped out of the shadowy hall to stand upon the step.

Robson. She should have known he would have her followed, she thought flatly. Since she had refused his advances and he had purchased a debt against her, he had been trailing her like a carrion crow waiting for a sick beast to fall. Waiting, waiting until she had nothing left to pawn or sell, nothing left with which to feed Emily.

'Friend of mine saw you going off West all dressed up,' he said snidely, as his eyes travelled over her sodden, almost transparent muslin which clung to her like a second skin. 'What 'appened? Threw you out the back door, did they? Not that I'm complaining,' he added lewdly, as his button-like eyes came to rest upon her breasts. 'Why don't you come back to my house now, Miss Ross, and get yourself warmed up? We'll forget all about the fifty pounds—'

He broke off as she lifted her head, which had been bent against the stinging rain, and pushed back a swathe of dripping hair from her face.

'Get out of my way, Robson.' The words were clipped, cold, and sounded almost as dangerous as the expression in her dark eyes.

'All right, all right, no need to look like that—' He put up a warding hand and retreated a couple of steps to let her pass. 'I was only trying to help you out—'

'I will give you your money a fortnight from now as you requested, and until then I do not wish to speak with you, see you, or worse, smell you!' she added with ferocious contempt.

'You'll change your tune when the brat's starving,' he snarled. 'Your price won't be so high then! And where are you going to get fifty pounds? You'd be lucky to get half if you sold yourself to a duke in the Row.'

She stared at him contemptuously, but made no reply. With a curse he turned and left. She watched him go and then entered her lodgings. It was only after she had slammed the door and was in the narrow hall that smelt, as it always did, of overboiled mutton and cabbage that her anger gave way to despair. She sat down upon the bottom step of the stairs and put her face in her hands. She had as much chance of raising fifty pounds as she did of flying. There was nothing for it but to run, and where could she run with a four-year-old child and no money?

Startled by the noise of the outside door opening, she rose to her feet, her thin face ablaze with anger. If it was Robson again. . .

'Lallie?' The one soft word stilled her instantly. Stilled her heart, her breath, her mind as she recognised the tall, broadshouldered figure who blotted out most of what little light penetrated the dank and narrow hall.

'Lallie? May I come in?' He stepped forward without waiting for her answer.

The choking tightness in her chest kept her mute. She could only stare at him in disbelief, not even noticing his familiarity as her eyes took in the changes five years had made. He seemed taller, more muscled in the shoulder, leaner at the waist. Indian and Spanish sun had left streaks of gold in the rich dark brown hair which swept back from his brow. His face, burned to the colour of tanned leather, was harsher; the angled jaw, slanted cheekbones, the wide thin slash of his mouth—all seemed more defined. War had wiped out all traces of the boyishness that there had been in his face at twenty-five. There was a new dangerous hardness beneath the lazy aristocratic grace, a coldness in the blue eyes she did not remember—but all else was the same, down to the tiny imperfection in the long haughty nose, where he had broken the bridge in a hunting accident at sixteen.

And she still wanted to touch him, wanted to run to him and beg him to hold her, wanted it so much that it hurt— Dear God, how could it hurt so much after five years?

'I have brought your bonnet and shawl,' he said almost apologetically. 'You left them at Lady Carteret's house. I thought you might have need of them. . .' When she made no effort to accept the garments, but remained absolutely still and silent, not moving, scarcely even breathing, he came further into the hall and set the shawl and bonnet down upon the rickety sidetable.

'I—I found a ticket in the lining of the bonnet for a pawn shop in the next street,' he said slowly, after what seemed like an endless silence. 'They directed me here. . . If I have called at an inconvenient moment then I apologise.' He sounded embarrassed as a watery shaft of sunshine suddenly illuminated the dark hall, and his gaze flicked from her hair hanging wet and heavy down her back to her clinging muslin gown.

She dropped her gaze to the floor, afraid suddenly

that she would see pity in his eyes, where once there had been love. No, she told herself savagely, that had been her mistake. He had never loved her. It had been no more than lust, an amusing interlude in an otherwise tedious posting.

As she remained frozen and mute, he gave an exasperated sigh. 'Say something, anything, a greeting at least—'

'Good afternoon, Major Haldane.' The words came out of her mouth like stones, cold and hard.

'Good afternoon—is that all you have to say after—?'

'After five years?' She cut him off. 'I can think of nothing else.'

'Lallie.' He took a step forward and put out a hand as if to touch her arm, a gesture she recoiled from as if he had held a razor. His arm dropped heavily back to his side. 'I cannot blame you if you have come to hate me.'

'Hate you?' she said brittlely, her brows lifting. 'I feel nothing towards you, Major, except what I should feel for any old acquaintance.'

'An acquaintance?' His mouth twisted into a humourless smile. 'I suppose I have no right to think myself more than that.'

'None.' She was unequivocal. 'Now, if you will excuse me, I have to change my gown—'

'I can wait, or come back later,' he said stonily. 'I want to know what has befallen you—why you are in this place—' His voice was heavy with disgust as he gestured to the hall.

'I do not see why my situation should concern you now,' she said coldly. 'Suffice to say that much has

changed while you have been abroad, and we are
unlikely to have much to say to one another.'

He shook his head. 'I have a great deal to say to you,
things I should have said five years ago.'

'Really? About what?' she said flippantly. 'The
weather? The state of the exchequer? Or the infamies
of General Bonaparte?'

'I was thinking of Lady Cressida Penwyrth,' he said
grimly.

'Lady Cressida...I am not sure I recall—' She
frowned and then suddenly lifted her gaze and gave
him a bright, brilliant smile. 'Of course, your betrothed.
I wonder how I could have forgotten. So many people
took the trouble to show me the announcement in the
papers and inform me of all the details. They said she
is very pretty. You must tell me where the wedding is
to be so I may be sure to come and watch at the
church—or will it be in the country?'

'Stop it!' The words exploded from him with such
savagery that she flinched. 'I never meant to cause you
such hurt,' he said more gently.

'Hurt? Oh, no, pray do not give it another thought, I
have not in years,' she answered brightly, but avoided
his gaze. 'My infatuation with you was already waning
when you left, Major, you merely saved me the trouble
of telling you so. So you see, there is no need for
explanations. Now perhaps you will see yourself out?'
She turned away abruptly.

'Wait!' He caught her arm as she tried to pass him.
'Please?'

She was momentarily stock-still, aware of nothing
but the warmth of his strong brown fingers burning
through the thin wet stuff of her gown, melting her

chilled skin, melting her so deep inside that she trembled.

'This has not changed.' His voice softened as he felt the telltale tremor run through her slight body. 'Has it?'

Her chin jerked up. She stared at him, her eyes almost black with fury. Five years before, a mask of complete indifference had been her only defence against the laughter, the sneers, the sudden silences when she had entered a room in which everyone had been talking a moment before. Now the anger and hurt she had been forced to suppress welled up in an unstoppable torrent. Her hand half lifted to strike at his lean brown face and then as she met his all-too-knowing gaze, she let her hand drop.

'Your arrogance has not diminished,' she said coldly, 'but it seems you have learnt some new manners upon the continent.' She dropped her gaze pointedly to where his hand still gripped her arm. 'Is this a Spanish or a French custom?'

'My apologies.' He released her instantly. 'Perhaps I am wrong—five years ago I wager you would have hit me—'

'Almost certainly,' she said tersely. 'But then I was very young and lacking in judgement about a great many things. Now, will you go?'

'I'm not going until you tell me why you were at my sister's house seeking a place, and why you are living here,' he said wearily. 'It is evident you are in some kind of difficulty and I should like to help you—'

'You may help me by leaving.'

'Lallie—' he began impatiently.

'And I should prefer it if you were less familiar, Major Haldane,' she cut in icily.

His wide mouth tightened into a thin line. 'As you wish, Miss Ross, but I shall not leave until you answer me—'

'Why were you so long? I'm hungry and Mrs Crouch would not give me anything and I don't like the thunder.'

The plaintive voice from the stairs made them both start.

'Great God!' His oath was barely audible, as he looked from Emily to her, and then back to the fair-haired child whose delicate face, with enormous grey eyes, was the miniature of her own. 'So that's it! Is that why you are here? Your parents have disowned you—'

'What does disowned mean?' Emily asked, eyeing Alexander Haldane with a mixture of awe and interest. 'Is it the same as dead?'

'No,' Lallie snapped, after one furious glance at Alexander Haldane. 'Now go back upstairs, Emily, I promise I shall not be long. Listen, the thunder is moving away now, it cannot hurt you.'

'Must I?'

'Yes,' she said firmly.

There was a silence that lasted until Emily had disappeared from sight and there was the sound of a door shutting far above.

'I did not mean to speak before the child,' he apologised abruptly. 'I was surprised—' He broke off as his eyes scanned her rigid white face. 'How old is she?'

'How old? She will be four this summer.' Her voice was blade-sharp. She knew not one of her neighbours believed her when she explained that Emily was her sister, a late child, who had caused her mother's death in childbed, but she had not thought that he of all people would assume Emily to be her child.

'Four.' He stared at her for a moment. 'Great God, for five years I've wracked my conscience over you and I can scarcely have been out of the door before—'

'Before what?' Her voice shook with all the anger she had never had the opportunity to vent on him. 'Before I was on my back? Is that not what you were about to say, Major Haldane?'

'I—' He floundered, shocked by her use of a phrase she would not have understood when they had last met. Great God! And to think he had actually come here with some half-baked romantic notion of beginning again—perhaps even making her his wife, as he had longed to do five years before. Wife! A sharp, outspoken young woman who had become little better than a— He baulked at the word that came into his mind. He did not want to believe that. He could not believe that. Not of Lallie... And the child, he asked himself cynically, where did she come from? Under a gooseberry bush?

'I never realised you had such a high opinion of my character, Major,' she said contemptuously as she read the thoughts that flickered through his eyes all too accurately.

'Who was it? Who has deserted you?' His voice was harsh. 'Hetherington? That damned mincing minister, he never could take his eyes off you—'

'Hetherington!' She gave a jagged laugh that went through him like a knife. ' If you will not allow me my honour, at least allow me some taste!'

'I cannot believe this,' he said, after a moment in which his blue eyes scanned her white set face. 'Not of you, not when—'

'Not when I would not make the ultimate sacrifice of my honour for you? I suppose it must be somewhat difficult for you to believe that Lord Alexander Haldane could fail where another man succeeds.'

'You are right—I find it difficult to believe, but only because I thought I knew you. It seems I was mistaken.'

'Not as mistaken as I was about you,' she retorted fiercely. 'Can you imagine, I actually believed you meant to marry me—?' Her voice cracked suddenly, and she had to look away.

'Lallie.' The colour left his face and the anger drained from his voice. 'Is that why? Because of me—?'

'Because of you!' She laughed brittlely. 'Do you really think being spurned by you so turned my reason that I threw myself at the first man who asked me?'

'No,' he said thickly.

'Good, because you overestimate your importance to me, Major Haldane. Emily has nothing whatsoever to do with you. Now, if you will excuse me, I am cold and I cannot think we have anything else to say, do you?'

'It would seem not,' he said, after an endless moment of silence in which he stared at her. 'But if you are in need of funds. . .I owe you that, at least—'

'You owe me what?' Her grey eyes blazed to silver as she spoke. 'A guinea for each kiss?'

'Damnation—I did not mean—'

'Didn't you?' Her dark brows lifted. 'Forgive me if I do not believe you.'

'Lallie—'

'Miss Ross,' she corrected him ferociously. 'Now go away! I do not want to see you now, or ever again.'

'Very well, Miss Ross,' he replied with equal ferocity. 'But at least satisfy my curiosity upon one point. Did you cheer when they posted the news of my demise? Or merely hang out the flags?'

She stared at him disbelievingly. He knew she had loved him. She had been too young, too much in love to hide it even if she had wished to, which she had not. She had never hidden her feelings about anything then. An adored only child, she had been showered with affection since birth. It had never occurred to her that if she loved someone, they would not return that affection.

'What?' His black brows slanted upward as she remained stonily silent. 'Not even a token denial. You've become a damned cold dish, Miss Ross. Good day. You need not fear I shall inconvenience you again.'

He inclined his head in the slightest of bows and then turned on his heel.

'Alex. . .' What made her say his name as he reached the door she did not know, but she regretted it the moment he halted and spun round, his eyes bright and cold as blue glass in his sunburnt face.

'What?' His voice was low and chillingly cold.

'I am glad the reports of your death were false,' she said flatly. 'I could never wish you dead.'

'Thank you.' His face softened fractionally. 'In the last five years it has felt at times as if half the world wished me dead. I am glad at least you were not among them. Goodbye.'

She stood motionless for several minutes after the

door slammed shut behind him, too numb inside even to cry.

'That was stupid, letting him go,' Mrs Crouch, her landlady, sneered, putting her head around the kitchen door from behind which she had undoubtedly listened to every word. 'Who are you saving yourself for, the Prince Regent?' She cackled at her own joke. 'A gentleman like that could 'ave set you up real nice with a house, a carriage, probably even a nurse for the little 'un.'

'Yes,' Lallie agreed dully as she picked up her shawl and bonnet. She knew she ought to run after him and gratefully accept whatever help he could give her. But she couldn't. She just couldn't. For tonight, at least, she would allow herself the luxury of pride. Tomorrow—tomorrow she would write and beg for his assistance.

CHAPTER THREE

FIVE days later, Lallie sat staring dully at the little heap of copper and silver coins in her lap. It did not matter how many times she counted it, there was not enough. Not enough even to feed them for a week, let alone pay the rent. And if she did not pay the rent by Friday—then she and Emily would be out upon the street. Friday. Three days in which to make five shillings. Even if by some miracle she managed to get some outwork that was not controlled by Robson, she would be paid nothing like that amount, not even if she sewed night and day.

There had to be something she could do, but her mind was clouded by panic as she glanced across the tiny attic room to the pallet where Emily lay sleeping. Emily was already too thin, too pale. Her heart twisted as she saw how firmly the little girl's arm was wrapped about the rather misshapen rag doll she had made her for her last birthday. At Emily's age she would not have given it a second glance. But then she had had a pony, books, dolls with wax heads and silken gowns, a garden to play in—

The clatter of hooves in the street below brought her to her feet in sudden desperate hope. She ran to the window, the coins falling from her lap and rolling across the boards about her feet. An answer, oh please let it be an answer from Alex. . .

The hope died almost as soon as it formed—it was

only the coal cart. She stayed at the window, staring out of the flawed glass. Five days. It had felt like a year as she had waited for him to reply to her letter, running to the landing, her heart thudding against her ribs at every knock upon the door, every footstep in the hall.

But he was not going to answer. Odd that it taken her until this moment to finally admit that to herself, she thought numbly, wondering why she had had such a ridiculous deep-rooted faith in a man who had already betrayed her trust. She made a sound that was half-laugh, half-sob. If he had not wished to continue the acquaintance five years ago, he would hardly wish to do so now. A few minutes' reflection had probably been enough to have him thanking the good fortune and judgement which had made him sever all connection with her and her family.

A glimpse of movement in the alleyway below sent a stab of fear slicing suddenly through her despair and anger.

Tyson, one of Robson's cronies, was lounging against the wall, staring up at her window. Her stomach knotted. These last few days she had not been able to take a step without one of Robson's men a pace or two behind her—they had followed her as she had trudged mile after mile, looking for work of any kind. One quiet word, one gesture from them, and her only answer had been a shake of the head. Even the pawnbrokers she usually used would not deal with her. And, by buying the debt her father had incurred in her name, Robson had her trapped as neatly as a fox who found every earth stopped against it.

'Try running,' he had warned her two days ago, 'and I'll have you in the King's Bench faster than a lighter goes under Tower Bridge, and then what'll happen to your little 'un?'

If it was not for Emily, she would have taken her chances of escaping Robson and his bailiffs and fled to the country in the hope that there she might find some farmer's wife willing to give her her keep in return for educating her daughters. But Emily would not be able to walk either far or fast, and she had no money for the stage or even a lift on a haulier's cart. And if they were caught and Robson carried out his threat—then Emily would be alone with no one to protect her.

She put a hand to her forehead and pushed back a strand of pale hair from her face. There had to be some way out, there *had* to be! To think of Robson even touching so much as her fingertip made her feel sick.

She turned to her own narrow bed where the lustrous blue silk velvet habit, and white silk ballgown with Brussels lace, which she had failed to sell to the brokers, lay glowing in the dingy room, looking as out of place as she had felt in Isabelle Carteret's silk-hung drawing room.

She ran her fingertips over the luxurious fabrics. Her other good clothes had been sold long ago, or washed and made over until they fell apart. The habit and the ballgown she had kept until last because there was cloth enough in them to make petticoats and gowns for Emily as she grew. No. That was not the entire truth, she admitted, as she picked up the rustling ballgown and touched the soft fabric to her cheek. This she had kept because Alexander Haldane had thought her beautiful in it—and she had worn it on the happiest night of her life. It seemed impossible now that she had once been so naïve or so happy— The folds of silk slithered loose and she dropped the gown abruptly back onto the bed as a letter fluttered to the floor.

She bent and picked it up, wondering, as she recognised the strong, black, slanting hand, why she had kept it. She knew every hurtful word of it by heart. Five years ago she had read it a thousand times, searching, searching for a reason, an explanation hidden in the coldly polite words. Searching for anything that might feed the stupid, stubborn conviction that Lord Alexander Haldane had loved her a little at least. Her mouth twisted. He had not even had the decency to tell her in person that he was engaged to Lady Cressida Penwyrth—instead, he had sent her this. A note regretting that he would not be able to call upon her in the foreseeable future. Call upon her— She gave a choked laugh. He had held her, kissed her, laughed with her, and let her think that he loved her— She crumpled the letter suddenly and flung it into the empty black iron grate.

Picking up the ballgown, she folded it and dropped it into the battered and scratched blanket box which served them as wardrobe and table and turned to do the same with the habit. It was only as she shook out the blue velvet folds that she realised that she did have one choice left. If she had to sell herself, it did not have to be to Robson. What had he said? 'You'd be lucky to get half if you sold yourself to a duke in the Row.' If she found herself a protector, a wealthy one, then she would at least be free of Robson. Utterly shaken by her own thought, she sat down upon her bed, clutching the habit as if her life depended upon it.

* * *

When Lallie and Emily entered the small shabby livery yard some two hours later, it was deserted except for a lithe young man, with unruly brown curls and an impish face, quartering a bay whose scarred chest proclaimed him to be an ex-cavalry mount.

'Tom! Tom!' Emily called out joyously, slipping from Lallie's hand like a hound from a leash to hurl herself at him.

'Hello, me dear!' Tom Mitchell turned and scooped Emily up from the ground. 'Come to see the horses again, 'ave you?'

'Yes,' said Emily. 'Have you a carrot I can give Toffee?'

'Over there—in that pail,' Tom said, setting her down and sweeping his brown curls back from his face with a grimy hand. 'And mind you keep your hand flat or he'll have your fingers into the bargain.'

'I know,' Emily threw back huffily over her shoulder as she sped nimbly across the yard.

'Well, haven't seen you for a bit,' Tom said, turning back to Lallie.

'I've been busy, looking for work,' she replied.

'But you haven't had any luck.' It was a statement rather than a question as his green eyes studied her too thin face.

'No. Robson has put the word out against me. Tom, I hate to ask, but I need some help. . .'

'There's not much I can do against Robson, Lallie, he knows too much about me. If he chose to put the finger on me, I'd be turned off quicker than I can blink. And if it's money you need—' he shrugged '—I'm out of funds myself at the moment. This devil eats money faster than I can make it,' he sighed, giving the glossy bay an affectionate slap upon the shoulder. 'Aye, and faster than I can drink it,' he said wryly as he caught the lift of Lallie's brows.

'He looks very well,' Lallie said, glancing at the bay who had begun to paw at the cobbles with an impatient foreleg, wondering, not for the first time, how Tom had come by a horse whose lines and breeding would have fetched a fortune at Tattersall's if it had not been for its scarred chest and rolling eyes which marked it out as one of the unfortunate beasts to have been used and discarded by some cavalry officer after it had become wounded and too terrified to be of use upon a battlefield.

'Aye, and just as well in my trade—my neck depends upon his speed and soundness.'

Lallie sighed. 'I'd hardly call highway robbery a trade, Tom. Why don't you give it up before you kill someone or they you?'

'Because I'd rather be hung for a sheep than a lamb.' He grinned at her. 'But don't look so prissy. I'm no murderer, and they've never caught me yet. Now tell me, how can I help you?'

Lallie cleared her throat. 'I was wondering if you'd lend me your horse, just for an hour or two tomorrow.'

'You! On this lad! He'd kill you.' Tom threw back his head and laughed.

'Please, Tom, I'll manage him, please,' she begged him.

'Where did you want to take him?'

'The Row,' she said flatly, after a moment's hesitation.

Tom was silent for a moment and his green gaze slid

away from her face. 'Decided to find yourself a rich protector then?' he said after a moment.

'Yes.' Her voice was barely audible. 'I have to get away from here, for Emily's sake, for my own.'

'It's all right. I'm not judging you,' Tom said quietly, running his hand down the restive bay's neck. 'I know you don't belong here, Lallie—and if you can do better for yourself than Robson, then I wish you luck.'

'You'll loan him to me, then?'

'Maybe,' Tom said wearily. 'You'd better give him a try this afternoon. Though what this devil will think of a side-saddle I hate to think. Come on, let's see what Flaherty's got in the harness room.'

'Oh, stop it!' Lallie groaned beneath her thick veil the following day, as Tom's horse threw up its head for what seemed like the hundredth time in as many seconds. The bay paid her no heed and continued to toss its head incessantly, paw at the ground and lash its tail irritably at the flies brought out by the sun. She grimaced as the animal danced skittishly, jarring her head. It was already aching from the heat. Tightening her grip upon the reins, she brought the horse back from a fretful jog to a standstill and tried to find a more comfortable position upon the side saddle which had been made for a lady of far ampler proportions and was sorely in need of restuffing.

Still stiff and bruised from her efforts to familiarise the bay with a side saddle the previous afternoon, she found the effort of holding him in check harder by the minute. It had been four years since her riding horses had been sold, and she lacked the stamina that came from riding daily. After a ride through Town during which it had reared or shied at every dog, street-seller, or flapping apron or petticoat, she had been exhausted long before she reached the Row.

It had been madness to borrow it. If Tom had not been so drunk this morning, she knew he would have changed his mind and refused to allow her to take the animal out of the yard. But beggars could not be choosers, she thought grimly, as the bay tried to sidle away from the bit.

She took a deep breath and lifted her heavy veil to look up and down the crowded Row, feeling horribly conspicuous as she realised she could not see another woman alone anywhere. A fair-haired dragoon officer, passing in front of her, turned his head to look at her, and smiled, his grey eyes appreciative.

She wheeled the bay away, her heart thudding against her ribs in sick panic. She wasn't ready. Not yet. She needed time to steel herself—

'Oh, be still!' she snapped at the bay as it regained her attention by snaking its head round and nipping ill-temperedly at the blue velvet skirt of her habit. She pulled its head back straight, muttering beneath her breath as it danced upon the spot and then surged into a half-rear, and shot forward, almost wrenching her arms from their sockets. Somehow, she kept her seat and circled it back to a fidgeting halt.

'Oh, well sat!' a male voice drawled from her left.

She turned her head and found herself being scrutinised by heavy-lidded brown eyes belonging to man riding a flaxen-maned chestnut.

The man's small and rather too feminine mouth curved into a smile. 'I've been admiring your equestrian skills for this last half hour,' he said lazily, 'but they are wasted upon such a beast. If you cared to accompany me to my house, I am sure I could provide a more amenable mount. Riding should be a pleasurable experience, if one is to profit by it, should it not?'

She stared at him, shocked into total silence by the blatancy of his invitation. This was what she had come for, to find a wealthy protector who would enable her to get away from Robson—and she could not do it— not for fifty pounds, not for fifty thousand, not even for Emily's sake.

The self-knowledge hit her like a blow, leaving her reeling with a mixture of despair and relief.

'Well, shall we go?' He mistook her silence for acquiescence and smiled confidently, showing small, very white teeth beneath his moist upper lip.

'I think not,' She replied with all the impassive haughteur she had learnt to hide behind when her father had made her go with him to the gaming hells; deliberately she let the bay swing its hindquarters threateningly towards the expensive chestnut.

'You disappoint me.' His tone was acid as he edged the chestnut out of range of the bay's hooves. 'And I do not care for disappointments. Another day would be more convenient, perhaps?'

'No.' Her reply was unequivocal.

'Oh, come now, if it is a matter of price—?'

'All the money in England would not persuade me to call upon you, sir,' she replied coldly. 'I should count it a great favour if you would go away.'

He laughed, his sensual Italianate features contorting into an unpleasant mask. 'If you change your mind, my name is Corton, the Marquis of Corton. Perhaps you have heard of me?'

She had—when she had accompanied her father to
the gaming hells. Corton had a reputation for duelling
and killing his opponents. There had been a scandal
about the last, a young man, barely out of school. 'Yes,'
she said after a pause, 'and none of it is good.'

'But being good is so very tedious, as I am sure you
know.' He inclined his head to her in an ironic bow,
before riding away.

His parting insult left her unmoved. She had heard
much worse in the gaming hells and she had more
pressing things to think about, such as how she and
Emily were to get away from Robson without a penny
to their name.

The bay's fretfulness intensified as a horsefly buzzed
about its ears. It was no use even trying to think clearly
here, she decided, as she fought to keep it from
throwing its head up again. She had better go back to
her lodgings. She drew down her veil and turned the
bay for home.

'Oh, Alex, did you have to be so rude to Lady
Bessborough?' Isabelle said crossly at the same
moment as she reined in her grey beside her brother's
large brown.

'Rude?' Her brother's dark brows lifted. 'I was
scrupulously polite.'

'Oh! You know perfectly well what I mean!' Isabelle
snapped, flicking at a speck of dust upon her green
habit skirt with her gloved fingertips. 'You really
cannot go on shunning Society like this, Alex. The
whole town is agog with the news of your return—and
there is a mountain of correspondence on my side-

board, half of which you have not even had the grace
to open and reply to—'

'I thought you were dealing with the invitations—'
he answered absently, his gaze fixed upon the slight
blue-habited figure some distance away, struggling to
control a large, mettlesome bay. 'I told you I have
some business to attend to for Lord Wellington.'

'Really?' Isabelle said tartly. 'I had the impression
that you have spent the last week sitting in the library,
drinking brandy all hours of the day and night and
brooding over that would-be governess, not to mention
growling at anyone who addresses a civil word to you.'

'I plead guilty to the brandy, but growling I don't
recall,' her brother said unperturbedly, his eyes still
fixed upon the bay. And then he laughed at his own
fancy. It wasn't possible. Goliath had been killed over
two years ago. He had heard the shot as Sergeant
Mitchell put the horse out of its misery after it had
been shot from under him within a few yards of their
lines. And yet. . .there was something so familiar about
the horse and rider that it nagged at him.

'Oh, look—' He turned his head away as his sister
prodded him with the handle of her whip. 'Isn't that
Lady Cressida over there? Why don't you go and talk
to her? She has called three times this week, and
Rutherstone would relinquish her in a moment if you
gave him the slightest intimation that you wished it.'

'Discovered his mistake already, has he?' her brother
drawled as he glanced at the young woman in a red
habit, amid a gaggle of dandies. 'Was this why you
were so insistent that I rode today, Izzy? Was this little
accidental meeting your scheme or Cressida's?'

'Mine, if you must know,' Isabelle sighed, her cheeks

flushing a little. 'Oh, do go and talk to her,' she wheedled. 'For my sake. I promised I should make you—'

'Making promises on other people's behalf seems to be something of a failing in this family,' he grated. 'I will not be manipulated by you or our esteemed father a second time, Izzy. If our dear brother is determined to ruin the family, so be it. I will not play the sacrificial lamb this time!'

'Whatever are you talking about?' Isabelle said looking at him blankly.

'It does not matter,' he sighed. 'It was all over long ago—' He broke off, an oath on his lips as he caught the near-side rein of Isabelle's grey, dragging her mount out of the path of the blue habited rider on the bay, who careered past them at breakneck speed, so near, the floating end of her veil caught and tore upon a buckle of the grey's bridle.

It *was* Goliath! The jagged scar on the left flank, left by a French dragoon's sabre, where the hair had grown back white instead of brown, was unmistakable. He stared after the charging bay in disbelief as he resettled his own mount with the unthinking, instinctive ease of the cavalryman. Then he sucked in a breath as the bay skidded and swerved, missing collision with a portly gentleman upon a sedate hack by a whisker. 'No brakes—why must women ride horses they cannot control?' he rasped, and then swore again as some of the other riders made frantic grabs for the bay's reins and only succeeded in making it veer wildly. 'I'm going to help—they'll be down and take someone else with them in a moment.'

'Oh, leave it to Corton, he's already going after her,

as I've no doubt she intended,' Isabelle said unconcernedly. 'She's been cruising the Row this last half
hour, Alex. A bolt is not an original method of gaining
attention, but it rarely fails.'

'That bolt is not contrived,' he said shortly. 'Damnation, that was close—' He exhaled sharply as the
careering bay took the rider beneath a stand of trees
and she had to throw herself flat along its neck to avoid
the low branches. 'She damn near lost her head along
with her hat and veil—' He broke off as the rider's pale
gold hair fluttered out like a banner. 'My God! It's
her!'

'Who?' Isabelle's question went unanswered. Her
brother was already yards away, galloping down the
Row, weaving between the carriages and riders with
the expertise that came from traversing the chaos of
the battlefield.

'Haldane abandoned you, has he?' a cheerful voice
said from beside her.

'It would seem so, General Houghton,' Isabelle said
turning to smile at the elderly man reining in beside
her. 'He seems intent upon rescuing that—demi-rep
who seems incapable of controlling her horse. I cannot
think why—Corton was already going after her—'

'All Curzon Street to ninepence, Haldane reaches
her first,' the General laughed. 'Corton never was much
of a judge of cattle. That chestnut of his is all show and
no substance—but Haldane always could pick a good
filly at a hundred yards, of the four legged or two
legged variety.'

Lallie flattened herself against the bay's neck as it took
her beneath another stand of trees, flinching as twigs

lashed across her face and caught at her hair. She dare not lift her head to look ahead. Her vision was restricted to the sun-dappled blur of ground and tree trunks as the horse sped on.

She saw the lightning-blasted tree lying across their path a fraction of a second before the bay and clung on grimly as the bay lurched into a huge leap and crashed over the obstacle without slowing and then swerved towards a gap between two trees. It was narrow—too narrow. The bay was allowing only for its own width, not its saddle and rider. She shut her eyes, bracing herself for the fall. There was a numbing, scraping blow to her right side, from shoulder to ankle, but somehow they were though and she was still in the saddle, though her right arm felt numb and useless.

'Stop, you stupid, stupid beast!' she sobbed, as she sat back and hauled upon the reins with her left hand. It was no use. She had ridden horses from the moment she could walk, but none of the skills she had acquired made the slightest difference. From the moment the guns of the Royal Artillery had fired the salute for some Royal birthday or the other, the bay had been uncontrollable. It had a mouth like iron and the strength of an ox.

She ducked her face behind her arm as another flail of twigs lashed against her face and then they were clear of the trees and out in the bright sunshine again, heading back towards the gravelled carriage track. A knot of riders scattered as the maddened bay cannoned through their midst, snapping at anything within reach as if it thought itself back upon the battlefield. With all her attention on staying on the bay, she scarcely noticed the chorus of oaths or the unsuccessful attempts of one or two gentlemen to grab at the bay's bridle.

Only the angry shouts of a curricle driver penetrated her growing terror. There was a tangle of carriages directly ahead of her. A curricle and a barouche had passed too close, the wheel of one becoming jammed behind the other. She used every means she knew with hand and legs to try and make it turn but, untrained to the side-saddle, the bay ignored her and charged on, head high and teeth bared, not looking or caring where it was going. They were going to collide with the carriages.

She wanted to shut her eyes, scream. But the desire to survive made her redouble her efforts, sawing upon the reins, trying to use her body weight to make the horse swerve—it was useless. She no longer had the strength left in either her legs or her body to have any real effect upon the bay. In sheer desperation she flung herself dangerously far forwards along the horse's neck and pulled on the cheek strap of the bridle, just above the bit. She hauled on it with all the strength she could find, dragging the bay's head around until it was almost looking at its tail. It would have to turn or fall—

'That's it! Turn!' Her breathless exclamation of triumph was cut off abruptly as the cheap, poorly oiled leather bridle broke. She was thrown forwards and would have fallen if the bay had not flung up its head as the bit fell from its mouth, pushing her back into the saddle. With one of her hands wound in its mane, she scrabbled frantically with the other for the trailing loops of reins. If the bay stepped on one and fell at this speed, neither of them were likely to survive. But then, perhaps it made no difference. Collision with the carriages was now inevitable unless the maddened horse came to its senses.

She was close enough now to see the panic on the face of the young man driving the curricle as he flung himself down from the box, and hear the screams of the ladies in the barouche as they scrambled clear in a confusion of petticoats and bonnets. If she had not been so exhausted, she would have screamed herself. She had not the strength to do anything but either hold on for dear life and pray the bay would swerve away or throw herself off— She looked down. The dusty gravelled ground was a blur. It would be hard as stone. There had been no rain since the storm a week ago.

'Hold on!' a male voice shouted furiously.

Alex. She recognised the voice instantly and with total disbelief. Stupidly it had not occurred to her that he might be here today.

'Hold on!' the voice roared again.

She could do nothing else. She could not have moved the fingers meshed in the bay's mane if she had wanted to. As she turned her head, her heart, mind and body had frozen, unable to register anything but the fact that it was Alex—unmistakably Alex. He was beside her. His brown was shoulder to shoulder with the bay, matching it stride for stride.

'I'm going to take you off,' he bellowed at her again. 'Get your habit clear of the horn and let go your stirrup—go on!' he urged. 'I won't let you fall.'

It was too late, the rational part of her brain told her. The carriage team was no more than a stride or two away. But she obeyed him, trusting him as instantly, as instinctively as she had five years before.

'Let go, now!' He pulled her sideways off the saddle.

For what seemed an endless moment she dangled in space, buffeted against the side of the brown with nothing between her and the rushing ground except his arm about her waist. Then everything was disjointed and confused as he pulled her up onto the pommel. She saw the bay slide into the rearing carriage team; heard it squeal in anger as one of the team reared in fright and came down on its back; saw it fall heavily, bringing down another of the team with it.

She felt the panic begin in Alex's horse as it tried to stop, its hooves skidding and sliding beneath it as it sought to avoid the mêlée of struggling horses. Alex was shouting, whether at her or the brown she was not sure. She clung to him as the brown took a bounding stride and heaved itself into the air, jumping throughout the tiny gap between the carriage and the plunging team.

She looked down. Two shafts, a skein of traces constantly shifting and moving as the bay and the carriage team milled in a tangled mess. It was no great height, but the brown was carrying a double load. She shut her eyes, expecting them to go crashing down in a tangle of horses and harness.

But there was only the jolt as the brown pecked a little upon landing, then, recovering itself, cantered on. They were over. Safe.

She let her head fall against Alex's shoulder and exhaled the breath she had been holding. From the moment his arms had wrapped about her, it was as if the last five nightmare years had dwindled to nothing. It did not matter that he had left her. It didn't even matter that he now so obviously thought her a whore and beneath his notice. He was here now and she felt

safe, safe for the first time in months, years. She felt
safe from Corton, Robson, safe from everything— The
illusion was shattered as he brought the brown to a halt
and vaulted down and lifted her after him.

'Of all the stupid, irresponsible, idiotic things to do!'
he ground out ferociously, his hands so tight upon her
waist that she half expected him to shake her. 'What
the devil possessed you to get upon that beast? You
could have killed yourself and someone else besides!'

He let go of her so abruptly as he gestured in the
direction of the bay that she had to clutch at the
brown's stirrup leather for balance as her legs
threatened to buckle beneath her.

She shut her eyes momentarily as a memory of
another time, another place, flashed into her mind. He
had come to her rescue before, when a newly broken
colt had bolted with her at his first sight of hounds. But
then he had laughed and had kissed her as he had lifted
her down. They had both laughed, being young and
utterly confident of their own immortality. And now he
was shouting at her and it hurt. Hurt inside and out—
or was it her arm from the collision with the tree? She
didn't know; her mind would not work properly.

'He was the most ill tempered, unreliable brute in
the entire Peninsula. His only saving grace is that he
was also the fastest—believe me, I know—he was mine
until he was shot from under me!' he went on fiercely
as she retreated from his towering figure a half-step
and leant against the warm silken flank of the brown.

His horse. She turned her head slowly to look back
towards the carriages. His horse. She felt too numb
even to feel surprise at the coincidence.

The carriage horse was up and standing on all four

feet. As for the bay—that was not only on its feet but evading all efforts to catch it and showing no more sign of their near-disaster than the broken bridle and the ruined saddle hanging upside down beneath its belly and the foam which flecked its heaving chest.

'More lives than a cat, that one,' he observed grimly as he too glanced at the bay. 'I didn't think he had a hope of surviving his wounds, but presumably, Sergeant Mitchell thought otherwise. I wonder how the devil he got him shipped home? The man was an inveterate scoundrel and a deserter but a genius with horses. How the devil do you come to be riding him?'

'I borrowed him—from a friend,' she said raggedly as she tentatively touched her right elbow with the fingertips of her left hand. Pain sheared along her arm, so intense it made her feel sick.

'No friend worthy of the name would have let you within fifty feet of that animal.'

'It was no-one's fault but mine,' she replied tersely, wondering what he would say if she told him the friend she referred to was a Tom Mitchell presently wanted in three counties for robbery on the King's Highway and, by the sound of it, for desertion from His Majesty's Army. 'He did not wish to lend him to me, but I insisted.'

'That I can believe—you always were reckless,' he said harshly as his gaze came back to her and skimmed over her from head to foot, taking in her thin ashen face with its too prominent cheekbones, and the slenderness of her arms and wrists beneath the tight-fitting lower sleeve of her jacket. 'Damn it, Lallie! One look at him should have told you he was no lady's mount!

Something which I intend to impress upon your "friend". Where is he?'

'I came alone,' she said thickly. The pain from her arm was getting greater by the moment. It hurt. . .hurt so much that she wanted to cry, and she was beginning to shake deep inside. And all he could do was shout at her.

'Alone—without a chaperon—' Despite their previous meeting, despite knowing about the child, he still felt shocked. There was only one sort of woman who came to the Row alone.

A chaperon! Whom had he expected her to bring—? Mrs Crouch, her large and slovenly landlady? Lallie would have laughed if she had not felt so sick and dizzy. Despite seeing where she lived, he still had not quite grasped the chasm which had opened up between their lives since they had last met.

'I came alone,' she repeated.

'I see.' His voice was heavy with contempt. 'And is this something you do often?'

'No. I have never been here before,' she said gratingly.

'Really?' His dark brows slanted upwards disbelievingly. 'Then what the devil made you choose to come today on that beast?'

'Oh, why do you think?' she said miserably, too tired and shaken to try and lie to him. 'I was hoping to find a—protector. . .' Her voice dwindled as his face froze into an unreadable granite mask.

He stared at her. It was one thing to guess, to surmise, but another to hear it from her own lips.

'I hadn't any money left,' she said flatly as the silence hung between them like lead and he remained as silent

and as frozen as a statue. 'No money for food, no
money for rent —' She gave up, choked by the lump
which had risen in her throat. He would never understand, not even if she tried to explain about Robson
and the debt he held against her. How could he
understand? When had Alexander Haldane ever gone
cold or hungry for want of money?

'Money!' The word exploded suddenly from his set
mouth. 'Are you telling me that a tradesman's daughter
could not think of a better way of getting it than this?'

'Oh, come.' She gave a jagged laugh. 'That is all you
and your noble friends have ever thought a tradesman's
daughter good for, isn't it?'

'That's not true—' the colour left his face '—and you
know it—'

'Do I? You gave me every reason to suppose it true,'
she replied flatly. 'Please credit me with some
intelligence.'

'Intelligence! When you would rather prostitute
yourself than accept my help! My God, I begin to think
you have lost your wits along with your fortune.'

'Oh, don't pretend, Major Haldane,' she said sickly.
'If you had ever cared for me in the slightest, you
would have answered my letter—'

'What letter?' he asked blankly.

'I wrote the day after you had come to my lodgings.
You did not answer.' Her voice was raw on the last
three words.

'You wrote—?' For a moment he looked puzzled
and then he exhaled heavily. 'Isabelle. She has been
sorting my correspondence for me.'

But she was not listening. She had turned away as
her eyes had filled with hot, blinding tears.

'Where do you think you're going?' he demanded as she took a shaky step away.

'To catch my horse—' she stumbled upon the trailing skirt of her habit as she spoke '—I want to go home.'

His hand shot out, catching her right elbow in a vice-like grip as he stopped her from falling. 'It's my damned horse,' he grated, 'and you don't look fit to catch a cold—'

'Let go of me!' Her plea was agonised, breathless, as renewed pain sheared through her body like a dozen newly whetted knifes.

'No!' he rasped, his grip tightening upon her arm. 'We have to talk—'

'Let go—my elbow—' she gasped sickly, as his face and the sun, sky, grass and riders began to spin and blur about her at ever-increasing speed. 'I hit my arm—the tree—'

'You're hurt!' At last and too late to stop the spinning darkness from dragging her down, he understood and released his hold upon her arm. 'Why the devil didn't you say—?'

He broke off, uttering an impolite Spanish oath as she crumpled so suddenly he barely managed to catch her before she hit the hard, dusty ground.

CHAPTER FOUR

'LALLIE. . .' For a moment he stood helplessly with her lolling in his arms. She was so light. . .lighter than he remembered. And, he thought grimly, as he stared at her hollowed cheeks, she looked as if she had not had a decent meal in a month. He set her down gently upon the ground, frowning as he gazed at her lying amid the pool of blue velvet. She looked so young, so damnably vulnerable.

Something inside him seemed to twist as he found himself remembering her as he had first known her, reckless, carefree, laughter always bubbling in her voice—she had been so open and generous with her feelings, so unafraid of anything or anyone. So unlike the woman who had wheeled to face him when he had stepped into that sordid lodging-house—he wished now that he had not mentioned her as a possibility to the General the day before.

'Is she hurt?' a Dragoon officer asked as the first of a knot of curious riders reached them.

'Yes!' he snapped. He stripped off his coat and bunched it beneath her head to make a pillow. 'Someone send for a doctor,' he added roughly as he gently stroked the dishevelled hair back from her chalky face and loosened the stock about her neck.

'No need, Haldane, I'll see to her.' A cheerful middle-aged man with abundant grey hair and a ruddy

58

complexion swung down from his saddle and knelt down beside Lallie.

'Sir John!' Haldane greeted the senior army surgeon with deep relief. 'I'm devilish glad to see you—damned horse scraped her against a tree. It's her right arm, I think—'

'Haldane! Haldane! You were so wonderful, so brave and I have treated you so dreadfully!' a crimson-habited young woman gushed as she spurred her roan forward. 'Please, please say you are not angry with me—you must let me explain—'

'I am not in the least angry with you, Lady Cressida, and there is nothing to explain,' Haldane said coldly. 'Now will you rein back—?' He caught the roan's bridle as its hooves came dangerously near to Lallie's still form. 'Have a care, will you?'

'You are cross! I knew you would be!' Tears came into the young woman's large hazel eyes. 'Please forgive me, Haldane, please—'

'I'll forgive you anything, as ever, if you'll be so good as to rein back and give Sir John and this lady some room—'

'Lady?' Lady Cressida's tears evaporated as quickly as they had come and she gave a stifled little snort of laughter as she glanced down at Lallie. 'Really, Haldane, surely you have not been abroad so long that you do not know the difference between a lady and a muslin? Surely you must have seen—?'

'I saw a lady having trouble with her horse.' His tone was icy as he put a hand either side of the roan's bit and pushed it backwards. 'Now, if you will excuse me, she requires some assistance.'

'Not in getting your attention. It seems she is expert

in that—!' the pretty brunette replied sulkily, her heart-shaped face losing its softness as he released her horse's bridle and turned back to kneel beside Lallie again.

'Lady Cressida, do as Haldane asks,' Isabelle Carteret said smoothly as she brought her grey to a halt beside the brunette and slipped gracefully down from her saddle. 'Sir John needs some room in which to work, and I'm sure we've all had quite enough drama for one day, don't you think?' She broke off as her gaze touched on Lallie for the first time. 'I might have guessed. . .' she hissed beneath her breath.

'Yes, you might,' her brother hissed back, 'since she wrote and told me of her circumstances. If it were not for you, she might not be in this situation.'

'Demi-reps are always in such situations,' Isabelle said dismissively. 'Really, Alex, I begin to think Lady Cressida is right, you must have had too much sun—'

'She's coming round,' Sir John said warningly, looking up from his deft probing of Lallie's arm.

Lallie's eyelids fluttered upwards.

'What. . .?' she began hazily as her eyes focused on Sir John's unfamiliar, but kindly, face.

'Be still,' Alex said from her other side as she began to try and sit up. 'You fainted.'

Alex—She shut her eyes again against the glaring sun, slipping back five years to Scotland. They had picnicked upon the sands at Rattray Head and had watched ships of the line sail along the horizon. It had been so hot, the sun so bright. . .

'Did you hit your head?'

The kindly stranger's question did not register, as a succession of images of sea and sunlight, and Alex writing their initials in the sand with shells, flickered through her mind like pictures seen by the light of a guttering candle.

'He said did you hit your head?' The voice was sharp, almost angry. Alex's voice.

'Alex, you are not talking to one of your Hussars now,' she heard a vaguely familiar woman's voice sigh disapprovingly. 'The girl's in shock—'

She opened her eyes again, wrenched back into the present. Lady Carteret! Full recollection came suddenly, and with it a sick sense of humiliation as she looked upwards to the part-amused, part-malicious expressions upon the faces of the riders crowding about them.

'Don't look so glum,' the middle-aged man said to her with a smile. 'You'll do—it's a nasty knock but there's no lasting damage. However you'll need to rest that arm for a day or two. Now, where's the rest of your party?'

'I—' she began inaudibly, wishing the ground would open and swallow her. She had never felt so alone or ashamed in her entire life. 'I—'

'She was supposed to be joining us.' To her utter astonishment Alex came lazily to her rescue as he stood up and placed himself between her and the crowd. 'Her groom's horse became lame and, instead of going home with him she was foolish enough to think she would find us in this crowd.'

Lallie stared upwards at him, a lump rising in her throat. He had always been kind, always quick to champion the underdog, but she had not expected him to go so far to try to save her from complete humiliation. Not when he believed her a whore.

'I—I—did not think it would be so busy,' she

picked up his cue shakily in the ensuing, startled silence. 'I'm very sorry for the trouble I have caused.'

'Oh, pray do not apologise, Miss Ross,' Isabelle Carteret said acidly, after giving her brother an astonished and furious look. 'Even the best of us, it would seem, make extraordinary mistakes from time to time.'

'Yes, we do, don't we, Izzy dearest?' her brother returned even more acidly, glaring at his sister. 'Especially in matters of correspondence.'

Isabelle's creamy complexion flushed to rose pink and she became silent.

'Ahem!' Sir John coughed loudly as brother and sister glowered at one another. 'Time enough for explanations later. This young lady has had a nasty fright, Haldane—the sooner she is home and safely put to bed the better.'

'Couldn't agree more. She might even be grateful enough *not* to make you pay for the privilege, Haldane.'

Lallie shut her eyes as a ripple of laughter followed the Marquis of Corton's clearly audible aside. She wanted to die. Now.

'I think I misheard you, Corton.' Alex's voice was like a steel blade, slicing into the laughter that died abruptly as one after another of the onlookers was treated to the cold blue stare which eventually came to rest upon Corton.

'I was just saying it was a damned fine piece of riding, Haldane, damned fine,' the Marquis drawled, letting his brown eyes linger upon Lallie. 'But then you cavalry fellows always do ride so well,' he sighed, still looking blatantly at Lallie. 'Just wish I knew how you afford such fine mounts on army pay.'

There was another nervous ripple of laughter punctuated by a giggle from Lady Cressida, which she hastily turned into a cough as Haldane's ice-blue gaze flicked to her before returning to Corton.

'I'd be delighted to enlighten you, my lord. Perhaps you would also appreciate some instruction in the art of shooting?' Haldane went on blandly, his eyes never leaving the Marquis's face, which had become a little pale. 'At a time and place of your choosing, of course.'

There was a sudden frozen silence, broken only by the clink of harness as the horses shifted fretfully at a distant rumble of thunder.

Lallie sat up, oblivious to Sir John's restraining hand and the pain from her arm. She wanted to shout at him and tell him not to be such a stupid, quixotic fool, tell him that what little was left of her reputation was never worth his life, but her voice was stuck in her throat.

'Alexander—' she heard the same mixture of fear and disbelief in Isabelle Carteret's barely audible whisper '—have you gone quite mad?'

'Haldane! Enough of this nonsense!' A portly, grey-haired figure, clad in a distinctly shabby if well-cut black riding coat, suddenly spurred his horse through the knot of onlookers. 'You know Lord Wellington does not allow his officers to duel, a fact of which I am sure you are well aware, my lord.' He gave Corton a withering glance from beneath bushy eyebrows.

'I was simply complimenting Haldane on his equestrian skills, General Houghton,' Corton said smoothly, shrugging his shoulders as far as the skintight fit of his azure coat would allow. 'It is scarcely my fault if he misunderstood. But if I have offended Miss Ross, then

I apologise wholeheartedly,' the Marquis finished
languidly.

'You have not,' Lallie blurted too quickly, flashing
the Marquis the most placating smile she could manage.
'Not at all. I am not in the least offended.'

'Well, Haldane? The lady's satisfied,' General
Houghton barked.

'So it would seem,' he replied, with a contemptuous
glance at Lallie that made her flinch.

'Apology accepted?' the General said firmly.

'If you insist, sir.' The words were clipped to the
point of insolence.

'Consider it an order,' the General said, giving him a
meaningful look from beneath bushy grey brows.
'Plenty of time for private quarrels after we've beaten
Boney, what!'

Haldane inclined his head to Corton. 'Apology
accepted, for now. . .'

Lallie exhaled the breath she had unconsciously held,
praying that her simpering to Corton had been enough
to defuse the situation. Alex was an excellent shot, but
she doubted he would aim to kill and Corton, so they
said, always did.

But Corton's attention was still on her. 'I should
deem it a favour to call and make my apologies
properly when you are recovered, Miss Ross.'

'And I should deem it a favour if you would not.
Ever.'

It was exactly the answer she would have given,
Lallie thought, though she doubted if she could have
delivered it with quite the cold ferocity Alex had given
it.

'I was not aware Miss Ross is in your charge,' Corton

drawled as he flicked a fly from his horse's neck with his whip. 'Surely it is for her to say whom she wishes to call. Where do you reside, Miss Ross? I am acquainted with Sir Murray Ross of Cadogan Square—'

'He is no relation,' Isabelle broke in smoothly before Lallie could say a word. 'Miss—Ross's family are from Banffshire.'

'Banffshire, you say.' Corton's brows rose. 'I do not recall having met them—'

'Miss Ross's parents are both dead,' Alex put in quickly.

'But surely you are not living alone in Town?' Corton addressed Lallie with a silky smile.

'Of course not,' Alex said dismissively as Lallie hesitated. 'She is staying with her guardian, Lady Ashton.'

'Lady Ashton is your guardian?' Corton's brows lifted as he continued to stare at Lallie. 'You must tell her to take you about more. I have never had the pleasure of seeing you with her.'

'Haven't you?' Isabelle said with an acid smile. 'They were both at the Prince Regent's reception which he gave upon his last birthday. Absolutely everyone was there. . .'

'I was indisposed,' Corton replied, a faint angry flush staining his face.

'Yes,' Haldane drawled. 'The lack of an invitation can bring on the strangest of maladies, so I have heard.'

'You go too far, Haldane!' Corton spluttered as there was a ripple of laughter from the other riders.

'Enough, gentlemen, enough—!' the General said warningly. 'Enough of this squabbling, there are ladies present and I am sure Miss Ross is in no condition to listen to it.'

'Quite right, quite right,' Sir John said cheerfully, 'Ah! Here is my groom with my carriage. If we could just get everyone to stand clear—'

'I'll see to that,' said the General. He waved a hand at the onlookers. 'No need now for the rest of you to hang about. Go on, off with you. No blood and gore to see here—plenty of that in Spain if you want it. No, didn't think you'd fancy it,' he guffawed as Corton and the others dispersed rapidly. 'Damned popinjays—Corton's waistcoat's enough to frighten the horses!' he growled. 'Go on, shoo—!' he roared at Lady Cressida, who was hanging back from her companions and casting meaningful glances at Haldane, which he was studiously ignoring.

'Oh, really! If this is how you speak to your men, General, I wonder they do not mutiny!' Lady Cressida complained petulantly.

'Speak to 'em!' replied the General cheerfully. 'I flog 'em if they disobey orders. Now take yourself off, and stop being a nuisance, gal.'

'*Really!*' Lady Cressida's pretty face flushed to a red which clashed unflatteringly with her habit. 'Haldane! Are you going to let him speak to me like that without a word?'

'It would seem so,' Haldane agreed lazily.

'I see,' Lady Cressida said peevishly gesturing to where Lallie sat, white and still. 'I may be insulted with impunity but when it comes to that—' She broke off as Haldane's black brows lifted warningly.

'Don't make a cake of yourself,' he said quietly in a

tone which almost made Lallie feel sorry for Lady Cressida. 'I will call upon you soon. Good day.'

'You promise?' The whine in the brunette's voice was replaced suddenly with a girlish lisp.

'I don't break my word, not even when it is given for me. You should know that, Lady Cressida.'

'Yes.' The brunette looked suddenly embarrassed. 'I look forward to seeing you, Major Haldane. Sir John, General, Lady Carteret.' She nodded to the others, but pointedly ignored Lallie before jerking her roan around and spurring it into a canter.

Lallie stared after her. So *that* was Lady Cressida Penwyrth, his betrothed. And he did not even seem to like her. There should have been some comfort in that, some consolation, but there wasn't. She would have found it easier to forgive him if he had left her for love rather than for a title and social standing.

'Never did envy you that particular mousetrap, even if it did come so prettily wrapped,' the General said. 'The Penwyrth girls always were damnably spoilt.'

'Not to mention damnably rude,' Haldane replied grimly, as he glanced at Lallie's set white face and she turned her head to avoid his gaze.

'Really ought to get her home,' Sir John said. 'Think you can stand, m'dear?'

'I'll carry her to the carriage,' Haldane replied before Lallie could even begin to answer the surgeon.

'No, I can walk—' Her protest was lost as he bent and scooped her up into his arms.

And then, for a moment, her mind was blank. Empty of everything but the clean masculine smell of his skin beneath his billowing linen shirt, empty of everything except the sense of belonging. And then, as she saw the stiff disapproval upon Isabelle Carteret's face, the curiosity upon Sir John's and the cold scrutiny of the General, the illusion vanished.

She did not belong in his world any more—she had stepped outside and society would never let her back in. His future lay with Lady Cressida and hers—hers was anywhere but here in his arms, and the sooner she recognised that the better.

'Put me down.' She jerked out the words, wriggling in his arms.

'Be still,' he said mildly, adjusting her weight, 'or you'll hurt your arm.'

'Put me down!' she repeated more loudly.

'No,' he answered softly in a tone she remembered all too vividly. 'I don't want to.'

Her eyes flashed up to his, wide, dark, disbelieving.

'Why are you doing this?' she groaned.

'Doing what?' he asked blandly.

'Carrying me! Challenging Corton...' Her voice tailed off as his dark brows lifted, mocking her.

'Acting as your protector,' he replied evenly, as he halted beside Sir John's carriage and lifted her in. 'You said you needed one, did you not?' he continued calmly, as he tucked the trailing skirt of her habit out of the way of the carriage door. 'Well, as of this moment you may consider that you have found one.'

He was asking her to become his mistress! For a moment shock held her rigid as she stared fixedly at his hand which had stilled upon the silky velvet a scant inch from her ankle. If she said yes, then she would still be able to see him—laugh with him—touch him. For a moment the temptation was overwhelming as her memory threw up a sudden image of his fingers upon her skin, the passion in his eyes and voice as he had held her and promised never, ever to let her go.

And he thought she was a whore, to be bought as carelessly, as easily as a new coat. The thought sliced through her like a knife as she lifted her gaze to his impassive, unreadable face. How could he think that of her—how could he want her on such terms?

Because he had never loved her, as she had him. That was a truth she had never really faced until this moment. To him she had only ever been an object he desired, wished to possess. Something inside her seemed to curl and die as she slowly shook her head.

'No. I will not be your mistress, Alex. I should rather starve.'

'That would be foolish in the extreme.' His eyes came snapping up, capturing her gaze, seeing, reading far too much. 'If you came here willing to take some stranger into your bed, why not me?'

'A thousand reasons.'

'Name one,' he said silkily, still holding her gaze.

'Because, because—' She cast about in her mind for a reason, any reason she could admit to and retain a grain of pride in the midst of her crushing misery.

'Because?' he mocked.

'Because you are a younger son, you cannot afford to keep both mistress and wife in any style,' she said, hoping that she sounded hard, uncaring. 'I had hoped to do better.'

'Very practical,' he said coldly, 'But you don't seem to have succeeded very well to date. Any other objections, Lallie?'

'I. . .' She floundered helplessly, feeling as if she was

being crushed by the weight of her misery. 'I—don't love you any more.' She wanted to choke back the words the moment they had left her lips. Dear heaven, had she no pride?

'"Any more."' His dark brows lifted as he repeated her last word. 'You did once, then? I thought you said it was never more than infatuation.'

'Oh! You know I did! I did not exactly hide it, did I? The whole world knew it!' She jerked her head away, chokingly angry with him, with herself for once having been so young, so stupid and still so stupid!

'If you think love matters, you'll never make a successful demi-rep,' he said after a moment of silence. 'Not in a thousand years.'

'Nor a governess or seamstress either, it would seem!' she snapped. 'Now go away and leave me alone unless you have some sensible alternative to suggest!'

'I am trying to offer you one,' he said, 'one that you might find considerably more lucrative than any governess's salary and probably a lot more entertaining.'

She turned back to him, her great grey eyes brilliant with unshed tears. 'And do you think Lady Cressida would find it entertaining?'

'It has nothing to do with her,' he said with a calm that made her want to hit him again.

'It has everything to do with her,' she said through clenched teeth. 'You are betrothed to her—'

'Alexander!' Isabelle's tart interruption made them both start. 'General Houghton wishes to speak with you, urgently.'

'Not now—' he groaned.

'Apparently it is urgent,' Isabelle told him sharply.

'You will excuse me?' he sighed, as he glanced up at Lallie. 'I suppose this is scarcely the time or place for this conversation.' He turned away to his sister before she could say anything further.

'Isabelle, will you stay with Miss Ross?'

'If I must,' Isabelle said coldly. 'I suppose it will lend credence to our explanation.'

'It is not necessary,' Lallie said quickly. She felt utterly drained and not in the least capable of dealing with Isabelle Carteret's contempt hard upon the heels of her brother's.

'It is,' Alex said tersely without looking at her. 'Isabelle will take you home. I'll help our groom bring the horses back. He'll not manage four, at least not when one of them is Goliath!'

'Home?' Isabelle gaped at him. 'Her!'

'Izzy—' he said warningly and took her arm, propelling her away from the carriage.

'You do not mean to my house?' Isabelle said breathlessly, wrenching her arm free and coming to a halt.

'Where else? I can scarcely take her to mine, can I?' he replied impatiently.

'It would make no difference to her reputation!' his sister snapped. 'It is mine that will be ruined by entertaining muslins! The children are there: Are you mad?'

'Izzy!' he rasped. 'I do not like calling in favours, but I trust you have not forgotten that I extricated you from that engagement to Sefton so that you could marry Robert. Do this one thing for me, and I will never ask you for anything again.'

His sister was silent for a moment as her green eyes

travelled over his face. 'Oh, very well,' she gave in grudgingly. 'But you had better not involve me in a scandal, Alex.'

'Thank you,' he sighed with relief, 'and thank you for inventing the appearance at the Prince Regent's reception—that was positively inspired. There were so many people there; no one will ever know if she was there or not.'

'I had to do something. You don't think I was going to have it put about town that my little brother had offered to duel for a demi-rep's reputation, do you?' Isabelle said scathingly. 'You've come near enough to making a complete cake of yourself as it is! I am beginning to think you have taken leave of your senses.'

Her brother glanced at Lallie, who sat motionless as a statue in the carriage. 'You could be right,' he murmured beneath his breath. 'She always did have that effect upon me.'

'And any other man susceptible to a pretty pair of eyes, no doubt,' Isabelle returned acidly, before swinging on her heel and stalking back towards the carriage, her beautiful face a mask of frosty disapproval.

'You were right. She's perfect for the task, Haldane, perfect, and the introduction to Corton could not have been better if you had engineered it!' the General said as he followed the direction of Haldane's stare after the receding carriage. 'Or perhaps you did, eh?'

'No,' Haldane said tersely. 'I did not. It was pure accident.'

'Accident or no, we've got Corton hooked better than we could ever have hoped.' The General grinned.

'He won't be able to resist stealing your mistress. He'll be so damned pleased with himself that he won't question anything she does and as for the plans, I'll wager that young lady will get them. She's quick off the mark, picked up your cue in a moment—and she'll pass for a lady. With a little luck that tale of yours will hold and you'll be able to take her about with you to Corton's usual haunts. Think Lady Ashton would co-operate?'

'Possibly,' Haldane said after a moment, 'so long as she thinks my motive for the deception is honourable.'

'I am sure you can think of some explanation that will convince her.' The General grinned at him. 'You're a damned plausible fellow, Haldane. Now, I take it you don't anticipate any difficulty with Miss Ross? Offer her whatever you like to get those plans.' The General chuckled. 'Say, a thousand guineas—'

'Five,' Haldane said. 'I doubt she would do it for less. Corton is not the most attractive of men to any woman of taste.'

'Very well, five.' Houghton shrugged his broad shoulders. 'Let me have her answer as quickly as you can. The sooner we have those papers, the happier I shall be.'

'Yes, sir,' Haldane said heavily as he watched the General ride away, and wondered why he felt such a sense of self-disgust. Five thousand guineas—and an entrée into society where any woman with her looks could find herself a very comfortable niche—it was far more than he could ever offer her. It would set her up; she'd be able to live comfortably, respectably even— and she wasn't an innocent girl any more—so why did he feel like a Judas? It wasn't as if he was still in love with her. Only the worst of flats fell in love with a muslin, and he had never been that. It was unthinkable, laughable.

And he had never felt less like laughing in his life. Lallie and Corton. The thought was enough to make him feel as if he had been run through. He even found himself wondering whether it was worth it—even if it did mean saving Wellesley's army and perhaps all Spain and Portugal from Bonaparte's yoke.

'Where is she?' Haldane asked as he strode into his sister's sitting room and found it empty except for Isabelle.

'I neither know nor care,' Isabelle replied, without looking up from her embroidery. 'She demanded to be set down.'

'And you agreed! She was injured, Isabelle.'

'How do you suggest I should have stopped her? By force?'

'No. I suppose not.' He swung away on his heel.

'Where are you going?'

'Where do you think?' he fired back at his sister.

'Alex, why don't you let well enough alone?' Isabelle rose to her feet, her embroidery falling unnoticed from her lap as she hurried after her brother. 'She is nothing more than an adventuress. You said yourself she let you think she was a widow to lure you into the mousetrap—'

'I said nothing of the sort.' He shook off the hand his sister placed upon his arm. 'Her godmother was elderly and more than a little confused and introduced her to me as her sister-in-law. Not wishing to embarrass her godmother, she went along with it until she had the opportunity to speak to me alone!'

'And I don't suppose that took her long,' Isabelle scoffed, undaunted by her brother's thunderous expression. 'Really, Alex, she was beneath your touch five years ago, and she is a great deal further beneath it now! She understands that, even if *you* don't!'

'So that's what you said to her, is it?' Alex said hoarsely. 'Thank you, dear sister, thank you very much! I wish you would not interfere in things you do not even begin to understand!'

'Alex—wait—' His sister put a more placatory note into her voice. 'You cannot mean to set her up—not now—you'll ruin your chances with Cressida—'

'Damn Cressida!' His voice was ice as he strode for the door. 'Let her marry Rutherstone.'

'What the devil has got into Haldane?' Isabelle's husband asked a moment or two later as he came into his wife's sitting-room. 'He damn near knocked me over in his haste and then bit my head off when I asked about the *demi-mondaine* in the park—the club's a-buzz with it. I hear he challenged Corton?'

'Yes. . .' Isabelle said slowly. 'He did. And the *demi-mondaine* was the woman who came here for a position as governess.'

'Good God, was she?' her husband laughed. 'Well, that would certainly have put the seal upon Jeremy's education.'

'Robert, really!' Isabelle glowered at her fair-haired giant of a husband. 'This is serious. He has met her before, five years ago in Scotland—and the way he speaks about her, you'd think he almost meant to marry the girl.'

'Marry a muslin!' Robert threw back his head and laughed again. 'Haldane? Never, my sweet, so stop worrying. Cressida'll net him yet, you'll see.'

CHAPTER FIVE

'What do you mean, Emily is not here?' Lallie demanded of Mrs Crouch as her landlady put a bleary-eyed face around the kitchen door. 'You promised to mind her in exchange for the ballgown. Where is she?'

'Robson's,' the older woman said without fully opening the kitchen door. 'He took her, said he had a kitten to show her.'

'Robson! You let her go with him after what happened to Ann Harris's girl!' Lallie stared at her, her own misery about Alex forgotten and irrelevant in the face of this unthinkable danger to Emily.

'You'd have thought Ann Harris would have been grateful to have one off her hands,' Mrs Crouch muttered. ''Sides—yours is too young to be of use to his customers—if she were eight or so—'

'You are a monster—worse than him!' Lallie spat at her. Then she was running, stumbling out of the house, oblivious to the pain in her arm, her shoulder, her aching legs, cursing her cumbersome skirt, cursing Tom Mitchell as she cannoned into him upon the pavement.

'Lallie—Lallie, what the devil is it?' he asked drunkenly as he caught her shoulders. 'You've not lamed my horse, have you? God, girl, you look like death—'

'Oh, why do you have to be foxed now, Tom?' she blurted despairingly. 'Let me by—'

'Foxed? I wouldn't say I was foxed,' Tom said, regarding her with benign if somewhat bloodshot green

eyes. 'Next to Taunton cider, the stuff they call ale at
the Dragon is like horse's—'

'Tom, have you a pistol about you?' she interrupted
him as she struggled free of his grasp.

'Course I have—fine highwayman I'd be without—'

'Then lend it to me, please.'

'What for?'

'Robson.' she said breathlessly. 'He's got Emily—'

'Emily?' Tom looked at her blearily.

'Please—the pistol, Tom, there's not time to explain,'
she said desperately.

With what seemed like unbearable slowness, Tom
fished in his tail pocket and brought out a huge pistol.
'It's primed, so you'd better be careful—'

'Yes—yes—I will—' She snatched it from his waver-
ing grasp and tucked the barrel into the waistband of
her skirt.

'Robson's a dangerous swine,' said Tom, as the
gravity of the situation seemed suddenly to dawn upon
him. 'Just give me a minute and I'll come with you—I
just need to rest here for a bit—'

Lallie groaned as he subsided into an untidy heap
upon the pavement.

'Come when you're ready, I can't wait—'

'Lallie. . .' His voice drifted after her as she stumbled
on.

It was only when she reached Robson's door that she
realised she had no idea of what she was going to do
except demand that Emily be handed over to her
forthwith.

And then the door opened and a thin red-haired
woman in a grubby pink satin gown regarded her with

tired eyes. 'He said you'd be coming, now he's got your brat. He's waiting for you upstairs.'

'Where is my sister?' she said breathlessly. 'If anyone has hurt her—'

'She's all right, it's not her he's interested in yet, it's you he wants,' the woman replied wearily. 'I'll tell him you're here. And if you'll take my advice, be nice to him. If you put up a fight, you'll only get hurt.'

'Thank you,' Lallie replied breathlessly, the beginnings of a plan forming in her mind. 'I'm sure you are right. Tell Mr Robson I should like to see him, alone.' As the woman disappeared into the house she undid the buttons on her habit jacket, making sure the peplum covered the butt of the pistol, and loosened the strings at the neck of her shirt. Nice, she thought ferociously. Oh yes, she would be nice to Mr Robson.

'Let's have some more gin.' Lallie forced herself to smile some ten minutes later as she slid away from the arm Robson attempted to put around her waist. 'No, no, I'll get it.' She got up from the arm of his chair and weaved towards the table.

She came back unsteadily, clutching the jug, and started to pour, but stumbled upon her trailing habit skirt so that the gin went splashing onto his sleeve.

'Oh, dear—' She gave what she hoped sounded like a tipsy giggle. She had to keep him off guard, there would be only one chance.

Robson laughed and reached for her. 'I knew we'd get on just fine once you'd seen reason, Miss Ross— now just you come here—'

'*No!*' Her voice rose almost to a scream as he caught her injured arm and she reeled dizzily away from him, spilling gin upon the dully smoking fire which exploded into sudden life.

'Come 'ere, I said,' he growled surlily. 'And have a care, you'll have the place on fire.'

'Let's dance. Shall we dance, Mr Robson?' She laughed wildly as he lurched to his feet and took a step towards her.

'There's only one sort of dance I want, come here—'

'With pleasure.' She swung round with all the strength she could muster.

'You—' Robson saw the jug a second too late to prevent it colliding with his skull.

He went reeling backwards against a wood panelled wall, clutching his head.

Dropping the bottle, she wrested the pistol Tom had loaned her from behind her back and levelled it at the middle of his body.

'You bitch,' he snarled as he brought his hand down and saw the blood upon his fingers, and when he saw the pistol he swore foully.

'Move and I will fire,' she said shakily. 'Call one of your women and ask them to send Emily in. Do it or I will fire!'

'She's not 'ere. Kitty's taken her out to help with the marketing. They'll not be back for a half-hour.'

She dragged in a breath. Kitty's marketing consisted mostly of stealing, food, purses, whatever she could get. She would undoubtedly be using Emily as a cover and getting her to carry what she stole. People rarely thought to search a child. But at least that was better than what she had feared—but what should she do now? If she left and went to look for Kitty, but Robson's men found her first, then Robson would have the upper hand again, and she would not get him off guard a second time.

'I can wait,' she said coldly, her decision made. 'I said, don't move,' she warned as he straightened and took a step away from the wall.

He subsided into immobility. 'You'll swing for this, you bitch, attempted murder this is, that's a capital offence,' he muttered.

'So is kidnapping,' she snapped, praying that Tyson or one of the other men below could not hear what was being said and that Robson would not realise how difficult it was for her to hold the heavy pistol in her left hand, or that she could barely use her right arm at all.

A little longer, just a little longer, she told herself as the wheeze of Robson's breath and the thudding of her own heart seemed to go on for ever. A little longer and she would have Emily and they would be out of the house. And what then...? She did not dare even to think about that...

'Stop!' Alex's roar had his coachman reining back the horses on their haunches. A second later he was out of the carriage before the wheels had stopped turning and across the shabby street to where a child sat huddled in a doorway, sobbing inconsolably.

'Emily?' he said tentatively as he bent down to the child's level. 'Whatever are you doing here?'

'A man shouted and chased us. Kitty ran away and I got lost.' Emily hiccuped, raising a grimy tear-stained face to look at him. 'I want Lallie—I don't want to go to Mr Robson's again. I want Lallie—'

'Then you shall not,' Haldane said soothingly. 'Now,

I'm sure Lallie will be home by now. Shall we go and find her?'

'Yes. . .' Emily said on a heaving breath.

'Come on, then.' He took her hand and pulled her gently to her feet. 'Do you want to walk, or ride in my carriage?'

'Carriage.' Emily hiccuped again. 'Mr Robson might come and the—Kitty said he'd hit me and Lallie if we didn't do what he said.'

'Did she?' Haldane said, his frown deepening as he exchanged a glance with his coachman who had got down to hold the door for them. 'Well, she is quite wrong. I shall not let anyone hit you, or your—' He stopped wondering what the child knew of her parentage. 'Or Lallie,' he finished.

'Good.' Emily sniffed, as she halted upon the step of the carriage to stare at the horses. 'I don't want Lallie to die. My father died—'

'Your father—that is a great pity,' he said gently, while inwardly cursing himself for the remarks he had thrown at Lallie. Her lover was dead, her child fatherless—gradually he was beginning to understand a little of what had driven her to lie to Isabelle, to come alone to the Row.

'Yes. But it's all right because I still have Lallie,' Emily said as she clambered into the carriage and bounced up onto the blue silk squabs, her tears already drying. 'Do you like, Lallie?' she asked as he sat down upon the opposite seat.

'Yes.'

'I don't know if she likes you,' Emily said thoughtfully as she regarded him with faintly accusing eyes. 'She cried the last time you came.'

'Then I promise I shall not make her cry again,' he said and wondered if the promise had as hollow a ring to the child as it did to his own ears.

'Good,' Emily said with satisfaction as she knelt up on the cushions to look out of the carriage window. 'How fast can your horses go?'

'I don't know if she's back yet. I hope so, I don't hold with young women being out late. A respectable 'ouse this is, sir.' Mrs Crouch wheezed as she led Haldane up the final flight of woodwormed attic stairs. 'Not what a fine gentleman like you would be used to, but my lodgers all say it's very comfortable.'

'Comfortable!' Haldane grimaced as they reached the door of Lallie's attic, thinking that he had seen establishments with more comfort to offer after they had been looted by the French.

'I could let her room a dozen times over for twice what she pays.' Mrs Crouch sniffed noisily and wiped her nose upon her sleeve and gave no sign of having heard. 'It's only out the kindness of me heart and fondness for the little one that I let her stay.'

'I am sure she is very grateful,' he said acidly. 'And no doubt you have things to do, madam. Some cleaning, perhaps, would not go amiss?'

'Want to surprise her, hey, sir?' Mrs Crouch's large, formless shape rippled as she gave a cackle of laughter and tapped her bulbous nose. 'Well, I can take a hint —'

'Good,' Haldane replied, pointedly ignoring her grimy outstretched palm.

Sniffing, Mrs Crouch lumbered away, corsets and floorboards creaking at her every step.

'Lallie?' Haldane tapped upon the door which swung inward upon creaking hinges. 'Lallie—I have Emily in my carriage—' He broke off. The room was deserted, bare but for the bed, a pallet and a battered blanket box upon which stood a chipped china wash-jug and basin.

He swore softly beneath his breath as he ducked his head to avoid the low lintel and stepped into the room, his booted feet loud upon the bare boards. There had scarcely been a day in Spain when he had not thought of her, but he had never envisaged her living like this—

She had been right, he had not understood. Only now was he beginning to understand what had brought her to lie at Isabelle's and to the Row upon a half-mad horse.

The anxiety he had felt about Emily's garbled tale returned suddenly with full force. Where was Lallie? She should have been back by now. It had taken him an hour to make various arrangements after leaving Isabelle's, then another ten minutes to drive here in his carriage. She should have been here—if she had not collapsed upon the road— Now, what was he to do? he wondered, as he stooped to pick up Emily's faded ragdoll lying upon the floor.

'Well, sir, would it be Miss Ross yer looking for?' The slurred west-country drawl brought Haldane jerking upright, so fast he cracked his head upon a low oak beam and swore. Rubbing his head, he turned.

'Yes—'

'And what would you be wanting with 'er?'

'I am a friend,' he said coolly, meeting the green gaze of the man who lounged against the door jamb with a steely glare. 'Not that it is any business of yours.'

'A friend?' The newcomer's gaze travelled critically over Haldane's immaculately tailored plain blue coat and down to his mirror-polished boots. 'Well,' he announced as his eyes lifted to Haldane's face again, 'she be in need of friends like you, 'er and the little one.'

'So I see,' he said grimly as he glanced about the room again. 'I never thought her father would see her reduced to this, whatever their quarrel. . .' He spoke his own thoughts aloud.

'Her father was the *reason* they were reduced to this. Not that you should speak ill of the dead.' Tom Mitchell shook his tousled head sombrely. 'Terrible business that was, died in Newgate of the gaol fever.'

'What?' The doll dropped out of Haldane's hands unnoticed. 'How the devil did John Ross fetch up in Newgate?'

'Drink, cards, dice and one creditor too many.' Tom shrugged. 'The man wasn't right in the head after his wife died.'

'Mrs Ross is dead as well?'

'Yep,' Tom replied. 'Just as well, as her husband lost everything he had in a twelvemonth after burying 'er.'

'Then how have the family lived since?' Haldane asked grimly.

'The way most of us do, Major,' Tom said laconically, 'from hand to mouth, courtesy of the pawnbrokers, dodging our creditors and praying to the Almighty for a bit of luck at the tables. Lallie had the worst of it. He was too drunk to care how they lived most of the time, but she did. I used to see it in her face when he made her go the hells—'

'He took her to the hells!' Haldane's voice broke.
'What the devil for?'

'Because she has a better memory for the cards and
the odds of Hazard than any sharp you can name. I
remember the first time I saw her, Hanson Street it
was—there were half the drunks and rakes in London
propositioning her and her father too drunk to lift a
finger to protect her—'

'And you? Did you offer to protect her?' Haldane
bit out savagely.

'Of course, what man wouldn't have, faced with the
bonniest lass he'd ever had the luck to set eyes upon?'

'If you have laid so much as a finger—'

'Hold on to yer 'at.' Tom retreated a step, after
seeing the expression upon Haldane's face. 'The
moment she spoke to me I realised she was a lady. I
might take advantage of women, but not ladies. A
principle it'd do you no 'arm to adopt.'

'What the devil do you mean by that?'

'Oh, come on, sir,' Tom drawled. 'You be Major
Haldane, aren't ye?'

'You have the advantage of me.' Haldane's voice
was chill. 'And yet there is something familiar about
you. Have we met?'

'Met? Not unless t'was Dorchester Assizes and you
were on the bench.' Tom laughed, making a dep-
recatory gesture to his shabby frockcoat. 'It'll be me
brother William you're thinking of—'

'William. . .' Haldane stared at him, puzzled for a
moment, then recognition came. 'My God, you're
another damned Mitchell! I might have known, I
suppose it was you who lent her my horse, which your

rapscallion of a brother stole from me when he absconded from the army.'

'I lent 'er the horse,' Mitchell said in an injured tone, 'which you gave my brother out of gratitude for saving you from the Frenchies before he got his honourable discharge.'

'What?' Haldane's eyes blazed.

'Well, that's 'is story,' Tom conceded, 'and as for the beast being your'n, I don't know 'ow you'd be proving that.'

'From a painting which hangs in my drawing-room and a bill of sale,' Haldane said icily. 'And I still do not know how you recognised me.'

'She's got a picture, a charcoal sketch. I found her crying her eyes out over it not long after I first met her,' the west countryman shrugged. 'Can't think why, meself, when she had me, Thomas Mitchell, down on my knees offering her lifelong devotion and to reform my wicked ways, but then woman always have been a mystery to me. Then, the day before yesterday, I find her doing exactly the same—and she told me the whole tawdry little story, Major—'

'Where is she?' Haldane interrupted him brutally.

· 'Why do you want to know?' Tom taunted. 'Thinking of introducing her to your dear mama and papa and posting the banns this time? I wouldn't mention that her father died in Newgate, if you do.'

Haldane exhaled slowly and forced his clenched fist to unfurl. Much as he would like to knock Thomas Mitchell flat, he needed to find Lallie. 'Do you know where she is?' he repeated ferociously.

'I might.' Tom took a pewter flask from his pocket,

slowly unscrewed the cap and began to lift it to his mouth.

'Then tell me, damn you!' Haldane roared.

Tom took a long pull and swallowed slowly before replying.

'At Robson's place.'

'Who the devil is this Robson?'

'A brothel keeper, a thief, a murderer.' Tom shrugged. 'Take your pick. He's been after Lallie for months and last week he bought a debt against her and he's determined to be paid, one way—' he paused and shrugged again '—or the other.'

'Great God!' Haldane lunged forward and caught the other man by his grimy shirt front, almost lifting him off his feet. 'Are you telling me she is in the worse kind of danger and you are standing here drinking yourself stupid? Where is this place?'

'We can't all be heroes, Major,' Mitchell retorted. 'And as for danger, she's never been out of it for the last four years. Where were you, then, when she was being insulted by the drunks in the hells and breaking her heart over you?'

'Fighting the French in Spain!' Haldane hissed. 'Where is Robson's?'

'On the corner, the north end of the street—' The last word was choked off as Haldane dropped him abruptly.

'Wait—' Tom put a restraining hand on his arm.

'Get out of my way!' Haldane roared.

'All right, all right, but just take this, will you, you might be needing it—' Mitchell pulled another pistol from the tail pocket of his coat. 'It's loaded. And tell

Lallie I'll have the other back when she's finished with it—'

'You gave her one of these! The recoil could break her arm! For the love of God, let me by—'

'Not a word of thanks, you ungrateful noble bastard,' Tom muttered as he watched Haldane descend the stairs three at a time. 'And if you break her heart again, Major, I'll give you a jaw to match.'

The threat fell into silence. Haldane was already in the street, shouting an order to his coachman as he sprinted past.

How much longer? Lallie wondered, as she listened to doors slamming, and footsteps descending and ascending stairs. How much longer?

'Getting heavy, is it?' Robson mocked her as his dark eyes followed the pistol barrel's waverings. 'Why don't you just put it down like a good girl, Miss Ross? You know you won't use it, so this is all a waste of time, ain't it?'

'Be quiet!' She gasped, straining to hear as the sound of footsteps grew louder.

There was tentative tap upon the door. 'It's Kitty, Mr Robson.'

'About time,' Robson growled back as Lallie made a brief gesture with the pistol. 'Send the child in—'

'I ain't got 'er. We got spotted and I had to scarper. She couldn't keep up, so I lost her.'

'You stupid—' Robson spat out a foul word as Lallie took an instinctive step to the door, her mind racing from one image to another, each one successively worse than the one before as she thought of Emily on her own in the streets.

'I'm sorry, Mr Robson,' Kitty whined.

'You will be—' Robson muttered, taking a step forward and then freezing as Lallie swung the pistol back to cover him again.

'Tell her to go away!' she hissed.

'It don't matter, Kitty,' Robson growled. 'Go and get on with the supper.'

'Yes, Mr Robson.' Kitty's voice was heavy with relief.

Lallie listened to her footsteps receding and the sound of the doors shutting below in the house.

'I'm leaving,' she said to Robson. 'You go in front—move!' She gestured abruptly with the pistol.

'You don't really think I'm going to let you go now, do you?' he sneered at her.

'Move!' she hissed at him ferociously, her finger tightening upon the trigger. 'I shall be right behind you. If you call out, I shall fire.'

With excruciating slowness, Robson led the way out of the room and down two flights of stairs into the vestibule which reeked of gin, ale and cheap scent.

'Hurry up,' She snarled at him tensely as he unlocked the front door. What she was going to do once she was outside, she didn't know. All she knew was that she had to find Emily. Find her before Robson or his men did or—she could not let herself think about the other dangers. If she did, she would not be able to do anything—

'Having some trouble, Mr Robson?' Tyson's voice from behind her brought her twisting around.

But it was too late. A hand caught her wrist, crushing it cruelly until the pistol fell from her numb fingers into Robson's outstretched hand.

'Let go of me!' She struggled frantically, slipped out

of Tyson's grasp and made a dive for the partly open door.

'Oh, no, you don't!' Robson caught her by her hair, jerking her back and wrapping an arm about her waist as he dropped the pistol into his coat pocket. 'You and me have got some unfinished business, Miss Ross. Upstairs! Now!'

'No!' Her voice rose to a scream as she twisted, flailing, kicking at any part of him she could reach.

'Bitch!' He swore as she clawed at his face with her fingernails. 'Give us a hand, Tyson—'

She screamed again, as Tyson grabbed at her and tore the sleeve of her gown as they dragged her towards the stairs.

It was then that the front door exploded inwards, splintering off its hinges.

'What the—?' Robson and Tyson froze. And for a moment, as she stared in disbelieving relief at the tall figure filling the gaping doorway, holding a pistol trained unwaveringly at Robson's ample belly, so did she.

'Let go of her!' The voice reverberated around the hall like thunder and Tyson and Robson let go of Lallie so abruptly that she went sprawling across the floor. 'Against the wall, hands above your heads!'

Robson and Tyson moved slowly to obey as Lallie scrambled to her feet.

'He has a pistol—' she blurted out as she saw Robson's hand begin to drop to his pocket.

'Then he had better stay very still.' Alex said, his stare at Robson as unwavering as his aim. 'Can you get it while I cover them?'

'Yes.' Somehow she forced herself to take the step

towards Robson and reach into his pocket and extract the pistol.

'Good girl,' Alex said soothingly as if speaking to a child. 'Now come over here to me.'

'Bitch!' Robson lunged as she began to turn away and blocked Alex's line of fire.

'Lallie! Don't!' Alex's shout of warning was lost in a blinding flash and crash as she pulled the trigger and found herself hurled backwards against the wall as if she had been kicked by a cart-horse.

She slumped against the wall, while a wrought-iron candle-holder and plaster and lathes rained down from the ceiling upon a cursing Robson and cowering Tyson, who had flung himself flat upon the floor.

'Fire's a trifle high,' Alex said drily, as she turned her head slowly to look at him.

'Have I killed him?' Her own voice seemed to come from a great distance away as she looked again at Robson, writhing amid the debris upon the floor.

'No. Unfortunately,' he replied after the briefest of glances at Robson. 'I'd say he was merely stunned by the candle sconce which your shot brought down from the ceiling.'

'*My* shot—' She stared in horror at the pistol in her hands.

'No, don't—' his voice rose and fell as she dropped it as if it were made of molten metal '—drop it,' he finished heavily in the silence following a second explosion, which left a large hole in the skirting board at the other end of the hall. 'It has two barrels.'

'Sorry,' she said shakily, her face whiter than the plaster dust which coated them both. 'I am not usually so stupid. . .I don't know what is wrong with me—I'm sorry—I can't—'

'It's all right—' Suddenly he was beside her, his arm about her shaking shoulders. 'Let's go before these two recover and the screaming harpies upstairs descend upon us.'

Her legs moved like those of an automaton as he propelled her out of the house and into the street. She felt numb, incapable of thought except for—'Emily!' She came to a jerking halt upon the pavement beside Alex's carriage. 'Emily! I have to find her—'

'Get in,' he said gently, 'and don't worry about Emily—'

'No, no, you don't understand.' she tried to pull away from him. 'I have to find her—I have to—' She could hear her voice rising, cracking but she could not stop it.

'Lallie!' He held her tightly against him. 'Lallie—listen, it is all right. My coachman has already put her in the carriage. She's here—look.'

'Emmy! Oh, Emmy—' She flung herself into the carriage and gathered the little girl into her arms. 'Emmy, are you all right? They did not hurt you?'

'No. But I was scared.' Emily said. 'But then he came and I wasn't any more.' She lifted her small fair head from Lallie's shoulder to look at Alex as he coiled his tall form onto the opposite seat. 'And now I've been very brave, haven't I?'

'Very brave,' Alex agreed gravely, after rapping upon the roof of the carriage to signal to the coachman to move off. 'Just like Lallie.'

'Lallie isn't afraid of anything,' Emily said with absolute faith.

'I know, and it's just as well,' he said as his gaze met Lallie's eyes over Emily's head. 'Since I was almost too late.'

'Are you in the cavalry?' Emily asked.

'Yes,' Alex said, slightly taken aback by the change of subject. 'I am, as it happens. Why?'

'Well, you can't help it, then. Tom was a foot soldier once and he says the cavalry are always too late.'

'Really.' Alex's brows lifted.

'Better late than never, Emily,' Lallie said with the ghost of a smile. 'Thank you for coming, Alex.'

'Better late than never,' he repeated the words softly. 'I doubt that is quite the way the infantry would put it in Spain if I were five years too late. I wish—'

'Have you got more horses?' Emily said before Lallie could even begin to wonder what he wished.

'Several,' he said easily.

'Can I have a ride on one of them?'

'Emily—' Lallie groaned.

'Of course.'

'Tomorrow!' Emily bounced upon Lallie's lap. 'May we go tomorrow?'

'So long as you are not too tired and Lallie gives her permission.'

'Can I? Can I?' Emily squirmed upon her lap.

Tomorrow. She stared at him helplessly. She did not even know where they were going. How could she think about tomorrow? Her mind would not work properly, it was jumbled with pain and fear and—and Alex. Why had he come? After what his sister had said, after what he had said in the Park, she had not ever expected to see him again. And now—what must he think of her now, finding her in the midst of a brawl with a brothel keeper—?

'Well?' he prompted her softly.

'Please,' Emily wheedled.

'Yes, yes, whatever you like,' she said exhaustedly, as she let her head tip back against the blue silk squabs.

'Yes! Yes!' Emily bounced excitedly again on her knee, making her gasp as renewed pain shot through her arm and shoulder.

'Why don't you come and sit beside me?' She realised he had heard her as he spoke to Emily. 'And I will tell you all about my horse so that you will know how to manage him.'

Emily accepted the invitation with alacrity, diving off Lallie's lap to sit demurely beside Alex and gaze up at him with rapt attention.

Children were so resilient, she thought, but then Emily had no real idea of the precariousness of their existence—if Alex had not come to Robson's—if he had not been there in the park—her thoughts dissolved quite suddenly into a jumble of incoherent disconnected images: Goliath crashing into the carriage horse, the circle of superior faces staring down at her, the terror she had felt when she had discovered Emily was missing, and Robson pawing at her—

She shut her eyes trying to blot out the image. It was better not to think or move. Better just to wish that this journey could last for ever, and she could stay safe in this blue silk-lined nest, listening to Alex's velvety voice and Emily's laughter. She ought to ask where he was taking them, and why he had come after them— but she was too afraid of his answers, too tired even to ask. She just wanted to stay here, letting the soothing,

rhythmic clatter of the horses' hooves upon the cobbles
and the steady rumble of the carriage wheels wash
everything else out of her mind except the fact that
they were safe. Would always be safe so long as Alex
was there—that was her last conscious thought as she
slid into the deep, deep sleep of mental and physical
exhaustion. A sleep so deep she was utterly unaware of
Alex, easing her into a more comfortable position upon
the seat, and tucking a light rug over her. She did not
even stir as he touched his lips to her forehead in the
lightest, briefest of kisses.

CHAPTER SIX

ALEX set down the tray of coffee upon the sidetable beside his canopied bed and stared down at Lallie, wondering whether to wake her or let her sleep on. She stirred, flinging out an arm, murmuring something incoherent.

He frowned, wondering if she were in the grip of yet another nightmare. The first time she had screamed during the night had brought him out of the chair in which he had been dozing and reaching instinctively for his sabre before he realised that he was at home in England, not in some war-torn Spanish village.

He sat down upon the edge of the bed and said her name softly.

She did not hear him, she was locked in another time, another place, seeing only her bedchamber in her godmother's house. . .

It was shadowy, difficult to discern anything but her discarded ballgown hanging upon the pier glass, gleaming ghostly pale in the moonlight which filtered through the muslin drapes at the raised sash window. And so hot. Not a hint of a breeze, far too hot to sleep, even if she not been acutely miserable, her eyes gritty and heavy from crying.

It was not fair, she thought fiercely. She and Alex had only snatched a second or two alone; they had barely had a chance to exchange more than a word before her godmother had come in and ordered her to come home with her at once. And now she was here and he would still be dancing at the Urquharts' ball. Dancing with Lady Fiona Murray or the Honourable Caroline Fortescue or any of a dozen girls who were more eligible than she would ever be. It was not fair!

The rattle of gravel against the panes of the half raised sash window sliced through her misery.

'Lallie? Are you awake?'

The soft enquiry from below brought her jerking upright in disbelief. Throwing back her covers, she ran across the room, pushed up the window further and leant dangerously far out, her hair waterfalling forward over her shoulders.

'Alex?' she said incredulously, delightedly, as she saw him smiling up at her, the moonlight glinting off the silver braid of his uniform.

'Come down,' he said softly. 'Please—'

'The doors are all locked,' she said, her heart thudding crazily as it always did whenever she saw him. 'The housekeeper keeps the keys in her room.'

'The dining-room window is open; I saw it on my way through the garden. Hurry—I'll meet you there.' Blowing her a kiss, he began to run to the other side of house.

If she hesitated, it was not for more than a moment in which to snatch up a shawl, and then she was tiptoeing as fast as stealth would allow through the sleeping house.

'Whatever are you doing here?' She laughed breathlessly as she scrambled up onto the dining-room window-sill. 'How did you get here?'

'I rode across the moss.'

'Six miles across country in the dark?' Her voice rose. 'You are mad!'

He grinned. 'There is a full moon and how else was I to claim the dances you promised me?' he said, holding up his hands to catch her as she swung her legs over the sill which was some three or four feet above the lawn. 'Will you do me the honour, Miss Ross?'

'Oh, Alex!' She flung herself down into his outstretched arms, loving him hopelessly, helplessly. He caught her easily and whirled her away across the dew-wet grass, spinning her round and round until they collapsed in a dizzy, laughing heap upon the grass beneath the great oak at the edge of the lawn.

'Come here,' he murmured, reaching out and folding her into his arms so that they lay facing each other. 'Do you know that it is eight whole days since I have kissed you, eight days since we have had more than a moment alone—not being able to touch you, hold you—has been torture—?' He broke off as he bent his head to seek her mouth.

She shut her eyes as he kissed her, melting to the invasion of his tongue, and the hungry exploring sweep of his hands running down from her shoulders, caressing the narrow curve of her waist, lingering on the swell of her hips—and stilling as he discovered what she was already devastatingly aware of—that there was nothing between her flesh and his hands but the finest, flimsiest of muslins.

'Lallie,' he groaned against her mouth, his kiss deepening, as his hands brought her hard against him so that she could have no doubt of the effect her near-nakedness had wrought.

This was new, beyond their previous flirtation, said a

voice in her mind. This was dangerous—and all she wanted, all she ever wanted, her body replied, drowning out all reason. With one hand against the small of her back he held her close, as his other hand began an urgent exploration again, gathering up the folds of muslin until his fingertips slipped beneath the hem, found her bare thigh, cool and silky in the night air.

She trembled as his fingers glided upwards, over her thigh, the curve of her hip, feathering across the flat plain of her stomach and ribs, and then went into shocked stillness as his hand closed upon her breast, cupping her against his palm, and his thumb found its aching peak, brushing, circling until she gasped against his hungry mouth. She had never been touched like this, never felt so soft, so unbearably brittle at the same moment.

'Alex—' She moaned his name against his mouth, curling her fingers into his shoulders as the pleasure became close to unbearable. It was a plea, but she was not sure whether it was for him to stop or take her further into this unfamiliar, overwhelming desire.

His fingers stilled, and then he took his hand away, withdrawing from her with an abruptness that left her bereft, cold.

'Alex?' she said uncertainly, sitting up, as he got to his feet.

He was silent for a moment, but for his ragged, uneven breathing and then he sighed and held out his hands to help her up, holding her at arm's length.

'Your godmother is right, you know,' he said heavily as they stood facing each other, linked only by their hands. 'We cannot go on like this—people are already beginning to talk, and then there is Hetherington.'

'What has he to do with it?' she asked tightly, her eyes like great dark holes in her ashen face. In the weeks that they had been together they had never spoken of the future, the difference in their stations: it had been an unwritten, unspoken pact. And she had been living from day to day, kiss to kiss, refusing to think about what would happen at the summer's end when she would have to return to her parents' house.

'Your godmother wants you to marry him,' he said gratingly, 'and fears that I will ruin your chances, something she makes clear every time I call.'

She stared at him. He was going to say it was over. And she was not sure she could bear it.

'I know,' she said bleakly. 'She thinks he would be a good match for me and that it would spare my mother the expense and fatigue of a season.'

'And me?' he said, his hands tightening upon hers. 'What does she say about me?'

She sucked in a breath. 'That you are the son of an Earl, and I am the daughter of a brewer. And that though Haldanes might dally with trade. . .' she hesitated and swallowed as her throat seemed to close up. '. . .they will never marry it.'

The words seemed to hang in a silence. A silence in which the warm summer night air seemed to grow suddenly chill against her skin as she pulled her hands out of his. It was over, she thought, as she glanced at his face, which had set hard, mask-like. The dream was broken into pieces by cold reality. It was over. He was going to say it would be best if they did not see each other again. She knew it. She leant against the trunk of the oak, pressing her face to the gnarled bark, waiting for his words as if they would be blows.

'Lallie?' He followed her and leant against the tree beside her, frowning as she turned her head away. 'Look at me.'

He caught her chin, turning her face back to his. She dropped her eyelids like shutters, shutting him out as her misery seemed to solidify into a suffocating lump in her lungs.

'My God! You do not believe her?' He was incredulous, and then instantly, ferociously angry. 'How can you be here with me tonight if you believe I would stoop so low—?'

'Because,' she interrupted him with reckless passion, her gaze flashing up to his face again, 'because I would rather be your mistress for an hour than any other man's wife—'

'Oh, Lallie—in some ways you are still such a child—' With a groan he reached for her and engulfed her in a rib-cracking hug. 'What am I to do with you?'

'Love me,' she blurted out against his chest.

'Do you think I could do anything else?' He laughed softly, resting his cheek against the top of her head. 'You are mine, and I'm never, ever going to let you go. . .'

He loved her. Nothing else mattered, she thought, as he kissed her and she seemed to melt into the warm darkness of his mouth.

'Lallie.' He was murmuring her name softly.

She smiled and stirred sleepily in the tangle of feather pillows and crisp, lavender-scented linen, instinctively not wanting to wake up.

'Lallie?'

He was more insistent this time.

Alex. Alex who loved her. Slowly, still suffused with happiness, she let her eyelids lift.

He was leaning over her, a hand either side of her head, his arms braced against her pillows. Still in the grip of her dream, she looked up at him with drowsy eyes, grey and soft as summer rain, and smiled—a smile that lit her face to an almost incandescent beauty.

Alex's breath caught in his throat as he stared down at her heart-shaped face, framed by the strands of silky pale hair that had escaped from the long thick braid which lay across the pillow like a glistening rope. Five years of living from hand to mouth about gaming hells and dens of thieves had done nothing to dim her seraphic beauty or the shining, seeming innocence in her wide grey eyes. And he knew suddenly with a twist of his stomach that he did not care how many men she had had, or who had fathered the child. He wanted her now as much as he ever had. . .wanted her to look at him again as she had in that moment of wakening. That was how she had used to look at him that summer, her face lighting whenever he had entered a room.

But that was hardly likely, he told himself grimly, not when she found out why he had brought her here and what he was about to suggest. Suddenly he did not know which he dreaded most, her anger and contempt or, worse, that she had changed so much that she would simply shrug and ask how much she would be paid.

He swore a silent oath. What difference did it make? She hated him already, she'd made that clear enough hadn't she? And there could be no going back—no matter how much he wanted it.

'Alex. . .?' She said his name uncertainly, the radiance fading from her face as the dream receded and the unexpected coldness in his blue gaze brought her snapping back into the present.

He straightened and folded his arms across his chest.

Lallie found herself staring at her fingers, lying a scant inch from his lean muscular thigh which his nankeen breeches covered like a second skin. She looked away hastily, her gaze flicking from the tawny brocade hangings of the bed in which she lay, to the straw coloured silk hung walls of the elegant bed-chamber, the muslin-draped pictures and furniture swathed in calico. It was all utterly unfamiliar to her. All of it except for him. After the vividness of her dream, he was all too familiar. She knew exactly how lean and firm his body would be beneath the fine linen and nankeen, knew how his skin would feel beneath her fingers if she were to reach out and slip her hand into the open placket of his lawn shirt.

She shut her eyes again, wishing that she could slip back into the dream, back into the past. Back to a time when she had believed he loved her.

'Lallie, don't go to sleep again, we need to talk,' he said tersely.

'About what?' she answered, without opening her eyes.

'Your future,' he said, making a decision not to mention Corton yet; there would time enough for that after she had agreed to take the house he had leased.

She sighed and sat up, wincing at the stab of pain from her elbow. She glanced down and touched it tentatively with the fingers of her right hand, and then her fingers stilled upon the linen sleeve. It was a man's shirt, the twin of his, and she discovered, as she shifted slightly in the bed, that she was wearing nothing else.

And would shortly not be wearing that either, she thought, as she felt the open neck of the shirt begin to slide off her slender shoulders. She grabbed at the neck in sudden panic as she saw his eyes flick downwards and darken. Where were the ties—or the buttons? She fumbled, her fingers impeded by the overlong lace-edged cuffs, and then winced again as her fingers found another tender place at the base of her throat where Robson had grabbed her about the neck.

'Let me.' He reached out to catch the ties and then, as she let her hands drop away and he noticed the marks, his hands stilled.

'Robson, I suppose,' he said grimly. 'He did not. . .' he looked away from her as he paused '. . .he did not hurt you in any other way?'

'No.'

'But he tried?' he said as his gaze came back to her throat.

'Yes—but I dissuaded him,' she said tersely. 'I hit him with a gin jug.'

'A gin jug?' His brows lifted. 'You have added to your accomplishments of late.'

'It was a matter of necessity.'

'Yes, I suppose it was.' The amusement that had briefly flickered in his blue eyes vanished as he pulled up the strings of her shirt.

She found herself transfixed and Robson entirely forgotten as she stared at his hands as he tied the strings—a hair's breadth was all that separated his deft fingers from grazing her breasts. She swallowed, her mouth suddenly dry as the image from the dream returned with devastating clarity.

It was only as the last bow was neatly tied and his

hands dropped away that she remembered to breathe and inhaled raggedly. He was right, she thought bitterly. This had not changed. She could not be near him and not want him to touch her.

She dragged her gaze from him and looked about the room again. 'Where is this—?' she began.

'My bedchamber, in my town house,' he said shortly.

'Your bedchamber?' Her voice came out as a dry croak.

His house. His bed. In the eyes of the world that would make her only one thing. And told her all too clearly that he now regarded her as a muslin, a demirep—a whore. Five years ago he would never have brought her here in such circumstances.

'There is no-one here except my old nurse, my housekeeper and the coachman,' he said, as if following the direction of her thoughts. 'And I promise you none of them will blab, so long as we are discreet for the next few days. No one need know you are here.'

'I see,' she said flatly.

'I am afraid I could think of nowhere else to bring you last night. I'm sorry about the dust sheets—' he made a brief expansive gesture with his hand '—everything has been shut up while I have been abroad and my bed is the only one which has been aired so far.

'Fortunately,' he added a little awkwardly as she remained silent, 'Emily is small enough to have slept comfortably upon the sofa in the dressing room.'

'Emily.' She sat up straighter. 'Where is she?'

'Enjoying a large breakfast with my old nurse in the kitchen. Then my coachman has promised her a tour of the stables so she might decide which pony she wishes to ride. I assure you she is quite safe.'

'Thank you,' she said. 'It is very kind of you.'

'The pleasure is mine. She is a delightful child.'

'Yes, she is,' she agreed, at the same moment feeling a guilty sense of relief that, just for once, she was free of the responsibility of looking after her.

'I trust you slept well,' he said as another silence stretched between them.

'Yes. Did you?' she replied, thinking how odd it was that they were conversing like polite acquaintances at the breakfast table when she was sitting in his bed, with less than a foot between them, wearing nothing but his shirt.

'No,' he confessed. He had been awake most of the night, struggling between the dictates of his conscience, duty and desire.

'Was it because of us—?' she said apologetically. 'If I had the bed and Emily the sofa, where did you sleep?'

'Next to you after half the night in a chair,' he confessed. 'On top of the covers and fully dressed but for my coat and boots,' he added drily as he heard her slight catch of breath. 'And, in case you are wondering, it was my housekeeper who attended to your clothes.'

'I see. Thank you,' she said stiffly. 'I hope you were not made too uncomfortable upon our account.'

'Uncomfortable!' He made a sound that was somewhere between a laugh and a sigh of relief. 'Is that all you have to say upon discovering you have spent a night in my bed?'

'What is there to say? Emily and I had nowhere else to go last night, and I can state from experience that your bed is infinitely preferable to the street.'

'The street?' He looked at her in horror.

She gave the smallest of shrugs. 'I learnt long ago

that beggars cannot be choosers. Sometimes when my
father had lost heavily at the tables we would leave our
lodgings in the middle of the night and spend the rest
of it beneath a bridge arch or in a doorway—anywhere
that offered shelter.'

'Did that happen often?' he said slowly, struggling to
envisage her in such a situation.

'Often enough for me to discover that hysterics do
nothing to improve a situation,' she said, staring down
at the quilted silk coverlet again, glad of the soft wings
of her hair which had escaped the braid and fell forward
to curtain her face from his gaze. She could bear most
things, but not his pity.

'I still cannot understand why you did not write to
me,' he said heavily as he looked at her. 'You cannot
think I should have abandoned you to such a life—all
you had to do was pick up a pen—'

'Would you have written to me, begging for my
assistance, if our situations had been reversed?' She
lifted her head abruptly, and regarded him steadily.
'Would you? I doubt it. Not if I had been the one to
send you such a note—if you had read of my engagement to Hetherington in a paper scarcely a week after
I had told you I loved you and only you!'

'No,' he said after another heavy silence. 'I suppose
not. But surely there was someone...your godmother—'

'My father had exhausted the patience of his friends
and family within a year of my mother's death,' she
said without rancour. 'And as for my godmother, we
quarrelled shortly after you left Scotland.'

'Over what?'

'Nothing of importance.'

'It was over me, wasn't it?' he rasped as she looked away from him suddenly. 'Tell me!'

She sighed. 'There was talk after you left so suddenly. People said that I had tried to entrap you. Then my mother died and my father turned to drink and the tables for comfort. Within a few months his business and our properties had to be sold, so there was no question of my coming out. It was then that Hetherington made an offer for my hand. My godmother urged me very strongly to accept because, with no fortune left to inherit and the damage to my reputation, she did not think I should ever receive a better offer. She said if I refused him, she would have no more to do with me or my family.'

'And you refused him.' He gave a stifled laugh. 'Was that not very foolish in your *particular* circumstances?'

'Very,' she replied tersely, knowing he was thinking of Emily. It was stupid not to tell him that Emily was not her child, stupid to want him to know without being told that she could never have gone so quickly, so easily into another man's arms after he had left. But she could not help it. If she told him the truth and he still did not believe her—she did not think she could bear that, not at this moment.

'Then why didn't you marry him?' he asked a little harshly. 'Was it—was it because of Emily's father?'

'Emily's father?' She gave a jagged laugh. 'No. It had nothing to do with him. I did not marry Hetherington because I did not love him. And I was too young to realise that, while you can live without love, you cannot live without shelter and food upon the table.'

'Love always was all to you,' he said only half-audibly.

'No.' She gave him a bleak, fleeting glance. 'Not love, Alex—*you*. You were all to me then—all I wanted—'

'And now?' he cut her off harshly, almost angrily. 'What do you want now, Lallie?'

'Now?' For a moment she stared at him, and then she sighed. 'What does it matter? You have your life, and I have mine. Our paths are not likely to cross again. Now, perhaps you will leave me to dress—'

'Why? You cannot mean to go back to that slum!'

'I have to get my things, few as they are. If Mrs Crouch has not pawned them already—'

'You are not going back there,' he rapped out. 'You're staying here.'

'Here?' She shook her head. 'I cannot stay indefinitely in your house and you know it.'

'No,' he said after a momentary pause. 'Yesterday, before I came to find you, I took the liberty of leasing a house. It is not large but it faces onto the Regent's Park. I think you will be comfortable there.'

'A house—' She gave a ragged laugh as she lifted her head to look at him. 'Alex—I cannot afford a room in a lodging-house, let alone to run a house!'

'You must consider yourself my guest.'

'Your guest?' Her brows lifted. 'I do not think that is the word that others will use to describe me. And how exactly am I to repay you for such hospitality?'

His hesitation gave her the answer to her question.

'I see,' she said acidly. 'You would expect me to become your mistress.'

'Not if you do not wish it,' he said through clenched teeth. 'I simply want you to be safe and not so desperate that you are at the mercy of men like Robson or reduced to touting for custom in the Row.'

'How very considerate of you,' she said sharply, wondering why it still hurt her so much that he seemed to think that her foray into the Row was far from her first such experience. 'But on the whole, I think I should rather not be a pensioner upon your charity—'

'Lallie,' he groaned, 'I am trying to help you—make some amends for the hurt I did you five years ago.'

'You saved my life yesterday in the Park,' she said with a half-laugh, 'and rescued me from Robson—I think that more than makes amends.'

'I don't,' he said firmly. 'So, will you take the house? Please? Surely we can be friends, if nothing else—?'

'Friends—?' She gave a ragged laugh. 'The son of an Earl and a penniless demi-rep? And for how long may I expect this friendship to last? How long before I receive another cold little note informing me that you will not be calling again? Upon your wedding day, perhaps?'

'No!' he said in grating tones as he swept back his hair from his forehead. 'I'm sorry about that damned note. At the time I thought a clean cut would be kindest. I told myself you were young, that it would allow you to forget me and make a good match—'

'Well, you were wrong!' The words burst from her lips and she almost hit him. 'It might have been that easy for you, but not for me!'

'Giving you up was not easy,' he replied harshly. 'It was the hardest thing I have ever done.'

'Then why did you?' The anger, and the question she had so wanted an answer to, spilled out before she could stop it. 'Why did you leave me for her?'

'Because I loved you!'

'Because you loved me?' Her silver gaze flashed up
to his face and she laughed derisively. 'Surely you mean
because you loved her title and wealth!'

'I have never loved anything about Cressida,' he said
rawly. 'And I never, ever wished to marry her! How
could I when every word she uttered, every gesture she
made only served to remind me that she was not you.'

'Then why—?' she said helplessly, her anger fading
into confusion because she knew suddenly that he was
telling her the truth. It had been no easier for him than
for her. 'I don't understand, I never did understand.'

'Because my foolish, drunken brother lost heavily at
the tables with the result that our estates had ended up
mortgaged to Lord Penwyrth. And then my brother
seduced Cressida Penwyrth—or she him, I have never
been certain which—and she told her father. Not
unnaturally, her father went to see mine, threatening
to foreclose on the mortgages—but it was decided that
if I made an honest woman of Cressida, then there
would be no foreclosure. The betrothal was announced
by them, without my knowledge, on the very day I
arrived in London, intending to ask my father's permission to marry you.'

'But why did you have to make amends?' she said,
frowning as she struggled to take in what he had told
her. 'Why you? Why couldn't you brother marry her?'

'Because he was already married to Cressida's elder
sister, which should give you some idea of my elder
brother's character and Cressida's,' he said heavily. 'At
first I was determined not to honour the betrothal and
to marry you. Then my father pointed out that I should
be embroiled in a breach-of-promise suit, your name

would be dragged through the mire of scandal, Penwyrth would foreclose upon the estate and I should be required to resign from my cavalry regiment. Even if I had been lucky enough to pick up a commission in one of the less fashionable regiments, how could I ask you, an heiress who had never lacked for anything in her life, to marry me and live upon an officer's pay that would not even keep one charger, let alone a family?'

'I should not have cared as long as I was with you,' she said, half to herself. 'And if you had told me, I could have asked my father to help us—'

'I did speak to your father,' he said flatly. 'It was he who finally convinced me that you would be much happier married to the respectable Mr Hetherington, rather than the impecunious son of a nobleman who could bring you nothing but disapproving relatives, debts, scandal and probably grief when I was foolish enough to stop a French musket ball. It was after seeing him, that I realised he was right—if I loved you, I must give you up. And I did love you, Lallie. Believe *that*, if nothing else.'

There was a raw note in his voice, almost a plea as he held her gaze with his blue eyes.

He had loved her. He had given her up because he loved her. She dropped her gaze, staring down at the swirling pattern on the bronze brocade, the breath seeming to stop in her lungs. He had loved her. It changed everything—and nothing. The past had nothing to do with now.

'You do believe me?' he asked as she remained silent.

'I don't know,' she replied wearily without looking at him, concentrating upon tracing the pattern on the brocade with her fingertips as if her life depended upon it.

'Then let me prove it to you,' he sighed, sweeping back a stray lock of hair from his forehead in a gesture that was so familiar to her, that five years seemed nothing. 'Take the house, let me take care of you and the child—'

'No,' she said grittily. 'It would not work, Alex. Not when you are about to marry Cressida Penwyrth,' she added in an undertone.

'No. I am not,' he said succinctly. 'As I was about to explain to you in the Park, she became betrothed to Harry Rutherstone after the news of my death was posted. I no longer have any obligation to her.'

Her fingers stilled on the coverlet and her silver gaze flashed up to his face.

'You aren't going to marry her?' she found herself saying stupidly. 'Not ever. . .?'

'Never.' A fleeting smile touched the corners of his mouth as he saw the relief light up her face. 'So why not take the house, Lallie? Would being beholden to me be so terrible that you would prefer to go back to the life you are living? Or getting some ghastly place where you would be at the beck and call of spoiled brats and cantankerous old dowagers? At least with me you would be safe.'

Safe. She almost laughed as she stared at him. Oh yes, she would be safe! Protected from everything but falling in love with him all over again. Not that there was any danger of that, was there? It was not as if she were still the romantic fool of eighteen who dreamed of marrying him and living happily ever after. He might not be going to marry Cressida Penwyrth. But sooner or later he would marry someone. Someone eligible, with an impeccable pedigree, a large dowry and vouchers for Almack's—

'Please, Lallie,' he said softly as he watched her lips begin to shape a refusal. 'In a month or so I will have to go back to the war. I might—we might never see each other again.'

That was not fair, she thought as she looked away. Not fair at all to remind her that he might be killed, that if she walked away from him now, she might never see him again, ever... Dear God, why did that thought still freeze her to the marrow?

'Would a month of my company be so hard to bear?' he said drily as he read her stricken expression.

'There's only one way to find out,' she said wearily. 'I'll take the house, Alex. Emily and I have nowhere else to go.'

'I see.' He stared at her, wondering why he felt such an acute sense of disappointment. It was not as if he were still in love with her. He had loved a generous, impulsive, passionate girl, not this cynical, mercenary stranger. 'Any port in a storm? Is that it, Lallie?'

'Why else?' She shrugged, her face carefully expressionless as she answered him. 'What would you have me say? That I still love you?'

CHAPTER SEVEN

HER question seemed to hang and echo in a silence that threatened to last forever. Yet somehow, as the silence between them lengthened, it lost its scathing edge.

'No, of course not,' he said at last. 'After five years it would be ridiculous for me to expect anything of the kind.'

'Quite ridiculous,' she agreed, the words as clipped and cold as the disappointment which flooded through her. He could not have told her more clearly that a business arrangement was all he wished for, his money in exchange for his pleasure.

'Yes. . .' he said slowly, then, as he caught and held her gaze for a moment before she dropped her lashes abruptly onto her cheeks, the colour drained suddenly from his face. He ran a hand over his unshaven face, feeling utterly shaken.

After an almost sleepless night he had reconciled himself to the fact that there could be no going back to what had been. He had told himself she was a stranger now, a demi-rep who was prepared to sell herself for money, and one who no doubt would be grateful of the opportunity he was going to offer her. But now, for a moment, just for a moment, he had glimpsed something in her face and eyes that had sent doubt stabbing through him like a blade. Supposing she had agreed only because she did still care for him. . .?

He dragged in a breath. What was wrong with him? He was beginning to think like some romantic addle-pated flat! He had to tell her about Corton and the plans—the sooner the better—before the stupid impossible hope that he had been nursing since he had first seen her at his sister's house sprang up in his mind again. He must be going mad, he told himself, to even think that the past could be recaptured, let alone think of any kind of future.

'Lallie,' he began crisply, 'there is something I must make clear.'

'What?'

'This arrangement of ours. . .' The words dried on his lips as she lifted great grey eyes, swimming with unshed, unexpected tears, to his face.

'Yes?' She waited for him to put into words what she already knew. Whatever had happened in the past, there was no room for sentiment in their new relationship and no promises of permanence.

He stared at her helplessly. Sitting in his bed, her slight form swamped by his shirt, she looked so vulnerable, so unlike a demi-rep, so unlike the laughing, impulsive girl he had loved five years ago, that his heart twisted beneath his ribs. He wanted to reach out, sweep back the silver-gilt hair that tumbled about her fragile face, kiss away the fear and hurt that was written in her eyes.

'I—' he began again, and stopped as he saw her swallow hard and bite down on her soft lower lip. He could not tell her about Corton and the plans, not now, not yet. Not when she was looking at him like that, and he found himself overwhelmed with new tenderness for her. 'You are sure it is what you want? If you have changed your mind—would rather I found you a position somewhere—?'

She shook her head, not trusting herself to speak.

'You are still tired,' he said softly. 'We will talk about this later. You had better get some more rest. I've asked for your breakfast to be sent up and hot water for your bath.'

'Thank you, you are very kind.' She swallowed back her tears. Breakfast in bed instead of a trip to the market to bargain for a burnt loaf and bruised fruit and half-rotten vegetables; a hot bath instead of an icy strip wash with cold water from a cracked jug and basin—she could hardly believe she was not dreaming—or that she had hesitated at all about accepting his protection.

'It is nothing,' he said brusquely as guilt sliced through him again. 'I thought if you felt strong enough this afternoon, I should have my housekeeper send for a dressmaker. You will need clothes. You can hardly go about in a habit all the time.'

'I suppose not,' she said. 'I will not need a great deal.'

'You will,' he said firmly. 'I mean to take you everywhere—and you must be sure to order for Emily as well.'

'I do not like the thought of your spending a great deal of money on me,' she said, frowning. 'It does not seem right.'

'Can it be wrong for old friends to help one another?' he queried more gently. 'If our situations had been reversed five years ago, would you not have done the same for me?'

'I doubt you would have let me,' she said wryly as

she traced the pattern on the bronze coverlet with her fingertips.

'Do you think pride would have kept me out of your bed, if I had been given the opportunity for any reason?' He grinned suddenly, the wicked slanting grin she remembered all too well.

'No.' She laughed, slipping momentarily back into their old familiarity as their gazes met and held. 'As I remember, it took all my godmother's time and determination to keep you out of it—' She stopped as he stared at her with sudden intentness. 'What is it?'

'Nothing. It is just the first time I have seen you smile and laugh as you used to...' he said after a moment. 'There is nothing I want more than to see you happy again.'

'Nothing?' She gave a jagged half-laugh as she dropped her gaze to the coverlet again and began to pleat the silk between her fingers.

'Well, perhaps not quite nothing.' He exhaled, his eyes suddenly very dark as he studied her downturned face. 'And what do you want of me, Lallie? Name your price. Within reason you may have anything you desire.'

What I want is for it to be five years ago. I want you to love me as you used to—I want you to want me for your wife. That was what she wanted, she thought, as she let her gaze come back to his face. She wanted to be loved by him, be able to see him, hear him, touch him...for the rest of her life. That was impossible now. She knew that. But she could have him for a little while, a month. And that was better than never...

'Lallie?' he prompted her softly.

'I want—I wish we could begin again.' Her voice was no more than a whisper. 'At the beginning.'

For a moment he was transfixed, staring at her with an expression she could not read. And then he exhaled slowly and reached out to still her hand.

'The beginning,' he said quietly, 'was when your shawl caught on a rosebush—'

'And you kissed me—' Her voice shook a little and she could not look at him as he began to stroke her hand with his fingertip, very gently, as if she were made of glass.

'Yes. . .' He sighed as very slowly he leant forward and lifted his hand to cup her chin, tilting her face up so that she had to look at him. 'I kissed you, like this. . .'

She shut her eyes. His lips were hard, dry and warm as they brushed over her mouth, once, twice and then, as she made a tiny incoherent sound of protest, stayed.

With a ragged sigh she lifted her hands to his shoulders as his arms wrapped around her. Her fingers curled into his hard, lean flesh, holding him to her, inviting the deepening of his kiss as her body melted in its old, instant response to his mouth, his hands. This had not changed. This would never change, and nothing else seemed to matter at this moment. He might not love her any more, but while he was holding her she felt loved, and that was better than nothing.

He turned with her in his arms, drawing her down with him into the soft mound of feather pillows, kissing her, caressing her with almost frantic urgency until she was lost in a fiery darkness, with no thought but to give him kiss for kiss, touch for touch.

She did not register the polite tap on the door until he lifted his head from hers and muttered something incomprehensible and, she was sure, quite impolite.

'That will be your breakfast and the first of a succession of housemaids bearing hot water, no doubt,' he said wryly as she opened dazed grey eyes to look at him, and then sat bolt upright at the second tap.

'Go away! Quickly!' she said, pushing him off the bed. 'Hide in the dressing room or something—there is another door into the corridor, is there not?'

He straightened and watched her with speculative eyes as she straightened the neck of her shirt, smoothed the bedclothes.

'Go on,' she pleaded as there was another tap upon the door. 'Please!'

'You are blushing,' he said coolly, 'Didn't anyone tell you demi-reps don't blush? Not even when caught with their lovers in the bedchamber.'

'No,' she snapped, her eyes flashing up to his face. 'Now please leave—'

He laughed suddenly. 'Very well, I have some appointments, but I shall be at home for dinner. Will you dine with me?'

'Anything you like, if you will just go,' she hissed, as the door handle began to turn.

With a grin he moved discreetly into the dressing-room, and drew its door shut a moment before the bedroom door opened to reveal a maid, bearing a large butler's tray loaded with silver covers.

Lallie sank back against her pillows, her face burning and her heart pounding. She was never going to make a demi-rep, she thought bleakly, not in a thousand years. She still cared far too much about what people thought of her.

* * *

Miss Roden, the dressmaker, was a small grey-haired woman, in a dark grey dress, who arrived with a plethora of boxes and bags, the contents of which soon covered almost every available piece of furniture in Alex's bedchamber.

There were chemises, spencers, petticoats, pelisses, nearly all of which, to Lallie's surprise, appeared to be quite finished. Dressmakers did not usually carry such a stock.

'A trousseau,' Miss Roden confided in her low whis-pery voice. 'Weeks of work and then unfortunately it was not required. The young lady in question eloped—' her voice dropped still lower upon the word 'eloped' '—with another, her family have disowned her and said the clothes were not required. Perhaps you would like to try the pink silk, Miss Ross—'

Miss Roden proffered a petticoat of palest pink silk with an overdress of delicate lace.

Lallie slipped on the petticoat first. It was a near perfect fit, though not to Miss Roden's eyes.

'Such a misfortune, to lose your boxes in such a way, and having travelled so far, too,' she tutted as she fluttered about Lallie, pinning and tweaking at the silk and lace. 'You cannot trust anyone these days.'

'No,' Lallie agreed vaguely. Presumably Alex's housekeeper had told Miss Roden that their boxes had been stolen while travelling to spare her any embarrassment.

'Much better...' Miss 'Roden gave a little sigh of satisfaction as she deftly placed the last pin in the lace. 'I thought you were much of a size with the unfortunate young lady—but you are a little more delicately made. Now, do you think you could try the white spencer and then the primrose muslin? If I pin them, I understand from the housekeeper that she is skilled enough with her needle to make the adjustments while we try on the rest. Then at least you will have something to wear while the others are adjusted.'

Miss Roden was as good as her word. By the end of the afternoon Lallie found herself in possession of chemises, the pink silk petticoat, the lace gown, the yellow muslin, a lavender muslin and the white spencer, a plum silk wrapping-robe and numerous other sundry items that Miss Roden had had the foresight to bring with her upon hearing of the theft of her boxes.

'I have a friend who is a stocking maker,' she whispered to Lallie as she bought out several paper-wrapped packets of silk stockings. 'You will not find better in all London. She supplies Lady Jersey. I also took the liberty of asking for some ribbons to be delivered; I thought you might need something with which to dress your hair. I hope you do not think I have been too presumptuous. I know Lady Carteret always appreciates having ribbons to match her gowns.'

'And so do I.' Lallie smiled at her and wondered what Isabelle Carteret would say if she knew that her brother had hired her dressmaker to garb his mistress. She was beginning to realise that Miss Roden was probably one of the most sought-after dressmakers in the capital, and probably one of the most expensive. But as she surveyed her reflection and saw how the simple elegance of Miss Roden's primrose muslin enhanced her slight curves, she found that the knowledge did not disturb her quite as much as it ought.

'Now,' said the indefatigable Miss Roden, opening yet another box, 'this was to have been for the Countess of Essex's youngest, but she was in no hurry for it and I can soon make another.' She held up a small confection of white silk and lace with a wide blue ribbon sash around the high waist. 'Do you think your sister will like it? There is a velvet spencer to go over it as well.'

'I think she will like it a great deal,' Lallie said, thinking that she was probably never going to be able to prise it off Emily's back once she had it on.

Alex's servants were awesomely efficient, Lallie thought as she was ushered into the drawing-room early that evening by the butler. All traces of dust and dust sheets had vanished in the space of an afternoon.

The room was luxurious and warm, despite its elegantly high ceilings. There was a rich blue and red turkey carpet upon the floor, the four tall sash windows were draped in blue damask trimmed with gold tassels and fringes, and the walls were also a deep blue, setting off the elaborately carved and gilded frames of the many pictures which hung upon them. She sat down on a golden silk sofa beside the Adam fireplace, plumped a blue and gold cushion and then got up again. She was too nervous about the prospect of seeing Alex again to sit still. She paced about, looking at the pictures without really seeing them, until she came to one of Mars embracing Venus while Cupid looked on. She looked away hastily, something tightening in the pit of her stomach as she remembered how he had kissed her that morning, and her own response. And then, glimpsing her own reflection in a window, she started for a moment, hardly recognising herself in the elegant column of pink silk and lace with its low neck and scrap of a sleeve which just clung to her shoulder. Her hair did not do the gown justice, she thought, as she put up a hand to tuck a wisp into the coronet of braids. But it was the best she could do by herself; she had not liked to impose further upon Alex's servants. They had enough to do in opening the house.

She went back to the sofa and sat down again, picking up a book from a small circular table beside it. It was some treatise on military tactics and she went to put it back down again, but her hands stilled in mid air as she heard the door open. Then she exhaled the breath that she had held as she saw that it was Emily, resplendent in her new gown, her hair washed and brushed into shining curls, with Mrs Brown smiling behind her.

'She just wanted to say good night, miss,' Mrs Brown, said. 'I'll wait for her in the hall.'

Emily flung herself forward to be hugged, careless of damage either to her gown or Lallie's.

'Do you know how many rooms this house has?' she asked excitedly as she settled herself beside Lallie on the sofa.

'No,' Lallie said truthfully. 'I have no idea.'

'It's got more than a palace!' Emily said. 'Well, at least more than thirty. I lost count after that. I got lost as well, but Mrs Brown found me almost at once. And there are dozens of horses and a chestnut pony which is just right for me—the coachman said so. And there is a piano and a ballroom with thousands of mirrors, Mrs Brown let me dance in it in my new dress.'

She chattered on excitedly in a similar vein for the next ten minutes.

'Emmy,' Lallie said gently when the little girl paused

for breath, 'you do know we are not going to live here for ever, only for a day or two.'

'I know that, Major Haldane told me this morning,' Emily said disdainfully. 'But I am allowed to visit whenever I wish, so long as you agree,' she added as Lallie's brows lifted. 'You will let me, won't you?'

'I expect so.' Lallie sighed, her attention so focused on Emily that she did not hear the door open, or see the relief on the face of the man that stood there at finding them both still safe under his roof.

'Good.' Emily smiled and got on to her feet and executed a pirouette of joy. 'Do you think I look like a princess? Mrs Brown says I do.'

'I think you both look like princesses.'

Lallie started, the colour leaving her face. 'Major Haldane, I did not hear you come in.'

'I know.' He smiled at her, and she felt her insides dissolve suddenly. Dressed in a severe black coat and breeches with the finest, snowiest of cravats, he was impossibly handsome. And she felt an odd stab of envy that Emily could run to him, hold up her arms to be picked up and spun around without the slightest reservation. And then another pang as she thought how at ease he was with children and how she had once daydreamed about the children they would have.

'I think Lallie is too old to be a princess,' Emily announced, breathless from laughing after he had finally put her down. 'She is almost as old as you.'

'Not quite,' he laughed. 'Now off to bed, your highness, or I will not take you riding tomorrow.'

'Goodnight.' Emily ran back to Lallie, kissed her, bobbed a curtsy to Alex, which had more than a little defiance in it, and then waited pointedly for him to open the door for her.

'I always wondered what you were like as a child,' he grinned as he shut the door behind Emily and turned back to Lallie. 'Now I think I know.'

'I am sure I was more polite,' she said ruefully, her heart beginning to race beneath her ribs as he came to halt in front of her.

'Possibly, but I rather think I prefer Emily's greeting to yours,' he drawled, his mouth curving. 'If you did not look so utterly beautiful in that gown, I should exact a penance for that "Major Haldane"—' He broke off as his gaze, which had travelled downwards from her almost severely arranged hair, reached her stockinged feet. 'Shoes—I forgot about shoes,' he sighed.

'I did not think riding boots are quite the thing for the drawing room,' she explained, blushing slightly.

'That would depend upon what else you were or were not wearing,' he said blandly.

She looked at him blankly for a moment and then as understanding dawned, blushed.

'You are really going to have to do something about that blush,' he mocked her gently as he reached down and caught her hands. 'Whenever I see it, it makes me want to kiss you.'

'Does it?' she stammered slightly as he drew her to his feet.

'You are trembling,' he said, frowning slightly as he looked down into her face. 'Are you afraid of me?'

'No.' She shook her head.

'Good. So, now are you going to greet me properly?' he murmured softly as he put his hands on her waist and drew her closer in a rustle of silk.

She went on tiptoe and kissed him lightly, shyly, upon his cheek, her heart pounding as if she had just run a mile.

'Properly, I said,' he growled and kissed her back. A long lingering kiss that made her forget everything but the wonder of being in his arms again, of having him close enough to touch, to kiss after so long.

'I hardly think that would pass as proper,' she said raggedly when the ringing of the dinner bell finally penetrated their mutual absorption in each other.

'For a mistress you still have a remarkably well-developed sense of convention,' he laughed softly as he released her and offered her his arm. 'It needs curbing—but I suppose that can wait until after dinner.'

She swallowed, her mouth and throat dry. She should tell him, explain that so far as being a mistress went, she lacked some rather essential experience. But she could not find the words with which to begin such a subject.

The dining-room was on a scale and magnificence to equal the drawing-room. She gave a slight gasp of surprise as she looked along a polished mahogany table which was at least twenty feet in length. At the far end, in front of the fireplace, two places of the finest silver and crystal were laid opposite each other.

'I had not expected to be dining in such state,' she said as he led her down the room.

He smiled as he pulled out her chair for her. 'It's hardly state. I told the servants we would serve ourselves from the sideboard. I don't want to share tonight with anyone but you.'

She gave a small sigh of relief. She was nervous

enough about this evening, without having to contend with the curious, hastily hidden glances of his servants.

'Champagne?' he asked softly, as he took a bottle from the sideboard.

She nodded. She could feel herself shaking again inside, a shaking that intensified as he came around to stand behind her. As he poured the sparkling wine into her glass, so close that if she moved a fraction— She exhaled as he moved away, not sure if she were glad or sorry.

He sat down opposite, filled his glass and lifted it. 'Shall we drink to us, Lallie, and the future?'

'No, not the future.' She shook her head. She did not dare let herself think ahead to when he would have to go back to Spain, or further still to the day when he might marry.

'Tonight, then?' he asked softly, his gaze catching and holding hers.

'Tonight.' She lifted her glass with a slightly unsteady hand and touched it to his, knowing that she had just accepted that they would become lovers, that it had been inevitable since that morning, perhaps since the day he had coming riding up her godmother's drive.

The dinner was light, delicious, but she barely registered what she ate. She was too aware of him—too aware of the blueness of his eyes as his gaze followed her every movement; too aware of the mobility of his mouth as he talked, the strength and deftness of his long, elegant fingers as he peeled an apple for her at the end of the meal.

And then he glanced up, caught her gaze fixed upon his hands. He dropped the apple and the paring knife abruptly on to the blue and gold plate with a clatter and got to his feet.

She stared down at the table as he came around and gently pulled back her chair.

She swayed slightly as she stood up; the crimson walls of the dining-room seemed to tilt, the floor to become spongy beneath her feet.

'I am not used to champagne,' she stammered and then winced as he caught her arm to steady her.

'I'm sorry,' he apologised, transferring his hand to the small of her back. 'How is the elbow? Perhaps we should have Sir John look at it again?'

'It is nothing which a little arnica will not mend,' she said as his arm curled about her waist and she glanced up at him.

'Arnica?' His mouth curved in a way that sent a prickle along her spine. 'I can think of a better cure for bruises. But perhaps you don't remember my remedy?'

Forgotten. If she had, looking up into his craggy, brown face with its mocking blue eyes and wide, half laughing mouth would have brought it all back a thousandfold.

'Forgotten what?' There was the slightest of betraying catches in her voice. She remembered all too well.

'That day at Rattray Head when we picnicked with the Russells and watched the fleet sail along the horizon.' His voice was like velvet now, stroking down her spine—or was it his hand? She could hardly tell as her body seemed to melt and pool into a growing heat.

'You lost your hat—'

'Did I?' Her voice was barely a whisper.

'Yes. A breeze came scudding in from the sea and sent your straw hat cartwheeling into the dunes. You and I chased after it, you tripped at the top of a dune, I tried to save you and we both fell, and your arms and shoulders had a dozen tiny bruises where we had rolled over the pebbles and shells —'

'Yes, yes—I remember,' she said thickly as her body threw up the image of his lips, dry and hot as the blazing July sun against her skin, kissing each tiny mark on her white skin. Kissing her throat, her shoulders and—shockingly—her breasts. Oh, dear heaven! Remembered pleasure came in an exquisitely painful rush, making her breasts achingly tight and heavy beneath the pink silk, and her legs hopelessly weak.

'Come here. . .' He caught her as she swayed again, and then picked her up as if she were no more weight than Emily and carried her upstairs.

After he set her down on his bed and she gazed up at him, looking so young, so uncertain, he found doubt came flooding back. Yesterday it had all seemed so simple. She had needed money and protection, he needed someone to get close to Corton and get the plans and, if they enjoyed some mutual pleasure, well, that was a bonus for them both. . .but now as he stared down at her he knew he had been fooling himself. It was never going to be that simple between them. He turned away from the bed abruptly and walked over to the window. Pushing aside the curtain, he stared out into the deserted and dusky street. He wanted her so much it hurt, but how could he make love to her and then ask her to give herself to another man for money? Whatever she had become, he was not sure he could do that, not even if it meant handing Spain to Bonaparte upon a golden platter.

Lallie stared at his back. She did not know what was

wrong, she only knew instinctively that if he did not make love to her now, he never would. . .and that she wanted him for her first lover, perhaps her only lover.

Slowly, quietly, she got off the bed. Standing in the centre of the candle-lit room, she began to undo the three buttons which held the bodice of the lace overgrown in place. In a matter of seconds it had drifted to her feet in a soft light cloud. The silk petticoat was a little more difficult. She had to reach behind her head. But at last it was loosened and she was able to slide it off her shoulders and let it float downwards in a rustle of silk.

The sound made him turn. He stood transfixed, staring at her as she stood in the candle-light naked but for her stockings. She was all ivory, gold and rose.

'Lallie?' he said in a choked voice as his gaze travelled over her. 'What are you doing?'

'Keeping to my part of the bargain,' she said huskily, thinking that if he did not come and take her in his arms she would die of humiliation. 'You do still want me, don't you?'

'Want you!' He stared at her helplessly. Demi-rep she might have become, but this was the Lallie he remembered. As reckless, as impulsive, passionate and even more bewitching than she had been at eighteen, offering him everything with her eyes, her mouth. . .her heart. . .

Dear heaven! How could he have been so blind for so long? How could he have failed to see through her anger, her coldness, her pride, until this moment?

'You do want me?' The doubt in her eyes made his heart twist beneath his ribs.

And then he was across the room and she was in his

arms. What the devil, he thought as he picked her up and carried her to the bed. Conscience could wait until the morning. In a month he would be back in that hellish war, in two he could be dead of a wound or the fevers that killed more men on both sides than were lost in any battle. Why not make love to her and lay the ghost of the girl he had loved five years before? he thought with sudden bitter humour.

What had she done? Lallie wondered, as she lay on the silky coverlet and listened to him tear off his clothes with what sounded like a complete disregard for buttons and seams. What had she done? She tensed as she felt his weight upon the bed. Then there was nothing. Just silence. She opened her eyes. He was lying upon his side, leaning upon one elbow, staring at her with an intentness she found almost frightening. Her hands moved instinctively in the age-old female gesture of modesty to cover her breasts, the gold down between her thighs.

'Don't—' He stopped her gently, putting her hands aside. 'I have dreamed of seeing you for so long and you are so beautiful. . .'

And so are you, she wanted to say as she stared back. She had seen him stripped to the waist before when there had been a fire in one of her godmother's barns and he had helped the hands put it out. But she had never seen him utterly naked, never realised how different his body was from her own female softness and curves. He was all muscle and sinew and long rangy lines like a thoroughbred. And she wanted to touch, but did not quite dare.

She gasped as his hands began to trail over her, melting away her fear, creating a new tension in her body. From shoulder to waist, waist to hip, hip to thigh. They were brown, weathered, deliciously rough against the satin smoothness of her skin. She watched with a kind of fascination and then, unable to bear the distance between them, she reached out to him, stabbing her fingers into his thick dark hair.

She gasped as she felt his skin, burning with heat against her own, the silky satiny unfamiliar hardness of him against her stomach. And then he kissed her. Kissed her tenderly, gently, on her mouth, her eyelids, her throat, while his hands continued their devastating exploration, tracing her curves from shoulder to the indent of her waist. Stroking her, teasing her with his hands and mouth until she was utterly pliant in his hands and the tension growing in her had nothing to do with fear, only desire.

She dragged in a breath as he cupped her small breasts in his hands, remembering, anticipating the sweet, almost painfully exquisite pleasure of the night in her godmother's garden. Oh, why was he teasing her like this, circling, stroking but never quite touching the rock-like tips of her breasts until she thought she would scream with frustration?

She moaned, pushing against him impatiently, wantonly.

'No. . .' He caught her wrists, holding her a little distance from him. 'Not yet. I want this to last forever — so that you forget that there has ever been anyone but me.'

'There has been no one like you.'

'Nor for me,' he groaned. 'Never.'

'No, you don't understand —' She gasped as he bent his head with shocking suddenness to her breast, biting softly, then sucking until she was writhing, helpless, her whole body falling and dissolving into some fiery inner darkness. She cried out a protest as he suddenly lifted his head.

'Please. . .' she begged him incoherently, her hand sliding down from his chest, to the flat plane of his stomach and lower in sheer female instinct.

'Patience,' he laughed softly. 'Let me love you first. . .'

She lay back quiescent, shutting her eyes again and giving herself up to each touch of his lips against her burning skin as he moved down and down. Kissing her lips, her throat, her breasts and still further down over her stomach to the soft mound between her thighs.

She jerked away from him, utterly shocked at such unimaginable intimacy. But he held her hips, stilling her as his lips and tongue found what seemed to be the very centre of her. And then she was lost, totally lost, in wave after wave of exquisite pleasure, and instinctive need to have him inside her, a need that was so intense she could not bear it any longer.

'Alex—please. . .' she begged him, sliding her fingers into his thick dark hair and lifting his head, saying with her eyes what she could not put into words.

His answer was to bring his mouth back to her breasts, and then her lips as he moved over her, parting her legs with his.

She should tell him, she thought in sudden panic as she felt him begin to push into the moistness between her thighs. Tell him that Emily was not her child, that she had never done this before—

But it was too late, a brief moment of resistance, of tearing pain, and he was sheathed in her, and staring down at her, shock momentarily overriding the desire in his eyes.

'I am the first.' It was more of a horrified statement than a question.'Why didn't you say—I thought—?'

'You thought I had become a whore,' she said, her eyes filling with tears.

'No,' he groaned. 'Never that—I thought you must have had lovers. And the child—if you are not her mother—?'

'Not now—' she said helplessly. 'Just love me—please.'

'Oh, Lallie—' With a groan he began to move in her, gently, slowly, at first, as if he were suddenly afraid she would break. Too slowly for the explosion of heat that was building in her body.

'Please—' she begged him, the irises of her eyes dark and enormous in her flushed face as she stared up at him and pushed her body against his in age-old instinct. 'Please—'

And then with an oath he was thrusting into her savagely with all restraint gone and the pleasure seemed to pound her in waves, sweeping her closer and closer to some inner precipice.

'Alex—' she gasped out his name. He juddered uncontrollably and drove into her one last time and she went tumbling over that edge, feeling as though she was falling into a bottomless void of darkness and heat.

'Alex...' she said his name again, shakily, minutes or seconds later, she did not know which, she only knew that he was her anchor in this disintegrating, melting world.

'It's all right, my love.' Holding her tightly, he rolled onto his back, taking her with him, cradling her against his chest until their ragged breathing slowed and became even.

His love. At this moment she could let herself believe that he loved her as much now as he had before and it made her want to weep.

'I did not hurt you?' He was utterly tender, anxious, as he stroked her hair back from her face.

'No, no,' she said slowly, her lips against his heated skin which tasted salty. 'I just did not know that it would be like that—so overwhelming that you cease to be yourself—'

'No, you did not,' he said soberly as he reached down and dragged the brocade coverlet up over their heated bodies. 'Why didn't you tell me?'

'I don't know,' she said helplessly. 'I was just so angry that you could think that of me—and the way you assumed Emily was my child—and I wanted to hurt you back—make you jealous.'

'You succeeded,' he admitted wryly. 'The idea of you and anyone else—' He broke off. 'Emily?'

'She is my mother's child,' she said. 'It was a childbed fever, that is why she died. Emily is my sister.'

'Your sister...' He exhaled heavily. 'How could I have been so blind? She is the image of you.'

'Yes.'

'I am sorry,' he said, his face grim. 'The things I said to you—about Hetherington and Corton—' His voice died abruptly on the last name. He had not given a thought to the plans, the General or Corton from the moment he had touched her.

'It does not matter,' she said, letting her head fall against his chest again.

'It does.' He sighed as his hands began to caress her

again. 'I should have known you better than that. Lallie, there is something I have to tell you, something I should have explained before we made love—'

'If you are trying to tell me that you cannot marry me,' she interrupted him roughly, suddenly unable to bear to hear him say it, 'I know. We were ill matched enough before, but now—' she grimaced '—it would be impossible. I am not asking you for promises, Alex.'

His hands stilled on the curves of her back. Marriage. It had not crossed his mind since his first visit to her lodgings. 'That was not what I was about to say.'

She lifted her head to look at him, her grey eyes veiled as she struggled to hide a half-formed, fragile dream. 'Wasn't it?'

'No—no, I was going to say—' He stopped. He still could not bring himself to tell her about Corton. How could he when she had just given herself, her innocence to him, so generously, so completely? 'I was going to say that I love you. I have always loved you.'

The dream broke and died. But she did not care as he caught her face between his hands and brought her mouth down to his again. Nothing mattered if he loved her. Nothing. She would rather have this month of being loved by him, than a lifetime with anyone else.

He was a coward, Alex thought the following morning, as he got out of his carriage and glanced up at his house and saw her silhouetted against the window, still for a moment and then lifting her hand to wave to him. He should have told her about the General, Corton and Wellington and the plans before he had gone out that morning. But he hadn't been able to bring himself to destroy the happiness that had shone from her face.

No, it could wait for a day or two. Wait until he was sure she would understand how important the plans were.

He glanced up at the window again, and felt a twinge of disappointment as he saw that she had turned away. And then the door was flung open, and she was running down the white steps towards him, smiling and breathless, wearing nothing more than her plum silk wrapping-robe, not caring who saw her or what his servants thought.

This was the Lallie he remembered. Exuberant, reckless, passionate, brave and utterly indiscreet, he thought with a twist of his insides as he moved to catch her in his arms before she tripped upon the trailing hem of the wrapping-robe. And no better at hiding her love for him than she had ever been. A few days and she would do anything he asked. It had all worked exactly as he and the General had planned—except that she was an innocent who loved him, and that he'd rather die than ever let her know he had contemplated flaunting her as his mistress solely to make her irresistible to Corton.

There had to be another way of getting those plans back before Corton could sell them. There had to be. At this moment, as she smiled up at him, he'd have handed all the world to Bonaparte upon a gold platter if it meant she would never find out. Having her here, waiting for him, this was what he had dreamed of five years ago, and through all the hot dusty months in the sierras of Spain and freezing mud of the mountain passes—and he was not ready to give her up, not yet. And certainly not to Corton. Lallie and Corton. The thought was like a sabre thrust to his belly.

'What is it?' Her smile had faded as she felt his sudden stillness and saw the coldness in his eyes.

'Nothing,' he said as he made a sudden decision and kissed her lightly upon the mouth, before putting his arm about her waist and drawing her back up the steps. 'Nothing of any importance.'

CHAPTER EIGHT

'I THOUGHT Isabelle said the doctor had forbidden you to ride,' Alex said two days later as he helped his great aunt down from the mounting block in her stable yard.

'The man's an interfering dolt! And your sister not much better,' Lady Lucinda Ashton said disgustedly, as she gave her elderly grey an affectionate slap upon the neck. 'Stiff joints and old bones don't mean I've forgotten how to manage a horse. I've not fallen off in thirty years and I don't intend to start now. You,' she snapped to her hovering groom, 'make sure she is rubbed down properly, none of your airy-fairy dabbing!'

'Yes, m'lady,' the groom acquiesced hurriedly, taking the grey's reins and leading it into the stables.

'And who, may I ask, is that?' Lady Ashton said as her piercing blue gaze swept over the immaculate cobbled yard and settled upon Emily, who was hanging by her fingertips from a half-door in an effort to see the horse inside, the toes of her boots a good two inches above the ground.

'Miss Emily Ross,' Alex said slowly. 'I am giving her some instruction in the art of equitation.'

'Ross?' Lady Ashton's brows rose as her gaze came back to her great nephew. 'As in a certain Miss Ross whom I advised you not to marry?'

'Yes. She is her sister.'

'So she's not yours, then?' Lady Ashton said bluntly,

141

looking back at Emily as she ran across the yard to where her plump chestnut pony was tethered and kissed it upon its nose.

'No, though I would not mind if she were,' he said wryly. 'She is enchanting, don't you think?'

'Yes,' said his great aunt drily. 'Like her sister, I suppose—I gather she's beautiful enough to risk dying for. Really, Alex, what were you thinking of, to challenge Corton of all people? And for a demi-rep!' his great aunt finished with a snort of disgust.

'Ah. . .' Alex sighed. 'I was hoping that I might have been the first to break that news to you.'

'No doubt,' Lady Ashton said crisply, 'since I gather that you claimed this Miss Ross is my ward.'

'You have not denied it to anyone?'

'Of course not. I knew you must have had a reason for doing it,' Lady Ashton said. 'You should have asked me first, though.'

'I know and I apologise.' Alex exhaled with relief. 'I am afraid it was all I could think of at the time to salvage what I could of her reputation and protect her from the maliciousness of Corton and others.'

'Still so fond of her after five years?' Lady Ashton's brows lifted. 'Even when you know her to be a demi-rep—?'

'She is no demi-rep, you have my word on that.'

'My dear boy, your sister told me Miss Ross was touting in the Park for custom!'

'Yes, because she had no money to keep food in the child's mouth or a roof over their heads. Since her father's death six months ago she has been trying to find respectable employment—but to no avail.'

'That does not surprise me,' Lady Ashton sighed. 'A

beautiful young woman without family connections, with a child she claims is her sister—what sensible woman would invite that into her household?'

'The child is not hers,' Alex said tersely.

'Oh, really, Alex—how do you know that? You have been abroad for five years—'

'I know for a certainty the child is not hers,' he said tersely. 'And that is why I have come to beg your help.'

'Oh,' said Lady Ashton after a moment. 'So that's the way of it. You have finally seduced her and now feel you must make amends. What do you want me to do? Find her a position as a companion or some such thing?'

'I want you to introduce her to Society as your ward,' he said after a pause. 'And I was wondering if you would consider staying in a house I have taken for her, to act as her chaperon. As a favour to me.'

'Introduce her to Society! Chaperon!' Lady Ashton laughed and then, as she saw his expression, sobered. 'You mean it, don't you? Why—?' Then she shook her head in disbelief. 'You are not still thinking of marrying her? It would be an impossible match.'

'I know that,' he said heavily.

'Then why go to such lengths to lend her respectability? Unless—' His aunt gave him a swift look. 'Unless it is something to do with this business you are engaged upon for Arthur Wellesley?'

Alex started as if he had been stung. 'How the devil do you know about that? No one is supposed to know.'

'I don't know,' his aunt said, 'it was an inspired guess. It's not like Wellesley to let one of his best officers go home on leave for no reason, and it's obvious your wounds are well healed and not causing you' the slightest inconvenience. And then your sister said you were spending half your time in General Houghton's company, and you were engaged in some military business for Wellesley—'

'I see. . .' Alex exhaled with relief. 'I'd rather you did not mention that to anyone else, Aunt.'

'I am not a half-wit,' Lady Ashton snorted derisively.

'I have never thought that for a moment, which is why I am asking you for help,' he replied. 'So, will you do it?'

'I don't know. . .' Lady Ashton said doubtfully. 'I shall have to meet the girl—be certain she knows how to behave. I don't want to be a laughing stock, Alex, not even for you.'

She broke off as Isabelle Carteret appeared suddenly in the arch which led into the stable yard. 'I am popular this afternoon, I was not expecting your sister. She looks a trifle out of sorts.'

'I might have known I should find you here, Alex. I do not know how you have the nerve, after using Aunt Lucinda's name like that,' Isabelle said, addressing her brother as she reached them. 'And you, Aunt— surely you should be indoors resting, it is still so very hot.'

'You look decidedly hotter than me, my gal, perhaps you should take your own advice,' Lady Ashton replied tartly. 'Now, if you do not mind, your brother and I were having a private discussion.'

'About that woman, I suppose. As if that episode in the Park was not bad enough, do you know what he has done now? Only installed the hussy in his town house! My maid had it from his kitchenmaid at the market!'

'I'd have thought you had better things to do than listen to servants' gossip,' her brother retorted. 'And the situation is only temporary, I assure you, so perhaps you will do me the favour of discretion, Izzy.'

'That hardly makes matters better,' Isabelle snapped back at him. Then her face froze in horror. 'You have not asked Aunt Lucinda to take her in?'

'And if he has?' her aunt said frostily. 'What business is it of yours?'

'Oh, Alex!' Ignoring her great aunt, Isabelle rounded furiously on her brother. 'How could you? Aunt Lucinda is not well, she is too old to be embroiled in this—'

'Great God, Isabelle!' Lady Ashton snapped. 'I swear you will not be happy until you have me confined to my bed upon a diet of pap and water and have me die of boredom! I am quite well, except for the odd creaking joint, and I shall decide what I shall or shall not do!'

'You don't know what you are saying,' Isabelle replied. 'Stop grinning, Alex,' she said furiously and then lowered her voice fractionally. 'Her wits are going, she doesn't understand the implications—'

'I understand them perfectly,' her aunt informed her in a tone sufficiently acid to strip veneer. 'There is nothing wrong with either my ears or my wits! And no doubt it will please you to know that Miss Ross will not be staying here.'

'Thank God,' Isabelle said with feeling.

'But I shall be visiting her in the near future,' Lady Ashton added with a wicked grin. 'Once Alex has set her up in her own establishment.'

'You cannot mean it!' Isabelle's coral mouth dropped open.

'It should be preferable to visiting the family; at least Miss Ross will have no interest in hurrying me into my grave.'

'Just what do you mean by that?' Isabelle asked fiercely.

'That you do not think it would do much harm to Hetty's prospects if people think it will not be long before she inherits my fortune. Well, I'm right, aren't I?'

'That's ridiculous,' Isabelle protested. 'You know it is.' Her green eyes filled suddenly with tears. 'All I care for is your health and Alex's happiness—'

'I am quite happy,' her brother said blandly.

'Well, I am not! To set that woman up now! It's just not fair. I had such hopes for Hetty and the Duke of Bressington's son—'

'So that's what you are in such a flap about,' Lady Ashton cackled. 'Getting a ducal coronet for Hetty. Well, if you looked beyond the end of your dainty nose you'd know that Hetty has been in love with Viscount Horsely's boy for the last year. And, since she is your daughter through and through, I should not try to change her mind or she'll be away to Gretna before you can blink.'

'You do not think she would—?' Isabelle's creamy complexion went white as milk.

'No,' Lady Ashton said patiently. 'I've promised her a very substantial dowry so long as the pair of them do things proper and above board, which they will so long as you do not interfere, as I recall your parents tried to do with you. I trust you remember that if it had not been for Alex, you would have created enough family scandal to last a lifetime.'

'That was quite different,' Isabelle said tersely. 'I was in love.'

'I remember,' her great aunt said heavily. 'You'd have thought you had invented the condition. Now as you said, Isabelle, it is very hot and I am going in to get some refreshment. Now, where is that child of yours, Alex? I am sure she would like some lemonade.'

'Child!' Isabelle said weakly as Alex strode off across the yard and leant over a door to lift Emily out from a loose box which contained a foal. 'You do not mean that little moppet is Alex's—'

'Only by proxy,' Lady Ashton said with a grin. 'She belongs to Miss Ross.'

'I think the sooner we have that lemonade, the better,' Isabelle said, flicking open the fan which hung from the loop upon her wrist and fanning herself.

'Lemonade is for children!' Lady Ashton snorted. 'You can have it if you want. I had a good claret in mind, one that my sister Charlotte sent me from France before the Revolution—'

'Claret? Do you think you ought to? The doctor said—'

'The doctor can say what he pleases,' Lady Ashton said, scooping up her habit skirt and striding off across the yard. 'I intend to enjoy my cellar while I still can.'

Later that afternoon, Lallie stood in the centre of the drawing-room of Rosemount House, staring about her in delight. The room was light, airy, with three tall windows in a bay which overlooked the Park. With the straw-yellow carpet, eggshell-blue walls and the green of the trees visible from the windows, it felt like being in the country, she thought delightedly. So different from the lodgings she had inhabited during the last five years that it was like being in a different world. She wandered about the room, studying the portraits and landscapes upon the walls, touching the veneered tables, the elegant chairs, the elaborately draped Chinoiserie chintz curtains. The long elegantly-legged sofa, which was upholstered in the same wonderfully patterned green and blue chintz as the curtains, she decided she would move to the other side of the Adam fireplace. Her mouth curved as, glancing down out of the window, she saw Emily and Mrs Brown exploring the garden. Her smile widened as she watched the plump grey-haired nurse stoop to pick a snapdragon and show Emily how to squeeze the flower to make the dragon's jaws snap. She could hear Emily's delighted laughter floating up. She could not have found a better nurse for Emily if she had interviewed a hundred applicants, she thought; as Alex had told her yesterday, Mrs Brown was delighted with her new charge.

'So? Do you like the house? You do not find the decor too old-fashioned?'

She started as Alex came up behind her and put his arms about her waist, pinning her arms to her sides.

'Do I like it?' She sighed as she leant back against him, her body, still half-aroused from their love-making earlier that morning, tightening with instant antici-pation. 'It is perfect—'

'Mmm,' he murmured huskily against her throat as he watched her reflection in one of the pier glasses which flanked either side of the central window and saw her nipples harden beneath her lavender muslin, her lips part as one of his hands moved down over her skirts to find the parting of her thighs, the other up to cup her breast. 'I rather think it is—I want to make love to you right here and now—so that I can watch you.'

'Alex!' she said, half shocked, half intrigued, as she too stared at their reflection in the pier glass, watching his intent face as he caressed her through the layers of muslin, watching herself yield to his hands like some wanton stranger as she began to melt inside. In the last two days she had begun to realise that the passion between them was like a drug—the more they learned of each other, the more they wanted.

'We can't. . .' she groaned, trembling slightly as he increased the pressure with the heel of his hand and she felt the now familiar heat begin to build in the pit of her stomach. 'Not now—not here—'

'No, I suppose not,' he growled against her ear. 'But there must be somewhere—that French bedchamber with the Egyptian couch. . .'

'The one with the Chinese wallpaper has a very fine glass—opposite the bed,' she said slowly, raggedly as he continued the inexorable movement of his hand between her thighs. 'Oh—' Her knees buckled suddenly as she felt what she now knew to be but the first small explosion of pleasure.

'Wait—' he groaned.

Catching her up in his arms he almost ran with her out of the drawing-room, across the hall and up the broad, shallow stairs.

'Which way—?' he gasped upon the landing.

'Left,' she half sobbed, half laughed, her arms wrapped about his neck. 'At the end of the corridor.'

* * *

'I am beginning to think we have gone mad as the King,' she said breathlessly, as a half-hour later she sat upon the corner of the crumpled bed in her equally crumpled muslin, fastening the buttons on her bodice, while Alex struggled back into his knee breeches and attempted to repair the damage to his cravat. 'Whatever will Mrs Brown think?'

'Mrs Brown thinks that I should make a respectable woman of you,' he said as he shrugged into his silk waistcoat. 'She told me so yesterday in no uncertain terms. I think having been my nurse she still sees herself as being in *loco parentis*.'

'I hardly think your parents would express the same sentiment.' She tried to laugh, as she fastened the uppermost button of her gown, but it came out wrong.

'No,' he said, serious suddenly. 'I had a letter from my father yesterday begging a loan and telling me to find myself another heiress with all speed as my brother has run up yet more gambling debts.'

'And will you?' She stared at him, her grey eyes darkening as a lump rose in her throat.

'No,' he said, holding her gaze. 'I am going to marry you, if you will do me the honour?'

'Honour!' She gave a helpless ragged laugh.

'I should count it so,' he said as he dropped on to his knees before her and caught her hands.

And he meant it, she thought. Five years of war had not changed him as much as she had thought. He was still quixotic, Alex, who had cared little more than she for conventions. She stared back him, her eyes, her face, incandescent with happiness. To marry him— there was nothing in the world she wanted more. And then reality came flooding in, cold as a millstream in December.

'You can't marry me—not now—you know I have no fortune—no expectations—'

'I told you, I had an inheritance from an uncle. My income is more than adequate to keep us both.'

'According to society I have no reputation. . .' she went on desperately.

'Which puts you on a par with most of the daughters of aristocracy,' he said unconcernedly.

'You don't understand,' she groaned. 'My father died a debtor and accused of theft in Newgate, Alex. And before that we lived amongst highwaymen, pickpockets and every kind of rogue.'

'I know,' he smiled, and drew one of her hands to his mouth to plant a kiss upon it. 'Tom Mitchell told me, and that your father made you go to the hells with him. I gather you have a talent for the recalling the odds of Hazard and remembering cards.'

'Scarcely ideal accomplishments for your wife, Alex,' she said despairingly. For them to marry was impossible. He must know that. As a mistress she would be acceptable as his companion in certain situations, perhaps even approved, since she had the manners and education of a lady. But as a wife—with her background, his friends and family would never accept her. And she loved him too much to ask him to choose between them.

'Far more useful than netting purses, or warbling in Italian, I'd say.' He smiled at her—the smile that had always stopped her heart in mid-beat. 'And the ability to wield a gin jug or wine bottle would not go amiss at some of Prinny's rowdier receptions.'

'Alex,' she said despairingly, 'you would not be asked to Prinny's receptions if you married me. You know that you would be cut by everyone you know, and your career, your regiment—'

'I can live without all of them, but not without you.'

'You would come to hate me—'

'I shall die first,' he said simply. 'I love you. Marry me.'

He loved her. Loved her enough to want to marry her against all conventions. That knowledge was like stepping off a cliff and finding the air supported her. But she could not let him ruin his life—

'If you won't, I shall never marry anyone else,' he said. 'You will be denying me a wife, a family—'

'That's blackmail,' she gasped. 'You're being quite unfair.'

'Yes,' he grinned at her.

'Oh! Ask me again in a month,' she said helplessly. 'I want to be sure you are not speaking out of—'

'Lust? Passion?' He grinned at her again as she hesitated. 'Do you really think we are going to exhaust that in a month?'

'At this rate, yes,' she groaned as he got to his feet and pulled her into his arms.

'Then perhaps we should increase the rate?' he murmured against her throat. 'Because I have no intention of waiting a month for your answer.'

'You are impossible,' she sighed as his lips found a particularly sensitive spot on her throat and she felt herself begin to melt inside.

'Miss Ross? Major Haldane?' Mrs Brown's voice echoed from somewhere in the house.

'Oh, heavens!' She pulled out of his embrace

abruptly, and tried to smooth the creases out of her muslin and pat her dishevelled hair into some sort of order. 'There, do I look respectable?'

'Respectable?' His wide mouth curved lazily at the corners as he studied her still-flushed face, her slightly swollen and reddened lips, and noted that at least three buttons of her bodice were in the wrong holes. 'No, but you look delicious—'

'Oh, not now!' Half laughing, half exasperated she backed out of his reach as she heard Mrs Brown's footsteps ascending the stairs.

'Quickly—put your coat on—oh, Alex, the key is not in the door! Where did you put it after you had locked the door?'

'I don't know, ' he whispered back. 'You'll have to help me with my coat,' he added as he eased one arm into one of Weston's inimitable pieces of tailoring, which fitted him like a second skin.

'Oh, hurry up!' she begged him as she moved to hold the coat for his other arm and helped him pull it onto his broad shoulders. 'We cannot be discovered locked in here. Where is the key? In your pocket?'

'No,' he said after patting them.

'On the mantelpiece ?' she suggested in an agonised whisper.

'No,' he said, after crossing quickly to it and looking behind the blue and white jars.

'Oh, think! Quickly! She will be here in a moment.'

Suddenly, as his gaze travelled over her panic-stricken face, he began to laugh. 'Listen to us! It is as if we were back in your godmother's house, snatching kisses behind the library curtains again! This is your house. And we are both old enough to do as we please in it. We shall be down in a moment, Mrs Brown,' he called out cheerfully. 'Perhaps you could put Miss Emily into the carriage?'

Mrs Brown acquiesced and Lallie exhaled with relief.

'Now,' he said, still smiling, 'where the devil did I put that key? If we can't find it, we shall have to stay here while Mrs Brown goes and finds us a locksmith.'

'No, we won't,' she said after a moment. 'I don't know why I did not think of this in the first place.' With a smile, she took a pin out of her hair, and crossed the room. A moment or so later and the lock was undone.

'Your new accomplishments never cease to amaze me,' he laughed as she turned to him triumphantly. 'Who the devil taught you that?'

'Tom Mitchell,' she said. 'He also taught me how not to get cheated at the market, how to mark cards and spot loaded dice.'

'A useful man,' he said thoughtfully after a moment. 'I don't suppose he is in want of employment? You said he is good with horses? You will need someone to run your stable.'

'Yes,' she said, slightly surprised by his suggestion, 'and I think Tom would do it very well.'

'Then I will send one of my men to him and offer him the position.'

'I am sure he will accept—if Goliath is to be kept here. He is very fond of the beast,' she said with a smile.

'He and his brother have always been over-fond of other people's horses,' he said darkly. 'But perhaps we'll make an honest man of him yet.'

'Perhaps,' she said without total conviction as she replaced the pin in her hair.

'When do you wish to move here?' he asked as they walked slowly down the stairs.

'Tomorrow,' she said after a moment. 'Discreet as your servants are, I cannot possibly remain at your house for much longer before it becomes known.'

'No, I suppose not.' He sighed, deciding not to tell her that his sister already knew. 'But for my part, I wish that you could stay. I hate the thought of missing a moment with you when there is so little time before I must go back to Spain.'

'Spain.' A cold black void seemed to open up beneath her feet. He had nearly died in Spain, along with hundreds of other young British men. He might never come back again. 'I wish you did not have to go back,' she spoke her thought aloud.

'I have to, Wellesley needs every man he can get,' he said softly, holding her close. 'That is one of the reasons I want us to marry as soon as possible. If something should happen to me, I want your future to be secure. My family would leave you with nothing if they had an opportunity to get their hands on my money. My brother James could scarce disguise his disappointment at my return.'

'Happen.' She made a small choked sound; she had taken in nothing since that word. 'You mean if you are killed, don't you?'

'It could happen. It would be foolish not to face that,' he said quietly. 'I am an exploring officer, I spend a great deal of time behind enemy lines gathering intelligence that they do not wish us to have.'

'I know,' she said, struggling to be as calm as he was. 'Tom told me it could be very dangerous. He said that galloping up and down behind French lines in full uniform was as good as sending Marshal Soult an engraved invitation asking him to use you as a target for shooting practice.'

He laughed. 'It is rarely like that. Most of the time it is very dull work, taking notes in the shelter of a bush about troop numbers and depositions—and if the French do spot me, ninety-nine times out of a hundred, I can out run them. Our horses are corn fed whereas theirs live on grass.'

'And the hundredth time?'

'If you have any sense, you surrender,' he said as she lifted worried grey eyes to his face.

'But last time you chose to fight,' she said flatly, thinking of the still livid scar which ran down from the base of his throat almost to his stomach.

'I had some information which could have saved Lord Wellington a great deal of uncertainty.'

'But was it worth your life?' she said fiercely.

'Perhaps,' he conceded. 'And I promise you, next time my horse puts its foot into a hole, and I find myself looking up at a very large and angry French dragoon, I will wave the white handkerchief faster than my sister can recite the name of the most eligible bachelor of the season.'

'You promise,' she begged him.

'So long as you promise to be at home, waiting for me.' He hugged her suddenly, so tightly that she thought her ribs would crack. 'Now, come on, Mrs Brown and Emily will be growing impatient. Emily especially, I have promised her another riding lesson this afternoon.'

CHAPTER NINE

THREE days later, Lallie sank down upon the feather-filled cushions of the chintz sofa in the drawing-room of Rosemount House with a sigh of relief and smiled as she glanced at the gilt clock upon the white marble mantel. Alex would be back in an hour or so, and at last they would have a little time together that was not taken up with the hiring of servants, the purchase of linens and china and heaven knows what else—not to mention yet more fittings for herself and Emily with Miss Roden. She picked up a fold of the skirt of her new, silver-grey muslin and then let it drift back into place. A glance into the glass in the Chinese bed-chamber, which she taken for her own, had told her that the classical style with its Grecian overtones suited her perfectly. And that her new lady's maid, Jenny, the niece of Alex's housekeeper, had a touch of genius when it came to the arrangement of her hair. Lazily she twirled one of the spiralling curls which tumbled down from the classical braided coronet on top of her head, framing her face.

It was impossible not to take a delight in having beautiful clothes again, and knowing that she looked her best for Alex.

Though she had been uneasy at first at his spending so much money upon them. A point of view that Alex had dismissed by asking her if she would have objected if they had already been married. What difference did it make? he had asked her. If he bought things for her, it was because he loved her and took pleasure from doing so.

He loved her. Her mouth curved again and she leant against the arm of the sofa, rested her head on one hand and brought her feet up onto the cushions to adjust the cross-ties of her dainty silver kid sandals. She was only just coming to believe it, only just beginning to realise it was true. The only cloud upon her happiness was the knowledge that as much as he wanted it, marriage between them would never work. The difference in her father and mother's situations had not been half as great, but it had destroyed their love, leaving them both bitter and dissatisfied. Her mother had resented her father every time she had been slighted by the aristocratic acquaintances of her childhood. Her father had grown impatient with his wife's snobbery and refusal to mix with the wives of his fellow brewers. No, she told herself firmly. It was better to be a mistress and loved, than become a source of resentment.

A tap upon the door made her start and hastily lower her feet to the floor.

'Come in,' she called.

'There is a gentleman to see you, miss,' Fletcher, her rosy-cheeked housemaid, who was another more distant relative of Alex's housekeeper, informed her politely. 'General Houghton.'

'General Houghton? Are you sure he has come to the right house? I do not know a General Houghton.'

'He was quite definite, miss. Says that you met in the Row with Major Haldane.'

'Oh, of course,' she said sickly, knowing that the

episode in the Row was always going to cause her deep embarrassment. 'It must be Major Haldane he wishes to see. Tell him he is welcome to wait and show him in. When I ring, bring some Madeira and cakes.'

'Yes, miss.' Fletcher scurried away cheerfully to her bidding. Lallie breathed a slight sigh of relief. Servants could be as disapproving as their supposed betters, but not one of the staff recruited by Alex's awesomely efficient housekeeper had betrayed by so much as a glance that her situation was in any way unusual. And that she suspected she owed to kindly, sensible Mrs Brown, who seemed to be ruling the household with the same velvet glove that she employed with Emily.

'Miss Ross.' To her surprise, the General was beaming broadly at her as he entered the room as if she were his oldest and dearest acquaintance.

'I am sorry,' she began with as much composure as she could muster in the circumstances, 'if you are looking for Major Haldane, he is not here. Though he did say he would call later. I expect him within the hour if you would like to wait?'

'Not Haldane, I've come to see, m'dear,' the General informed her heartily. 'It's you. And I must say it is a pleasure to see you again. And looking so well, I am pleased to see, after your mishap in the Park. I trust your injuries are healing well?'

'Good! Good!' he barked as she said stiltedly that they were, while she wondered what on earth he wanted with her. 'I hope Haldane has found you a new horse—saw just the mare for you at Tattersall's the other day. A grey, mild as milk, and pretty as a picture.'

'Really?' she said, trying to gather her wits and wondering how and what the General knew of her

relationship with Alex. 'Won't you sit down?' she said
lamely, sitting down herself upon the sofa.

'Thank you.' The General sat in an armchair
opposite her, pulling it forward so that he was closer to
her. 'Now, then—shall we get down to business?'

'Business?' She looked at him blankly. 'I do not
know what you mean.'

'Good.' He grinned at her. 'I see Haldane has
impressed upon you how vital it is that no one knows
about this, but you need not worry, my dear, Haldane
and I are as one in this. We both want to bring Corton
down.'

'Corton. . .' She repeated the name, her confusion
growing by the moment. 'Major Haldane has not
mentioned the Marquis to me.'

'Didn't tell you who it was, eh?' The General nodded
approval. 'Well, I suppose that was wise until he was
certain you would accept the offer. You feel the price
is fair, I hope? A lease upon this place or any similar
establishment you fancy for five years, and a substantial
sum which, if managed carefully, will keep you in
comfort for some time, Miss Ross. That is, if you
succeed, of course,' he added. 'Not that I have any
doubts. Corton will not be able to resist settling old
scores against Haldane by stealing his mistress. I do
not anticipate that you will have difficulty in becoming
intimate with him.'

'I do not know what you are talking about,' she said
slowly, as ice seemed to form suddenly in the pit of her
stomach as she began to understand his implication.
'But I should very much like you to explain.'

The General stared at her. 'You mean Haldane has
not mentioned this to you? I assumed that since he'd

set you up it was all agreed—oh, well—' he shrugged '—I suppose he thought it better to leave it to me. But first I must ask you for your word that you will speak of this to no one but Haldane or myself, for your country's sake?'

'You have it,' she said, clasping her hands in her lap so tightly that her knuckles went white. Alex could not have betrayed her trust a second time. She would not believe it. 'Please go on, General.'

'Corton, as you may be aware, has a position in the War Office. He is also deeply in debt. So deeply in debt that he has apparently decided to sell his country's secrets to France—'

'Then why is he not arrested?' she interrupted with a frown.

'For two reasons—first, because we have no concrete proof of his treachery and we cannot move against a scion of one of the oldest families in the country without it. Second, the information he has passed before has been inaccurate and of little consequence, and it has suited us to mislead the French. But now, by mischance, he has obtained a set of plans of some fortifications which Lord Wellington has constructed in the greatest secrecy on the Portuguese border.'

'How can fortifications be secret?' Lallie asked bemusedly.

'Because our army has so far ensured that not a single French scout has got close and Lord Wellington has told no-one who does not need to know of them. The French intend to sweep us out of Spain and Portugal this summer, Miss Ross. They have far greater numbers and, if we meet their entire force in open battle, we would almost certainly be defeated. These fortifications are Lord Wellington's trump card, and I am certain will eventually win the game for us. But if the French learn about the obstacle in front of them before reaching Torres Vedras, half the effectiveness of the fortifications will have been lost, because the French will have had time to prepare and plan for a prolonged siege. So you see how essential it is that these documents are recovered from Corton before he can pass them to the French?'

'I think so,' Lallie said helplessly. She could not think straight. Alex could not have done this to her. It could not all have been lies just to get her to agree to this, could it? The questions revolved around and around in her head. 'These plans have great value to the French—' she said, struggling to find a reason, an explanation she could accept.

'An incalculable value.' The General sighed, leaning back in his arm chair. 'A fact of which Corton is fully aware. But the French are proving slow in arranging to pay him the sum he is asking for, possibly because they think he is exaggerating their importance, possibly because they are becoming dissatisfied with the quality of information that Corton is passing to them. Or perhaps possibly because they have decided they have paid Corton enough already and intend to take the plans from him by force. But Corton is no fool; he keeps the plans with him at all times, either in his coat or even, we understand, his nightshirt. He also takes very great care never to be alone, keeping two armed men near him at all times, except, of course—' he paused to look at her significantly '—when he is engaged in somewhat intimate activities. And that, my dear, is where you come in—it was Haldane who pointed out that a woman was far more likely to get below Corton's guard, and be able to appropriate the plans discreetly without an arrest and a court case that could lead to the publicity we so wish to avoid. Once we have them back, Corton can hardly shout that they have been stolen without destroying himself. So, my dear, you will do it? I assure you, you will have our eternal gratitude—'

'You said that it was Major Haldane's idea—' she said leadenly, beginning to shake inside. 'He wants me to approach Corton and become intimate with him!'

'Well—' The General gave a slight shrug. 'He gave me the impression that you are no longer exactly inexperienced in these matters.'

'But he has asked me to marry him!' she blurted out in disbelief. Surely Alex could not have discussed her with him in such intimate detail?

'Marry?' For a moment the General looked startled, then he smiled and nodded. 'Smart chap, Haldane. I was wondering how he was going to manage to throw you in Corton's path, but if people think you his great aunt's ward, and that he means to marry you, you'll be able to move freely in Corton's circle. And Corton won't be able to resist making a play for you, not if he thinks Haldane means to marry you—you'll hardly need to wink at him.'

She felt sick, as the General went on and on, explaining how generously she would be rewarded for success. She had been such a fool. Believing that Alex loved her, believing that he wanted to marry her when all the time he had been planning this—to give her to Corton like some common whore so that Lord Wellington might deceive the French and win their stupid war games in the Peninsula! A lump rose in her throat, choking her. She would get Emily and leave now. This minute. She never wanted to see or hear Alexander Haldane again, ever.

'You will excuse me,' she spluttered, getting up suddenly and running from the room and across the hall, almost cannoning into Alex as he opened the front door and laughingly caught her in his arms.

'Have you missed me so much already? I've only been gone an hour—'

He stopped as she remained rigid in his arms, and he saw that she was ashen.

'Lallie? What the devil is it?'

'Let go of me!' Her voice was like the ice around her heart. 'I am going to get Emily and then I am leaving. I never want to see you again! Not ever!'

'Lallie,' he said, half-amused, not taking her seriously for a moment. 'Whatever has upset you—?'

'I said, let go of me!' His hands dropped away from her as her eyes came up to his, glittering like sabre blades in her chalky face. 'I am leaving!'

'Leaving?' He shook his head. 'Don't be ridiculous. You cannot just leave without telling me what is the matter and—you have nowhere to go.'

He was right. They had nowhere else to go. And she hated him for it so much that it felt like a knife being driven into her.

Her hand came up without thought and she slapped his face so hard that the sound seemed to echo through the whole house, so hard that her palm and fingers burned from the impact.

He went very still, but displayed no sign of anger except for a flicker of blue ice in the depths of his eyes.

'Well,' he said as the silence stretched between them and she watched the colour seeping back into the pale imprint left by her fingers upon his cheek, 'shall we go into the drawing-room where we can discuss this calmly and you can tell me why I deserved that?'

'You know why!' she accused him so fiercely, burningly angry at his betrayal that she wanted to hit him again. But instead she turned upon her heel and went back into the drawing-room.

'Lallie—' He followed her in and then came to an abrupt halt as he saw the General and muttered something indecipherable beneath his breath.

'I am so sorry, General Houghton.' Lallie gave the older man a bright, brittle smile as she sat down again upon the sofa, straight-backed, her hands clenched in her lap. 'I felt a little unwell for a moment. It is so hot today, is it not?'

'Very,' said the General. 'Afternoon, Haldane.' I have just been explaining to Miss Ross how vital it is that we retrieve those plans discreetly and how grateful we will be for her help.'

'I see,' Alex said heavily.

'So do I—now,' Lallie said, keeping her gaze firmly fixed upon the General. 'Now, tell me again, what is the price if I succeed, General? Five thousand guineas, I believe you said? And the lease upon the house?'

'You have my word on it.'

'Then we have a bargain,' she said flatly. Five thousand guineas would give both her and Emily security for life. She need never be dependent upon any man's help again, least of all Alexander Haldane's.

'You do not!' Alex's voice was like a whip, cracking

across the room. 'Not if I am to have anything to do with the matter.'

'So far as I see, you need not. It is my decision, not yours,' she said coldly, her face as blank, as white as the Grecian marble bust which stood upon one of the side tables. 'You have nothing to do with it!'

'Haldane? What the devil is the problem? Miss Ross has agreed to help us.'

'The problem is that I no longer consider Miss Ross suitable for the task—as she should well know,' he rasped.

'Well, I do,' said the General firmly. 'And you can count that an order if you wish. There's no time to find someone else. Now, if you will excuse me, Miss Ross, I have an appointment with the Prime Minister at four sharp, so I must take my leave. Perhaps you and Major Haldane could decide upon where and when you can engineer your reintroduction to the Marquis? Good day to you both.'

'Sir!' Alex followed him to the door. 'We must discuss this further—'

'No time, Haldane, no time. Call on me tomorrow if you must,' the General said breezily. 'I'll let myself out.'

CHAPTER TEN

'LALLIE?'

'What?' she replied icily as she watched him shut the door behind the General and then walk slowly across the room towards her.

'I should like to explain—' He sighed as he sat down upon the sofa a little distance away from her and pushed back a lock of dark hair from his face.

'There is no need,' she answered, without looking at him, her hands clenched so tightly in her lap that her knuckles were white.

'Please, listen—'

'To more lies?' Her voice was cold. 'The General was admirably clear. Corton has some secret plans which must not fall into the hands of the French. I am to get them, by whatever means are required. When I think of it, I am ideally qualified as a spy, am I not? I know how to pick a lock and a pocket—and as for certain other skills, you have more than filled that unfortunate gap in my education, have you not?'

'Do you really think your education is what I have had in mind this last week—that I was training you for Corton's pleasure?' he retorted ferociously, and then, as he glanced at her mask-like face as she stared fixedly at the opposite wall, he exhaled heavily. 'Lallie, you must know that what has happened between us is no pretence—I love you, I want to marry you. How many times do I have to say it?'

'You do not need to say it ever again,' she said with
a ragged laugh, 'since I have already agreed to do what
you want. So tell me, when I am to encounter Corton?
What should I wear—this?' She gestured to the silver-
grey gown with which she had been so pleased because
she had thought he would admire it. 'Or something a
little lower, do you think? And perhaps I should wear
some paint—'

'That is enough!' he rasped, reaching out to catch
her chin in his hand and turning her head so that she
faced him. 'Look at me and listen! That day, after I
had been to see you in your lodgings, the General
asked me if I knew anyone who might be suitable for
the task of getting the plans. It had to be someone we
could trust—someone beautiful enough to appeal to
Corton—'

'Someone desperate enough to do anything for
money!' she cut in acidly.

'You would not take my help,' he said grimly, 'and
then, when you came to the Row like that—and Corton
was so obviously taken with you—'

'You and the General decided I should be perfectly
fitted for the task!'

'Yes—no—' He groaned. 'I was already having
second thoughts. But at that moment I was so damned
angry at finding you, apparently preferring to tout for
Corton's custom in the Row than accept the help I had
offered you, that I agreed I should ask you if you would
help.'

'So that is why you came after me and rescued me
from Robson's,' she said acidly as she lifted her eyelids.
'You were following orders.'

'I came because I thought that, if you would not be

my mistress, at least the General's scheme would enable you to make enough money to escape that damnable lodging. It was only when I saw how you had been living and spoke to Tom Mitchell that I began to realise just how hard things had been for you.'

'I am very grateful for your concern, but you need not put yourself out further upon my account. I am quite capable of surviving without your assistance.'

'It did not look like it to me when I found you brawling with a brothel keeper!' he snapped and then groaned when he saw the hurt in her eyes a moment before she dropped her lashes. 'For heaven's sake, Lallie—you cannot think after these last few days that I could let Corton anywhere near you!'

'I do not know what to think!' she flashed back at him. 'That is the whole trouble, Alex, when I am with you I have never been able to think!'

'Well, you certainly aren't thinking at the moment,' he agreed savagely. 'I did not tell you about all this, because I never meant you to find out that I'd contemplated involving you. It never occurred to me the General would call here, or, after we had made love that first time that you would ever agree.'

'Well, you were wrong, weren't you?' she said with a toss of her head.

'You cannot mean to go further with it?'

'Why not?' She was as cold as he had ever seen her.

'Why not—?' He floundered. 'Because you love me!'

'Do I?' She treated him to a haughty smile borrowed from an encounter in a hell with the infamous Harriet Wilson. 'Oh, it seemed best to let you think that, and you have proved very generous as a consequence. But like you said in the beginning, Alex, any port in a storm would have done!'

'You do not mean that.'

She shrugged. 'Wait and see. Corton is very rich, is he not?'

'In debts!' he snarled as his patience ran out. 'If you persist in this, everything is over between us. If you cannot bring yourself to believe that I love you, or that I am telling you the truth...' He made a helpless gesture with his hands.

'It was over the moment General Houghton walked through the door!' she snapped back.

'Very well,' he said, after a sharp intake of breath, 'if that is how you wish it.' He stood up, towering over her like a storm cloud. 'I shall tell the General that we shall both play our part. There is a ball tomorrow night at Lady Furney's. I shall call for you at eight o'clock.' His mouth twisted into a savage smile. 'Corton will be there, so be sure to wear something appropriately low.'

'As low as your behaviour has been?' she countered, glaring up at him. 'If I did that, I should be naked to the waist!'

'Then that should do very well...' He paused to look down his long nose at her with the aristocratic hauteur he had never used towards her before. 'Corton always did have a taste for the obvious.'

'Get out!' she hissed at him. 'Get out of my house!'

'Your house?' he taunted and bowed with insolent perfection and turned upon his heel.

When he reached the door, he hesitated and glanced back at her.

'I shall call for Emily at two o'clock tomorrow for her riding lesson,' he said quietly. 'Perhaps you will tell

Mrs Brown to have her ready at the stables? I see no reason to disappoint the child, do you?'

'No,' she replied grittily.

He still hesitated as their gazes clashed and held. 'Damnation! Do you find it so hard to trust me?'

'Hard?' She gave a jagged laugh. 'Impossible would be a more appropriate word. You lied to me five years ago—you have lied to me now. All your talk of marriage and love—you did not mean a word of it!'

'If you believe that, there is no point in continuing this discussion,' he rasped back at her. 'Let the past destroy the future if you must, but just remember this time that the choice was yours, Lallie, not mine!'

She stared after him as he strode across the room, doubt and hope surfacing suddenly in the midst of her rage. If it were not for what had happened before, would she have judged him so instantly in the wrong now? They had been so happy for the last few days, and he had shown her nothing but kindness, consideration and—love.

The click of the door as he shut it behind him jolted her out of her immobility. She ran across the room, threw open the door—

'Alex—wait!' He stilled in the act of picking his hat up from the table in the hall but did not turn to look at her.

'Why?' He was at his iciest. 'You said yourself that it is over.'

With that he put on his hat and walked out of the front door, pushing it shut almost in her face as she followed him.

'Damn you! You stupid, idiotic man!' She swore aloud for the second time in her life, striking the closed door with her fist. And then, furious, she wheeled away, and strode back into the drawing-room in a swirl of grey muslin. She was utterly tired of men turning her life upside down! Her father, Robson, Corton! All of them! Especially Alexander Haldane! She would get Lord Wellington's plans from Corton, wave them under his long aristocratic nose along with the General's money and tell him so!

At five minutes to eight the following evening, Lallie stared at her reflection in the pier glass in the drawing-room, not quite able to believe that the sophisticated-looking young woman reflected was herself. Using fine gold ribbons, Jenny had secured her hair in a Grecian style of spiralling curls, some of which had been allowed to escape to frame her face and brush her bare neck and shoulders. And there were more gold ribbons that crossed beneath her small high breasts and tied behind her back to make the high waist of the floor-length column of white silk gauze, which was otherwise absolutely plain but for a Grecian key pattern embroidered upon the hem in gold thread.

Aside from her pallor she knew she had never looked better, but the knowledge did nothing to diminish the sick feeling of anxiety in her stomach, which had been growing all day. It was one thing to decide in a moment of anger that she would get the plans, quite another to carry out the task. And if Alex had called that afternoon after Emily's riding lesson, if he had given the slightest hint of an apology, she knew she would have abandoned the whole idea. But he had not called, or sent a single word. And if all was over between them, then she needed that five thousand guineas. Needed it to make a life for herself and Emily which no man could snatch away from them upon a whim.

She lifted a hand to make a hundredth unnecessary adjustment to the scrap of puffed gauze on her shoulder that passed for a sleeve upon the ball gown, wishing that the fashion was not for such low necklines. The low curve barely covered her nipples and she could not help remembering the contempt upon Alex's face the previous afternoon when he had suggested that she should wear something of the kind. Frowning, she picked up a long narrow gauze scarf from the table in front of the mirror and began to arrange it about her shoulders.

'Good evening.'

Alex's cool voice brought her spinning around, the scarf stretched behind her head, between her half-raised hands.

He was standing in the open doorway, dark, lean and utterly male in a way that was emphasised rather than diminished by the skin-tight satin breeches, dark blue coat and foaming silk and lace at his cuffs and throat.

'I-I did not hear you arrive,' she stammered, as she let go of the scarf and folded her hands in front of her, wondering how long he had been watching her.

'Too busy preparing yourself for Corton, were you?' he drawled as his gaze travelled lazily down from her parted lips to the milky white mounds of her breasts. 'I have to say you look exceptionally well, like Artemis reincarnated. . .' he paused as his eyes came back up to hers, blue and cold '. . .or should I say Aphrodite — after all, the Romans equated Artemis with Diana, who was renowned for her chastity.'

She stared at him, momentarily stunned with disbelief. How could he level such an insult at her when he was her first, her only, lover and he *knew* it! She wanted to rage at him—to cry—to hit him! But that would only lay her open to more of his contempt.

'I will take your word for it,' she replied icily, her face and voice as composed she could make them as she wrapped the gauze scarf tightly about her shoulders. 'Your knowledge of these matters is so much more extensive than mine.'

'A deficit I am sure Corton will be happy to remedy,' he drawled. 'Are you ready? I do not care to keep my horses standing.'

'Then let us go.' She tried to sound uncaring, but her voice shook and she had to turn away from him abruptly as the ever-tightening knot in her chest threatened to release itself in tears.

There was a silence as he watched her arrange and rearrange the gauze scarf about her shoulders with short jerky movements, the reflection of her set face in the pier glass almost as white as her gown.

'You don't have to do this,' he said gratingly as he watched her. 'Stay here with me tonight and I will give you your five thousand guineas.'

'You mean be your whore rather than Corton's?' She gave a jagged laugh. 'No, thank you, Alex, I prefer the General's money. It is cleaner. At least he does not lie to me.'

'Oh, this is ridiculous!' He struck the door a sudden crashing blow with his fist that brought her whirling around in shock, her eyes storm grey and shimmering in her ashen face. 'Why is it that women are incapable of using their reason?'

'Probably because the behaviour of men has already

deprived them of it,' she flared back at him. 'Shall we go now—you said you did not want to keep your horses standing?'

'Damn the horses!' He stepped in front of her as she went to pass him and she found herself halted by the wall of his body, a scant inch from her own.

Her rage had crystallised now, had become as cold as his. She lifted her eyes slowly to his face. 'War really has led to a deterioration in your manners, has it not?' she said emotionlessly. 'Will you stand aside?'

'No.' He smiled at her. A smile that did not touch his bleak, blue eyes. 'I wanted to give you this—a little gilding for the lily.'

She watched numbly as he took out a silk handkerchief from his coat-tail pocket, and unfolded it to reveal a gleaming strand of pearls, fastened by a gold and turquoise clasp.

She recognised them instantly. They had been a much-loved gift from her mother upon her seventeenth birthday, the last gift she had received from her before she died. Of all the things she had had to sell, these had been the hardest to part with, except for her horses. She stared at them. The last time she had seen them they had been in the greedy, grimy hands of a pawnbroker in Petticoat Lane.

'Where did you—how did you—?' she mumbled.

'The brokers who gave me the address of your lodgings,' he said succinctly. 'It was not difficult to recognise them since you used to wear them all the time. I presumed that circumstances had forced you sell them and thought you would like them back. I meant to give them to you before—'

'As a bribe to do as you and the General wished!'

'As a gift! Believe it or not!' He snapped back at her.

'Not, I think,' she said stiffly. 'But it does not matter. As soon as I am able I shall pay you for them.'

'Oh, please, consider them a lover's gift, already paid for,' he drawled as his blue eyes held hers for a second. 'They are not worth five thousand guineas, of course, but they should cover the night before last, if nothing else.'

Her hand lifted to hit him, but when she saw his taunting smile, she knew that he was expecting, almost wanting, her to do so. She brought her hand back down to her side, drew in a breath.

'Well, shall I fasten them for you?' he asked with a mocking mildness that made her want to kill him.

'If it pleases you,' she replied dully. She wanted to hurl the pearls in his face. But she had nothing else of her mother's, nothing with which to remember her by except these. And she could not afford pride. The pearls were valuable. If she failed in her attempt to get the plans, they would keep Emily and herself for some time.

'It always pleases me to touch you,' he said bitterly as he picked up the strand of creamy pearls and lifted them to her throat. For a moment there was something in his voice, his eyes, that twisted her insides into a knot. 'That's the worst of it, is it not?' he added savagely as his coat sleeves brushed her throat and she flinched. 'Odd that you can despise someone, and still want to touch them, isn't it?'

She made no answer except to shut her eyes and wish that her treacherous senses were not so attuned to him that even the brush of cloth against her skin could trigger off a hundred memories of his mouth, his hands on her body. But shutting her eyes made no difference. She was still painfully aware of his warmth, the clean masculine smell of his skin, each rise and fall of his chest. It just was not fair, she thought fiercely. How could he make her feel like this when she knew him to be a liar—knew that he had planned to give her to Corton for his own ends?

The clasp fastened, he let the pearls drop abruptly into place at the base of her throat.

They felt cold and hard against her skin, more like a slave's shackle than a lover's gift, she thought, as she opened her eyes to find him staring at her.

'I hate you,' she said despairingly as their gazes met and held. 'I wish I had never met you and I never want you to touch me again!' She meant it. And yet she could not take the step back which would have put a safer distance between them.

'You need not have any anxiety upon that account,' he replied coldly. 'I can assure you I shall have no taste for Corton's leavings, however temptingly they might be wrapped.'

'Good,' she snapped as he stood aside and made her an ironic bow. 'Because I have no great taste for a liar and a pimp!'

By the time they had driven to Lady Furney's town house in a chillingly hostile silence, her head was aching and her eyes burning from the effort of not crying and she felt absolutely sick with nerves about the evening ahead.

Alex threw open the carriage door and leapt out almost before the coachman had brought the horses to a halt.

Lallie glanced out of the open carriage door at the impressive façade of Lady Furney's house, her nervousness increasing by the moment. Because of the still-suffocating heat, not a curtain was drawn and every sash window was open. She swallowed, and bit her lip as she gazed from window to window. Judging by the crowd, and the noise of chatter and laughter flooding out along with the candlelight, it seemed all society was there tonight. There were bound to be people there who had witnessed her humiliation in the Row, and Corton, no doubt, amongst them.

She had managed to put Corton out of her mind for a few seconds, but now the fear came flooding back. She dragged in a breath, and glanced at Alex, hoping, begging him with her eyes for understanding, for some way out. But his face was cold and hard as ice, his eyes dark and unreadable.

'Are you going to alight,' he said tersely, 'or do you mean to sit there all night? You need not worry, they won't dare cut you if you are with me.'

His casual arrogance made her angry enough to snap out of her fear. She stepped out of the carriage, ignoring both the hand he offered her and his impatient exclamation as she stumbled on the train of her gown.

She would have walked up the shallow steps to the door ahead of him, but he took her arm in what looked like a polite grip, but felt like claws of steel digging into her flesh through her long white kid gloves.

'Remember,' he said grittily, 'that the General desires Corton to think we are intimate.'

'Then stop holding me as if I were a felon you had just apprehended,' she hissed back at him.

'Your pardon.' He relaxed his grip a little as they

entered the lower hall. She came to a faltering halt, momentarily overwhelmed by the glittering ostentatious grandeur of Lady Furney's town house, with its overabundance of gilded plaster mouldings, gleaming marble and glowing brocades and brilliantly clad occupants. After her dingy lodgings, Rosemount House had seemed like a dream, but this was like stumbling into one of Grimm's fairy tales. Everywhere she looked there was the gleam of gold and silvergilt, the glitter of candle flame on crystal, the flash of diamonds and shimmer of silk, satin and pearls. She had attended one or two country balls in Scotland, but never anything as grand as this. Her gaze was drawn upwards, following the stately sweep of the broad marble staircase, skimming over the great painted panels of voluptuous nymphs and unlikely looking shepherd boys cavorting against pastoral backgrounds, to the great painted ceiling some three storeys about, where Zeus and his goddesses sprawled about a central sun from which hung the largest crystal chandelier she had ever seen, suspended from what looked like a frighteningly fragile gilded chain.

It made her feel dizzy and she looked away hastily.

'Go on—' Alex hissed in her ear. 'No one is going to bite you—'

She was not so sure of that, she thought, as she let him propel her across the blue and white marble floor towards the chattering, glittering line of people who were slowly making their way up the stairs to be greeted by Lady Furney. She felt her stomach contract with nerves, her mouth go dry. Even five years ago, secure in her position as an heiress to a wealthy brewer, she would have felt unsure of herself in the midst of this gathering. There were faces here she recognised from the Park, and one or two she half recognised from the hells. Faces which were already turning to look at her and Alex with something more than polite interest.

'People are staring at us,' she said.

'Don't worry. A new beauty always arouses curiosity,' Alex muttered in her ear. 'They will be wondering if your complexion is natural or assisted and what your dowry is worth, and if I mean to marry you.'

'Really?' She flicked a glance at him. 'Are you sure they are not saying there is that muslin from the Park! And how tasteless of Haldane to bring her here—'

'If they thought that, you would not have got past the footman upon the door,' said a dry voice from behind them. 'And whatever Haldane's myriad faults, I do not think tastelessness is one of them.'

They both turned as one, Alex with a faint smile, Lallie looking horrified at being overheard by the snowy-haired dowager who stood behind them, resplendent in diamonds and blue satin.

'So, this is my ward,' Lady Ashton said quietly as her sharp blue gaze travelled over Lallie from head to foot before flicking to her great nephew. 'You might have warned me you were to be here this evening, Alex. It would have looked better had we arrived together. But I suppose this is as good a place to start as any.'

'Start?' Lallie said uncertainly as she met the imperious dowager's stare. Surely Alex had not involved his great aunt in the scheme to get the plans.

'Haldane did not tell you that he has asked me to introduce you to Society?' Lady Ashton's finely curved brows rose.

'No, he did not,' Lallie said tersely as her eyes met Alex's blue gaze in a silent, furious question.

'My apologies,' he said coolly. 'Other considerations put the matter quite out of my mind.'

'Really, Haldane,' Lady Ashton sighed wearily. 'Next you will tell that you have not even told Miss Ross you intend to marry her.'

'I have told her on several occasions,' Alex answered drily as Lallie's lips parted and no sound came out. 'But I do not recall confirming my intentions to you, Aunt.'

'It was obvious the moment I thought about it, my dear boy,' Lady Ashton said blithely. 'I do not suppose anything I say will change your mind this time, so you leave me with little choice but to help, if the family's reputation is to be preserved at all.'

And pigs fly, Lallie thought bitterly. It did not surprise her that he had not told anyone else that he meant to marry her. 'You need not concern yourself, Lady Ashton,' she said thickly. 'He does not intend to marry me. It has been merely pretence—'

'A pretence!' Lady Ashton's brows lifted. 'My dear Miss Ross, do you think Haldane is some second-rate seducer who goes about promising marriage when he does not mean it?'

'I am afraid that is exactly what she thinks,' Alex said as his gaze met and held Lallie's. 'And that is only the least of it, isn't it, Miss Ross?'

Lallie glared back at him. He was being completely unfair. He knew she could say nothing of Corton and the plans.

'Don't be provocative, Haldane,' Lady Ashton said tartly. 'If Miss Ross really thought anything of the kind

she would not be here with you now. And may I
suggest that you both put aside whatever it is you have
quarrelled over and put your minds to the task in
hand.'

'What task?' Lallie asked.

'Repairing your reputation, Miss Ross,' Lady Ashton
muttered before taking her arm and drawing her into
an alcove. 'Now, I have had your father's unfortunate
history from Alex—so tell me about your mother. Who
was she?'

'Jacintha Reynolds,' Lallie said bemusedly as she
exchanged an accusatory glance with Alex. She did not
understand what had possessed him to involve his great
aunt.

'The Surrey Reynolds?' Lady Ashton asked sharply,
her grey brows rising along with her voice. 'Your
mother was the Honourable Jacintha Reynolds?'

'Yes, but we did not have anything to do with her
family. They considered she had married beneath
herself.'

'It does not matter, the less said about your father
the better.' Lady Ashton was dismissive. 'But the
Reynolds—well, that is far better than I had hoped.
Your grandmother Reynolds and I were great friends
in our youth. You even have a look of her.' Lady
Ashton smiled at her for the first time. 'Now, let us
make a start with Lady Furney—all you need do is
smile and say as little as possible.'

With that, Lady Ashton snapped open her fan and
headed for the great sweep of blue-carpeted stairs.

'Go on!' Alex prodded Lallie in the ribs as she
hesitated.

She wheeled to face him, her eyes blazing silver. 'Is she part of this scheme—?'

'No,' he said succinctly. 'I had asked her to assist in introducing you to Society, that is all.'

'To what end?' she hissed, remembering what the General had said about how much easier it would be for her to become close to Corton if she were able to move in society circles. 'So that I might meet Corton at every opportunity, I suppose?'

'Why else?' he said and smiled nastily. 'You had better hurry up, Lady Ashton is not renowned for her patience. And do try to smile at me. Corton is watching us from the half-landing.'

Involuntarily she glanced up to where the great crescent of marble stairs curled back upon itself. Corton, resplendent in a dark plum coat and richly embroidered waistcoat, was leaning languidly upon the marble banister, staring down at them. His smooth white face was impassive, but as he caught her gaze his plump mouth curved into a smile and he nodded to her.

She stiffened, jerked her gaze away, her heart thumping. There was something about Corton and his almost cherubic looks that nagged at her memory as it had when she had first seen him in the Park. Something in the cold dark eyes that frightened her in a way she could not even begin to explain. She did not want to go anywhere near him. Not for any amount of money.

Alex touched her arm.

She turned to him, thinking, hoping that he was about to relent and put out an olive branch.

But his face was cold, contemptuous. A stranger's face. She did not know this Alex at all. 'What's wrong?'

he drawled as his blue gaze travelled over her ashen face. 'Isn't he handsome enough to tempt you? You should have asked the General for a higher price to sweeten the pill. You still could—I do believe that is him over there.'

Very well, she thought savagely, if that was how he wanted it!

'Thank you for the suggestion,' she smiled at him with saccharine sweetness as their gazes clashed and held. 'But five thousand will suffice—for a start.' With that, her chin high, she began to climb the stairs in Lady Ashton's wake, ignoring the arm he offered her. She was too icily angry now even to feel anxiety about the introductions ahead. It did not matter if they cut her. Nothing mattered any more except getting the plans and the five thousand guineas which would buy herself and Emily independence.

She smiled her way through the introductions to Lady Furney and her family, made the necessary responses in a polite if faintly detached manner and was just breathing a silent sigh of relief when a young woman who was all too familiar greeted them.

She groaned inwardly. Lady Cressida Penwyrth was the last person whom she wished to encounter at this moment.

'Lady Ashton, what a delight to see you looking so well,' Lady Cressida trilled, 'and you, Major Haldane. Though you do not deserve my good wishes, since you still have not found time to call. I hope we shall have time to talk this evening. I should never forgive myself if I thought you had suffered a wound, albeit of a different kind, from my hands as well as those of the French.'

She gave Alex another significant look from beneath long dark lashes. A look which might as well have been cast at a granite wall for all the answer it got, Lallie thought, with a relief which she did not care to question. After all, she was done with Alexander Haldane, was she not? And she did not care if Lady Cressida wed him tomorrow! She was welcome to him!

'If you are referring to your engagement to Rutherstone,' Alex replied easily, 'you and he have my heartiest congratulations and I wish you every happiness. Now, I do not think you have been introduced to Miss Ross?' He gestured to Lallie, whom Lady Cressida had so far treated as if she were totally invisible.

'My ward,' Lady Ashton put in as Lady Cressida gave Lallie a cold glance.

'Of course,' Lady Cressida said languidly. Her blue eyes flicked over Lallie again and her petal-shaped mouth curled into a rather unpleasant little smile. 'I could hardly forget Miss Ross after her little escapade in the Row. Nor, I am sure, can half the gentlemen here. But then perhaps that is what you intended, Miss Ross?' The insult was spiced with a tinkling little laugh that set Lallie's teeth upon edge and did nothing to improve her temper.

'Oh, no,' she replied with deliberate innocence, eyes wide, a bland smile on her lips. 'It was entirely accidental. But then I have never had to seek attention from any gentleman, least of all Major Haldane.'

She had the satisfaction of hearing Lady Cressida's breath catch in her throat as her implication sank in, and Alex make a choking sound which became a cough.

'I do not doubt it.' Lady Cressida's pretty mouth was tight as she replied. 'Lady Ashton, Major Haldane, I hope to see you later.' With that she turned upon her heel.

'Not if I see you first,' Lady Ashton murmured in unexpected support, as she flashed Lallie a smile.

'Never did like her,' Lady Ashton confided. 'All simper, sugar and curls on the outside and more venom than a viper underneath. Ill treats her horses, too—I saw her beat a horse once that had a flint in its foot—Leicestershire it was—poor beast could scarce put its foot to the ground and she wanted to put it at a gate—'

'Aunt, I do not think this is the place for hunting memoirs,' Alex said with a trace of expasperation. 'Shall we get on? Cavendish is making frantic signals to me from over there which seem to imply that he and most of my brother officers desire to be introduced.'

He gestured to where at a tall, craggy-faced and faired-haired Hussar stood on the far side of the room amid a group of other officers, the silver braid on their uniforms glinting and glittering in the candlelight.

'Well done, my dear,' Lady Ashton whispered to Lallie a little while later after a bewildering round of introductions. 'You carried that off very well. Now for the rest. I doubt you will have trouble with any of the gentlemen present, it is the ladies we shall have to watch out for, especially,' she added ruefully as she glanced at Lallie, 'those with plain daughters. Now on no account are you to dance with any of the following,' Lady Ashton said, reeling off a list of names. 'They are all notorious rakes. Nor must you dance with that young gentleman over there if he asks you.' She made a gesture with her folded fan to a tall thin young man with mousy hair and rather more nose than chin who was staring at Lallie.

'He does not look like a rake,' Lallie could not help remarking, looking away quickly as the young man smiled at her.

'He isn't,' Lady Ashton said succinctly. 'He's heir to a dukedom and Lady Brewham has him down for her eldest daughter, and we do not want to upset her. In fact, we shall make a start with her. If she acknowledges you, it will make the rest think twice before cutting you—'

'You ought to be in Spain, Aunt,' Alex sighed from behind Lallie's shoulder. 'You plan a campaign as well as Wellington.'

'I rather think I shall need to,' Lady Ashton said with a frown as she glanced over Alex's shoulder. 'The Marquis of Corton seems intent on giving us our first skirmish. He is coming over here now. Remember, my dear,' she murmured to Lallie, 'you went to the Row alone out of ignorance and as for Corton's comments, you know they were no more than jests. And that goes for you, too, Alex,' she added as she glanced at her great nephew's face, 'I want no more duelling talk.'

There was little danger of that, Lallie thought fiercely. He'd only challenged Corton in the Park to make her more tempting bait!

'Good evening, Lady Ashton, Major Haldane,' Corton drawled as he reached them, making the most perfunctory of bows to Lady Ashton and Lallie, and nothing more than the stiffest of nods to Alex. 'And Miss Ross, is it not? But perhaps you do not remember me?'

For a moment she was frozen as the instant revulsion

she always felt upon seeing Corton flooded through her. She could not go through with this—but she had to—for Emily, for five thousand guineas.

'No one could forget you, my lord,' she said with what she hoped sounded like simpering admiration.

Beside her, she heard Alex exhale sharply and saw his mouth tighten into a grim line as Corton smiled and flashed him a mocking look.

'Nor you, Miss Ross, I assure you.' Corton turned his smile upon her and fear slid like ice along her spine. 'I have thought of you often since your adventure in the Row. You should take much more care in your choice of mounts, you know. These cavalry screws are such uncivilised beasts.' He looked directly at Alex as he spoke.

It was only as she saw Alex go white to the lips with unmistakable, barely suppressed fury, saw his right hand go for where he was used to carry a sabre and heard Lady Ashton's stifled gasp that she realised what Corton had implied. As Alex's pale lips parted to speak, she took a step between the two men and smiled brightly up at Corton. 'I could not agree more, but given the choice I should rather take to the dance floor with a cavalry remount than its rider, I swear they would seem to have fewer feet and better conversation.'

It was a poor enough sally, she thought, but it served its purpose in diverting Alex's furious glare from Corton to herself. She was, she realised as she glared back at him, almost beginning to enjoy herself. And so was Lady Ashton, she thought, as the elderly dowager gave her a sudden wicked grin that was oddly like Alex's.

'Then you must allow me to rescue you from such a fate, Miss Ross,' Corton laughed and drawled at her. 'May I have the honour of the first and fifth dances?'

'Oh, but the honour is all mine, my lord.' She treated him to the best imitation of breathless admiration that she could manage.

'Great God,' Alex muttered at her contemptuously after Corton had left them, and Lady Ashton, after a faintly puzzled look at Lallie, had turned aside for a moment to speak to an acquaintance. 'If I had not witnessed that, I should never have believed that you could behave in such a way—you all but invited him into your bed!'

'Which is exactly what you and the General had in mind, was it not?' she retorted ferociously in a low voice, her eyes glittering like polished steel as she met his gaze.

'You cannot mean to go so far,' he rasped back at her.

'You or him? What difference does it make so long as I am paid?' she snapped back, wanting to hurt him as much as she was hurting inside because he had brought her here and was prepared to allow her to go through with the General's scheme.

'I cannot believe how you have changed—' He broke off as he stared at her and she met his gaze without flinching, her chin high and eyes steady. Then he shook his head as if in disbelief. 'And I thought I knew you!'

'How could I not change?' she returned thickly. 'You knew a girl who knew nothing of poverty and hunger or any danger greater than taking a fence upon the hunting field—a girl who believed that you loved her and nothing else mattered. If you must be astonished, it should be that I was still stupid and naïve enough to believe that you loved me a second time! And what of you?' she went on raggedly as he stared at her, ashen and set-lipped. 'Have you not changed? Five years ago, would you have considered asking me to become Corton's whore even if Bonaparte's defeat had rested upon it—?'

'No.' He cut her off flatly. 'I'd have run anyone through for suggesting it.'

'No,' she said slowly after an unguarded moment in which their eyes met and held and she found herself suddenly wanting to cry. 'You wouldn't,' she said miserably. 'You would not have taken it seriously for a moment. You would have laughed—and then you would have come and told me and we would both have laughed and thought the whole thing a ridiculous joke—'

'I suppose so,' he agreed with a bleakness that matched hers. 'We used to laugh at most things then, did we not? Perhaps it is a habit we should both relearn?'

'I wish you would now,' Lady Ashton interrupted them tartly before Lallie could even begin to decide whether or not he had just extended an olive branch or was telling her he did not care what she did any more. 'Do try and look as if you are enjoying yourselves. To look at the pair of you, you would think you were to climb the steps to the gallows! Lady Brewham might look like an executioner, but I assure you most people survive an introduction.'

The introduction to the formidable Lady Brewham and her four eldest daughters was followed by a flurry of others which left no time for her to dwell upon Alex's faintly wistful remark, or indeed to talk with him. She was swamped with requests for dances and sometimes friendly, sometimes hostile, enquiries about her health after her unfortunate accident in the Row, which she dealt with politely but firmly, earning nods of approval from Lady Ashton.

'I think you have been quite a success,' Lady Ashton told her with some satisfaction after Charles Cavendish, had begged her for her last remaining dance. 'Now I believe that is the orchestra striking up for the first set, so if you will excuse me I am going to find some refreshment and a chair. Haldane will look after you.'

'A success indeed,' Alex said acidly, killing any fragile hope she had had of reconciliation, of a way out of the whole stupid tangle. 'There does not seem to be one of my male acquaintances who does not wish to dance with you. I thought Charles Cavendish and Downey were going to come to blows over the gavotte.' His disdainful tone was like a knife, sliding under her skin. 'But then they do not know that you would oblige both of them for the right price, do they?' he finished silkily. 'Though they'd probably consider five thousand a bit over the top. But then, they don't know you as I do.'

She stared at him disbelievingly, wanting to dash her wine in his face, hit him, hurt him in any way she could—

'Oh, I shouldn't,' he said as he watched her hand lift, 'You don't want to undo all Lady Ashton's hard work, do you? After all, why stop at Corton? With your looks and an entrée into Society, you could probably get yourself set up by an Earl or even a Duke, judging by the way old Winchester was looking at you just now.'

Her hand stilled momentarily, the glass half raised, and then she lifted the glass slowly to her lips, and took a sip of the sparkling wine, which was almost, but not quite, as cold as her heart and mind, before replying.

'Then perhaps you will be so kind as to introduce me,' she said as her gaze clashed with his in a glitter of silver and blue like two steel blades. 'If there is one thing I have learnt this last five years, it is never to waste an opportunity for financial gain.'

She had meant to shock him, and felt a jolt of bitter triumph as she saw that she had succeeded. He returned her stare for a moment and then shrugged. 'If you wish it. Now or later?'

'Later,' she said too quickly.

'Saving your energies for Corton?' he drawled as he put down his empty glass upon a passing waiter's silver salver and helped himself to another.

'Isn't that what you want?' she returned. 'No doubt the safe return of the plans will earn you your commander's gratitude.'

'Undoubtedly,' he said a moment later, as blandly, as smoothly as if they had been discussing the weather. 'That's the orchestra tuning up. I suppose all your dances are promised.'

'Except one,' she said tersely. 'It was to have been with Captain Downey, but he has been called back to his barracks.'

For a moment as their eyes met again she felt a flicker of hope and wondered if he would ask her for it. Wondered if he remembered the last time they had danced five years ago. Remembered how they had relished every precious moment of being close, being allowed to touch. . .

Five years. It seemed more like a lifetime, she thought, as she gazed into his cold, veiled blue eyes. Five years ago when she had scarcely faced a problem greater than that of which gown to wear at dinner. Five years ago she had had all the certainty of youth that he loved her and that no quarrel between them would ever be too great to mend.

'Well, don't expect me to ask for it,' he said with a rasp of laughter. 'I am not in the mood for dancing. But I am sure Corton will oblige,' he said coldly as he looked away. 'It should prove an ideal opportunity for you to further the acquaintance.'

With the slightest of bows, he turned and walked away from her, leaving her alone amid the chattering crowd.

CHAPTER ELEVEN

SHAKING, her throat aching from the effort not to cry, she stared at one of the great Italian landscape paintings upon the opposite wall without taking in a single detail. Dear God! How she wished she had never gone to Isabelle Carteret's! Wished she had never met him again! Wished she had never, ever, met him! If it were not for Emily, there was nothing that would keep her here another moment. She would rather take her chances upon the street!

'Miss Ross? I do believe I have the honour of the first dance?'

She turned, her skin crawling and heart thumping as she recognised the drawling affected tones of the Marquis of Corton.

'You look somewhat out of sorts. I do hope Major Haldane has not upset you. These army fellows can be so rough at times. They have no appreciation of the finer things or knowledge of how they should be treated. Whereas I. . .' he paused as he touched a pudgy white fingertip to the bare flesh between the top of her glove and her puffed sleeve '. . .appreciate the rare, the beautiful.'

'One has but to look at you to know that, my lord.' She forced herself not to recoil from his touch, forced herself to smile. The sooner she had the plans, the sooner she need never go near the man again.

'Thank you.' His cold black eyes held her gaze as he

194

smiled, making her think of a snake she had once seen in the menagerie of a nobleman when she was a child. 'I like to surround myself with perfection, be it porcelain, a jewel, a horse or...' he paused '...a woman. When I see something I want, I must have it, whatever the cost.'

'Not everything is for sale,' she countered, dropping her eyelids demurely for fear she would not be able to disguise the loathing she felt for him. 'Some things have to be won.'

'Oh, I have always found everything to have its price, so shall we dance, Miss Ross, or should I say Miss Smith?'

'I don't understand you,' she said after a fractional hesitation, as they began a cheerful mazurka, hoping that her panic, the sudden race of her heart did not show in her face. She did not want Corton to know anything about her. Nothing.

He smiled again. 'Oh, I think you do. You see, when we met in the Park I knew I had seen you before. I confess it took me a little while to remember where—a gaming den, just off Hanover Street. You were in some distress, your father having just been taken off to Newgate—I offered you assistance but was most rudely put off by some gentleman of the road and his pistols.'

That had been Corton! Now she understood her instant aversion to him, her fear of him, that faint nagging feeling of familiarity. She stared at him, almost forgetting to move her feet in time to the music. Her nightmarish memories of that particular evening were incomplete and blurred.

She could remember her father's desperate face as the constable led him out and the fear she had felt as she had found herself alone amid a dozen or so men, all more than half-drunk, and most angry, because her father owed them money. Shocked and afraid, she had not resisted when a stranger had taken her arm, and hustled her out of the hell towards his carriage in the street, promising to take her home. It was only as he had opened the carriage door and she had glanced up into his cold black eyes, that instinct had told her that he was no friend. The rest was a blur.

She had tried to turn back, the stranger had sworn at her and tried to force her into the carriage. Then Tom Mitchell had appeared, an unlikely guardian angel, half-drunk but armed with his horse pistols and the stranger had leapt into his carriage and gone away at all speed, leaving her sobbing upon the pavement.

She had been in such a state of panic, of fear, that she had registered nothing about her would-be abductor. But now the memory came back, crystal clear. But she was not going to admit that to him. She had to brazen this out.

'You are quite mistaken—you are confusing me with someone else. My sister and I have been living in Banffshire until a month or so ago.'

Corton sighed as they executed a swift turn. 'Please do not try and cozen me with that tale. I know that you and your sister have been lodging in a house just off Petticoat Lane since last December. Before that I believe it was some rookery in the Seven Dials, was it not?'

'And if it was?' She was as offhand as she could manage as she realised there was no point in trying to lie further. 'What is it to you?'

'To me, nothing. But I rather think it might matter

to you, Miss Ross. A word in Lady Furney's ear and your little foray into Society would soon be over, would it not? So, tell me, Miss Ross, exactly what is Haldane trying to do in bringing you here?'

She was silent for a moment, making a performance of concentration upon her steps as she thought furiously. Corton knew she was not what she was pretending to be, but he was only guessing that Alex knew her true history.

'Why, escorting his great aunt's ward, my lord,' she said as lightly as she was able. 'Lady Ashton was a great friend of my grandmother's. As far as she and Haldane are concerned, I have never lived anywhere but Scotland until this last month.'

He gave a snort of laughter. 'Well, I always knew Haldane was a chivalrous fool, but I never took him for a flat.'

'Oh, please do not speak ill of the man I am to marry.' She also laughed, playing the demi-rep for all she was worth. 'He has his good points.'

'Marry!' Corton almost choked. 'You certainly do not lack for audacity, Miss Ross, but I scarcely think you will succeed there—'

'He has already proposed.' She smiled as Corton did not quite manage to mask his shock.

'He means to marry you, a woman who has been a frequenter of some of the worse hells in Town and has a father who died in Newgate gaol!' Corton shook his head in disbelief and then he laughed. 'Oh, this is delicious, Miss Ross. You cannot think how I shall enjoy putting this about.'

'I was hoping I could persuade you to keep silent upon the matter,' she said hastily.

'Really?' he drawled and looked at her speculatively in a way that made her skin crawl. 'How?'

'Once we are wed and I have access to his fortune—'

'No.' He cut her off with another smile. 'I don't think so, Miss Ross. I shall have money enough. The price of my silence is you. I made up my mind that I should have you in the Park, but the thought of cuckolding Haldane, well. . .that makes you irresistible. You have no idea how much pleasure that will add to our encounters.'

Or how much I will get from taking the plans from you, she thought with sudden cold anger. If only the General knew it, at this moment she would have been happy to act for nothing, simply to cheat this odious, evil man of his triumph!

'Oh, please don't worry,' Corton drawled, leering at her. 'I shall not tell Haldane, at least not until after the wedding. I want to see his face when he finds he has shackled himself to a. . .' he hesitated insultingly '. . .a common muslin.'

'Then I might as well tell him of what you have threatened now,' she countered, 'for I shall have little to lose.'

'Please do,' he smiled. 'He is obviously in love with you and will certainly call me out. And if one thing would give me more pleasure than cuckolding him, it will be killing him, Miss Ross. And then where will you be? Back in the Seven Dials?'

'Then you leave me little choice,' she said, deciding to let him think she was beaten.

'I was sure that you would see it that way, being a

practical young woman.' He smiled at her, his eyes black and snake-like as they held hers.

'And after you have had your revenge upon Major Haldane, what then?' she asked. 'Supposing he discards me? Will I still enjoy your protection then?'

'That depends upon how well you please me,' he drawled as the last chord of the mazurka was played and he let his fingers trail down from her shoulder and over her breast before releasing her. 'But I am sure you will not find it difficult to think of ways to do that, Miss Ross—'

'Badgering you for another dance, is he?' broke in a cheerful voice with a Scots accent. 'Well, you canna have this 'een, Corton, it's promised to me, so awa' wi you.'

'Macleod?' For a second an expression close to fear flickered through the Marquis's dark eyes as he stared at the tall, rangy Scotsman. 'I did not expect to see you here.'

'Ach, ye know me, my lord, I like to be where folks least expect me. Now if ye dinna mind, the lassie's mine.'

Bemused, Lallie found her arm taken by the red-haired Scot, as the Marquis bowed and ceded his place beside her.

'You are mistaken, I fear, this dance was promised to Captain Downey, Mr. . .' she began hestitantly.

'Macleod, Captain Alistair Macleod,' he supplied with a grin as she stared at him blankly. 'Captain Downey was called awa', a message from his Colonel.'

'I know—' she began. She did not want to dance—she wanted to find Alex.

'It seems they have to sail for Spain tomorrow, so he

asked if I would stand in for him,' Captain Macleod went on.

'Oh, I see. Thank you,' she said absently as they began the gavotte and she searched the room with her eyes for Alex. She had to talk to him, whether he wished to listen or not.

Captain Macleod seemed oblivious to her lack of attention, chattering on about the war, asking questions about Alex's exploits in Spain and Portugal and his miraculous return and how well she was acquainted with the Marquis of Corton. Questions that she answered mechanically with little thought as she looked in vain for Alex.

'I suppose a man like Major Haldane must find home leave very tame when he has been used to being in the thick of it,' Captain Macleod observed as they parted and then came back together to execute a turn.

'Oh, I think he is busy enough,' she replied thoughtlessly. 'He seems to have to go to the War Office most days to meet with General Houghton.'

'And wi' the Marquis, no doubt. I suppose they are great friends.'

'I do not think so,' she said, taken aback by his rather vulgar questions. 'If fact, Major Haldane does his best to avoid him.'

'Ach, weel, I dinna blame him for that—I suppose the Major prefers to be amongst fighting men. I had heard that Lord Wellington and his intelligence chief regard Major Haldane as one of their most useful men, whether on campaign or politicking at home.'

'Really?' she said a little frostily, as she was beginning to find his questions a little too intrusive, his Scots accent a little too overdone as if he were playing the

simple Highlander. 'And what do you do in London,
Captain Macleod? From your accent, you would seem
to be as far from home as myself.'

'You're not a child of the heather?' Red brows lifted
over his hazel eyes. 'You dinna sound like one.'

'My mother was English and I had English governesses,' she explained. 'But I did not set foot in England
until I was eighteen.'

'Weel, weel, I'd niver ha taken ye for a Gael!' he
exclaimed, and then whispered something in the Gaelic
which brought a rose blush to her face and, in spite of
everything, made her laugh.

'You understand the tongue?' he asked her.

'Enough of it to recognise a shameless flatterer,
Captain Macleod,' she answered lightly in Gaelic. 'And
no, I will not awa' to Gretna with ye.'

'Ach, I should have known you'd be spoken for—
from the look on your face it wasn't the Marquis, so I
suppose it's Major Haldane. The rest of us dinna have
a chance against the cavalry.'

'I am quite sure you get plenty of chances, Captain
Macleod,' she said with a half-smile, then added as she
glanced at the clever foxy face and sharp hazel eyes,
'Or should I say that you take plenty of chances.'

'Oh, cruel, cruel,' he groaned. 'How canna ye be so
cruel?'

'Probably because I am half-English,' she returned
self-mockingly.

He laughed. 'Weel, that would explain it right
enough.'

'Who was that impertinent young man you were
dancing with?' Lady Ashton asked her after the gavotte

had finished and Captain Macleod had evaporated into the crowd.

'A Captain Macleod. I thought you must know him,' she said, still looking about for Alex, Macleod already out of her thoughts..

'Never seen him before,' Lady Ashton said. 'He'll be one of the Furneys' Scots connections, no doubt.'

She agreed without interest, still looking for Alex, of whom there was no sign. And then Cavendish came to claim her for the next dance and someone else for the next and the next until she found herself back with the Marquis of Corton again.

It was only as she reluctantly let him take her arm that she finally saw Alex, entering the ballroom with General Houghton, deep in what looked like a heated discussion.

And then suddenly, as if feeling her gaze upon him, Alex turned his head to look at her. Despairingly, she saw his face contort with disgust as Corton, also seeing him, deliberately drew her far closer than was acceptable.

Her second dance with Corton seemed a hundred times as long as any other dance, not because she found the steps difficult, but because of her enforced proximity to the Marquis.

Again and again she had to grit her teeth and bear it as his hand, which should have rested lightly upon her waist, strayed upwards to her breast, or down over the curve of her hip. Caresses which had no effect but to make her shrink further and further away from him as he tried to draw her closer.

'I trust you are not always so modest, Miss Ross,' he

whispered into her ear. 'Has the Major taught you nothing of how to please a man?'

'I do not relish being mauled in public!' she snapped, forgetting for a moment that she dare not offend him or let him know that she would die before she take him as a lover. Whatever else, she must keep him on a string until the letters could be secured and she was sure Emily was safe.

Then, in the midst of the struggle to keep him at a decorous distance, her fingers felt something rectangular and bulky beneath his coat. What was it the General had said? That he kept the plans upon him at all times. Surely it could not be that easy?

She dragged in a breath and fluttered her eyelashes at him in what she hoped was an arch sort of way. 'You will find me different when we are alone.'

'I do hope so, I hate disappointments,' he drawled. 'Shall we say six o'clock tomorrow at my house in Portman Square? I will have my footman wait for you at the back gate, as no doubt you will wish to be discreet.'

'Tomorrow will suit me very well,' she lied with a bright smile, thinking that if she failed to get the papers now, it would give her another opportunity.

'Good.' He smiled as she yielded slightly to his embrace while she struggled to remember everything Tom Mitchell had told her about how a pocket was picked.

A collision, that was what was needed, something to distract the attention. Smiling up into Corton's smooth face, she let him bring her closer and whispered into his ear that she was looking forward to their next meeting in more intimate circumstances.

'So am I.' He smiled his cold smile at her. 'And even more to telling Haldane about it—after he has married you, of course.'

She wanted to punch him upon his pug-like nose, but somehow contrived to laugh. He was absolutely odious, she thought. No, not odious, but evil.

She chose that moment to stumble heavily, clutching his arm, almost pushing him into another couple while her right hand slid lightly under his jacket, found the inner pocket—and that it was sewn shut.

And then, to her horror, her wrist was caught in a crushing grip and she was jerked away. She looked up, her guilt written in her eyes, but Corton was not looking at her, but at Alex, who had caught her arm.

'What the deuce—?' Corton began coldly.

'Miss Ross looked unwell, I thought she had fainted and was about to fall,' Alex replied blandly. 'With your permission, I am going to take her out for some air.'

Before Corton could recover, or even begin to reply, Lallie found herself propelled across the dance floor.

'Let go of me!' she blurted out. 'You don't understand, I do not wish to offend him—'

'Are you trying to tell me you like him pawing you?' he snarled, dragging her back against him. 'Or was it the other way about?' he muttered beneath his breath before pushing her through the edges of the crowd, out of an open French window and onto a deserted lantern-lit terrace. 'You had your hand inside his coat!' he rapped out as she breathed in a ragged breath of soft summer night air, heavy with the scent of flowers.

'You cannot think I enjoyed touching him!' she flared back at him, shaken to the core by the fright she had had when he had caught her wrist. 'I was trying to get the plans—I am sure the General is right and he carries them with him.'

'Great God!' He swore as she jerked out of his grasp and began to descend the shallow stone steps down into the gardens. 'Do you mean you were trying to pick his pocket?'

'Yes! The sooner I get the papers, the sooner I will have my five thousand guineas and need have no more to do with him—or your precious General—or *you*!' she finished fiercely as she flounced down the last step.

'Is that really what you want?' he said harshly as he followed her. 'For us to have no more to do with each other?'

'Yes!' she retorted, as he caught her arm again, pulling her into the shadow of the terrace.

'You know that is not true,' he said exasperatedly as he felt her trembling. 'I love you and you love me, you must do—you would not have given yourself to me if you did not.'

'It was necessity, nothing more,' she said fiercely, jerking free again, her eyes glittering silver in the moonlight. 'Like you said, I had nowhere else to go!'

'Necessity!' She heard his breath catch in a disbelieving gasp.

'Yes. And as far as I am concerned, whatever debt I have to you has been paid in full. I do not want you to touch me ever again!'

He gave a ragged laugh, his teeth white in his shadowed face. 'I think you do protest too much, Miss Ross.'

'Really!' she said, flinging her head back to look him full in the face. 'Then why don't you try?' she taunted. Alex remained so still in the darkness that she could feel the tautness in his body, hear the tight rasp of his breath as he struggled with his temper. 'Or are you afraid that you might be wrong?'

She was silenced as he caught her to him and his mouth captured her parted lips in a punishing, searing kiss. A kiss that bruised her lips. A kiss that held nothing of tenderness, only the demand for possession as if he meant to stamp himself upon her for all time. And then, just as she would have struggled free of him, his mouth and hands gentled, offering the comfort that she had craved since they had argued the day before. And she was lost. It seemed like a lifetime since he had last held her and she had nowhere else to go, no other place where she belonged except here in his arms. Nowhere else where she was safe and nowhere else where she wished to be more—

'You are right,' he said as he lifted his mouth from hers, his breathing rapid and ragged like her own. 'This is necessity, isn't it? As much as breathing, you need me, Lallie.'

'Only until I have my five thousand guineas,' she blurted out, hating him because he was right. 'Now just leave me alone, Alex!' She twisted out of his grasp, snatched up her skirts and ran blindly from him across the lawn, the knot in her chest turning to choking sobs as she slid down the steeply banked edge of the lawn and onto a gravel path, which she followed without caring where it was going, so long as it was away from him.

'With the greatest of pleasure!' he shouted after her and strode back to the house.

His great aunt was waiting for him upon the terrace.

'Enough is enough, Alex,' she said frostily. 'I saw the

way you hauled Miss Ross off the dance floor. How am I to convince the world she is a lady when you treat her in such a fashion? Either you tell me exactly what is going on or I shall have no more to do with it!

'Well, of course she would accept the General's offer. What choice did she have?' his aunt groaned some minutes later. 'If I had been in her position, penniless, a child to support and apparently betrayed by the man I loved, I should have done exactly the same. For heaven's sake, Alex, the girl's life has been turned upside down by you, then her father's idiocy and then you again! No wonder she is desperate to have some financial independence!'

'I had not thought of it like that,' he sighed, pushing a hand through his thick dark hair. 'I could think of nothing but her with Corton. When she told the General she would do it, I could not believe it. I should have wagered my life that she would not give herself to any man she did not love, not for all the gold in Threadneedle Street.'

'Then for heaven's sake go and tell her so!' his aunt said in exasperation. 'That's if you don't want to lose her a second time.'

'Lallie!' He called her name softly as he halted at the foot of the bank where he had last seen her, and stared into the gloom. There were no lanterns in this part of the garden and it was dark and apparently deserted. There was a path, pale in the moonlight snaking off into what looked and smelt like a rose garden on the left, and a dark mass of shrubbery on the right. Which way had she gone?

Alex sighed as there was no reply. Where the devil

was she? He was about to start down the path when a
twig in the shrubbery cracked like a pistol shot.

'Lallie?' he said more softly.

There was no reply but silence. A silence that gave
him the same sense of unease as he often felt before an
ambush or attack in Spain. And then another unmistakable sound of a foot stepping on rotten wood behind
him, a foot that he knew instinctively was far too heavy
for Lallie.

'Who goes there?' he barked out the army challenge
out of habit gained upon the picket lines as he wheeled
around, reaching instinctively for the pistol that had
always been at his side for the last five years and
cursing inwardly as his hand encountered only the hilt
of his dress sword.

'Friend not foe, so dinna shoot—you're in England
now,' came a laughing Scots voice out of the darkness.
'Captain Alistair Macleod at your service, Major
Haldane,' the Scot added as he stepped out of the
shadow of the shrubbery. 'Like Miss Ross, I found the
ballroom a trifle too warm for my liking. I trust she is
recovered now?'

'I think so,' Alex returned coolly. 'I don't believe
I've had the pleasure Captain Macleod?'

'We have met, at Talavera,' the Scotsman replied,
'but I wouldna' expect you to remember me. You were
a mite busy at the time. A near thing that time, Major,
with those dragoons? You dinna step much closer than
that to death and walk away. I always wondered what
made you rush at them like that—you having such a
reputation for a cool head.'

'I'd just seen a particularly good friend killed.' Alex
shrugged. 'I lost my temper, always a stupid thing to do

in battle. You're not the rifle officer who came to my aid? If you are, then I owe you my thanks.'

'No, no!' Macleod shook his head and laughed. 'To tell the truth, Major, I was far too busy saving my own skin at the time—like you, I kept finding myself in the middle of the wrong army.'

'It's easily done, especially in the smoke.' Alex laughed politely. 'But if you will excuse me, Captain Macleod, I was looking for someone—'

'If it's Corton you're looking for, I saw him take the path for the carriage house. It's very dark, and a mite rough under foot, so, if I were you, I'd have a care.'

'Actually, it was Miss Ross I was looking for.'

'Lost her, have you? That's awful careless of you, Major.' Macleod laughed softly. 'She appears to be a very unusual young woman. I'd hold on to her if she were mine.'

'I intend to, Macleod.' There was a thread of ice now in Alex's voice. He was glad now that Macleod was not the rifle officer to whom he owed his life. It would not have been easy to be indebted to the faintly mocking Scotsman whom he found himself beginning to dislike.

'Then I'll say good evening, Major and I hope you find her quickly.' It sounded almost like a warning as the Scot turned away and walked off into the shadows, whistling a tune that was naggingly familiar to Alex, though he could not put a name to it.

He frowned. His sense of unease was growing, not receding, but for the life of him he did not know why. . . he only knew he wanted to find Lallie, make sure she was safe.

* * *

Lallie shivered and wrapped her scarf more tightly about her shoulders. She could not stay in the garden for ever. She had to find Alex, warn him that Corton knew about her, might even be suspicious... But she could not go in—not yet—not with her face streaked with tears.

She walled to and fro in the small garden which was bordered with high hedges. Why was she still clinging to the ridiculous hope that he loved her? she asked herself bitterly as she walked to and fro across the small circular lawn, so wrapped in her thoughts that she did not even flinch as the bats dipped and dived through the night air, skimming so close to her that she could almost feel the wind from their flight. Why did so much of her want to believe that what he had said about loving her, wanting to marry her, was true?

In the centre of the garden was a small circular fountain, the water spilling out of the cup held aloft by three nymphs, whose marble flesh gleamed softly in the moonlight. She dipped the end of her scarf in the cool water and pressed it to her tear-swollen eyes. She did not want Alex to see she had been crying. It would be the last humiliation.

'All alone, Miss Ross?' She gave a small gasp and wheeled at Captain Macleod's soft drawl.

She had heard nothing. He seemed to have materialised out of the gloom from nowhere.

'I did not mean to startle you—' he smiled '—you have my sincerest apologies.'

'It doesn't matter.' To her chagrin her voice was still husky from tears.

'I take it Major Haldane has been riding somewhat roughshod this evening?' he said gently.

'You could say that.' She managed a watery smile.

'I could not help but notice that he dinna seem very happy to see you dance with Corton, not that that surprises me. I shouldna' want the woman I loved anywhere near the delightful Marquis.'

'Major Haldane does not love me,' she said stiltedly. 'We are old acquaintances, that is all.'

Macleod laughed. 'Oh come, Miss Ross! I've never seen the Major as rattled as he has been this evening, not even with a troop of *chasseurs* upon his heels.'

'You have served in the Peninsula?' she said frostily, wanting to change the subject. She was beginning to take exception to Captain Macleod's habit of asking decidedly personal questions. 'Are you in Alex's regiment?'

'Ach no, we've never even spoken before tonight.' The Scot laughed again. 'But I've seen him at a distance from time to time. He has quite a reputation on our side of the lines—'

'Reputation for what?' she asked sharply.

'Impertinence, audacity, and a coolness under fire of which I've never seen the like.' The Scot grinned. 'I've seen him ride to within hailing distance of a French artillery regiment, stop, get his notebook out and begin to count the guns while the musket balls have begun to fly about him and the gunners take their range.'

She did not want to know that, she thought, with a lurch of her stomach, did not want to think about how often he must take such risks.

'Ach, I dinna meant to upset ye,' Captain Macleod said abjectly as he saw her stricken expression in the moonlight. 'Why not let me show you the rose garden to make amends—it's a rare sight even in the moonlight.'

'I don't think so—' she took a step back as he went to take her arm '—I think that will be Major Haldane coming to look for me.'

The Scot stiffened and listened momentarily to the sound of approaching footsteps on the gravel path on the other side of the hedge. Then he shrugged. 'I think you are right,' he said softly. 'Another time, perhaps? Goodnight, Miss Ross.'

With that he was gone, disappearing into the shadows as noiselessly as he had come.

'Alex. . .' she began tentatively and then her voice died as she heard his voice, and realised that he was with someone. She sighed. She wanted to speak to him alone. For the first ten minutes or so, she could hear nothing but the low murmur of his voice, and then as they moved closer suddenly, she identified the General's voice.

'What the devil did you think you were doing— hauling Miss Ross away from Corton like that? She was doing exactly what we wanted,' General Houghton snapped and stopped the greeting which had been upon her lips. She did not want to eavesdrop but it was going to be far too embarrassing to reveal herself at this moment.

'I was protecting my future wife's reputation, sir.'

'You do not really mean to marry her!' The General was incredulous. 'Surely that is for Corton's benefit?'

'I fully intend to marry her, if she will have me. She has not accepted me yet,' Alex replied tersely.

'She's hardly likely to turn you down, is she?'

General Houghton said with a snort. 'What demi-rep would throw away such a chance?'

'None,' Alex said in clipped tones, 'but as I have told you on several occasions, Miss Ross is no demi-rep.'

'No?' The General's voice was heavy with disbelief. 'She leapt at my offer of five thousand guineas quickly enough. What sort of respectable young woman would do that, eh?'

'One who is penniless with a child to support and thinks herself betrayed for a second time by the one person she should have been able to trust,' Alex said grimly. 'She only agreed because she was angry and afraid—and because I have behaved like a perfect fool.'

'And you're behaving like one now!' the General retorted. 'Damn it, Haldane! We need those plans. If one whiff of Wellesley's fortifications reach the French, his whole strategy for holding Portugal this winter could be destroyed. Bonaparte will have Spain and Portugal handed to him on a plate. Are you really prepared to let that happen because of some infatuation you have with a muslin?'

'No,' Alex said gratingly. 'But if you refer to Miss Ross in such terms again, I shall have no choice but to call you out!'

'There are people who will call her worse than that!' the General growled. 'Are you going to fight the whole world for her?'

'If need be,' Alex snapped. 'And you need not worry about the letters. I will get them.'

'You'd better,' General Houghton retorted, 'because it's probably the only chance you'll have of saving your career if you insist on making such a match!'

With that he turned upon his heel and marched off.

CHAPTER TWELVE

AND he *would* fight the world for her, Lallie realised, her heart leaping beneath her ribs as she heard him swear softly on the other side of the hedge. He would because he loved her. His anger, his bitterness, his contempt these last two days had all been because he loved her, not because he did not. And she had been such a fool to doubt it.

'Alex!' she called out to him, as she heard him begin to move away. 'Wait!'

'Lallie?'

'I am here on the other side of the hedge. Wait, I'll come round.' She picked up her skirts and ran, almost cannoning into him a minute or so later as he came running from the opposite direction to meet her.

They both halted and stared at one another in the pallid moonlight.

'You've been crying,' he said after a moment of silence.

'Yes.'

He sighed and offered her his arm. 'We need to talk.'

'Yes,' she said again as she put her hand upon his sleeve. 'But not here Alex, please can we go home?'

'Of course,' he said gently and drew her closer as they began to walk back towards the house. 'But we had better go make our farewells to Lady Furney and tell Lady Ashton. It will look better if we leave together.'

'I don't want to go in,' she said. 'People will see I have been crying and there will be questions—I'd rather go straight to our carriage. That path there leads to the stables, I'll get Tom to bring our carriage round to the front and tell Lady Ashton's man to bring hers.'

'Whatever you wish.' He turned and began to lead her down the path towards the stable block at the far end of the garden.

'Haldane! Haldane!' A voice hailed them from the terrace. 'A word, if you please!'

He swore softly and halted, releasing her arm. 'It's Downey. What the devil can he want?'

'Downey? I thought he had left,' she said, frowning. 'Why don't you go and see—and make our apologies to Lady Furney,' she said hastily. 'I'll meet you at the front with the carriages.'

'Are you sure?' he said, glancing at where the path disappeared into the trees.

'I am not afraid of the dark.'

'No.' A brief smile curved his mouth. 'You are not afraid of very much at all, are you?'

'Only of losing you again,' she said half-audibly, before touching him lightly upon the cheek with her fingers.

'Lallie—' She heard his breath catch as he caught her fingers and held them to his face. Then as Downey hailed him again, he released her.

'Five minutes. Not a minute more, promise? There is so much I have to say to you.'

'I promise.' Smiling, she turned away and began to walk rapidly along the path which disappeared into the trees. It was going to be all right. Somehow she knew it was going to be all right. Humming a snatch of a

Mozart aria she walked on, utterly oblivious to the man who waited beneath the trees, watching her approach and smiling to himself.

She was going to fall into his lap. Despite the last minute alteration in his plans it was all going far better than he had dreamed possible. Not only had he the papers without paying Corton a penny of the gold he could now keep for himself, but he had finally found the means with which he might damage Wellington's damnably efficient intelligence network. *Sacré Bleu!* If Haldane could be persuaded to deceive his masters— make an omission in a report here, an exaggeration there—Wellington would not even seek to confirm it, and then at last they might take that cool, canny Irishman by surprise and push him back into the Mediterranean. And the beauty of it was, they would not even have to pay Haldane—he was not the sort to be bought for money—but he'd do it to protect the delightful Miss Ross. MacLeod was certain of that after having seen them together in the garden.

'Haldane!' Captain Downey greeted Alex breathlessly as he stepped onto the terrace. 'You have not seen that Macleod fellow, have you?'

'Yes,' Alex said as he strolled into the ballroom, with Downey at his heels. 'What of it? You look quite out of sorts, Downey.'

'So would you if you had been sent on a fool's errand!' Captain Downey's pink-and-white Somerset complexion took on the hue of a tomato as he struggled to express his indignation. 'The fellow told me a deliberate lie—sent me back to barracks, simply so that he could steal my dance with Miss Ross. I do not know how he came to be invited here, for he is no gentleman.'

'How whom came to be invited?' Lady Furney put in, having come up beside them.

'Your Scottish cousin, Captain Macleod,' Alex said, beginning to frown a little. 'You say he lied to you so he might dance with Miss Ross?'

'Yes. Impudent fellow!' Downey snapped. 'I've a good mind to call him out!'

'But I have no Scottish cousins here,' Lady Furney said bemusedly.

'You mean you do not know him?' Alex said slowly, frowning. 'A red-haired gentleman, tall and slight but wiry—'

'Red-haired? Certainly not,' said Lady Furney huffily, as if it were some unfortunate defect. 'None of that in our family, I assure you.'

'An uninvited guest, no doubt,' snorted Downey. 'Told me he was an acquaintance of Corton's. I'm going to have word with Corton.'

'He's already left—' Alex began, but Downey had already strode off.

Macleod. Alex frowned. There was something nagging at the edge of his mind, an unease he could not put a finger upon. Something he had missed and it was something to do with Macleod. He went back over their conversation in the garden, and then, like a dash of icy water in the face, he knew what it was. The tune Macleod had whistled as he walked away, that haunting half-familiar tune. He had heard it whistled a hundred times on the lines in Portugal and Spain, whistled by French troops on French lines—but only once whistled in just that way, by a man whose face he had never

seen. A man who had sat calm and at ease, behind a
carved Moorish screen, while two Grenadiers had
beaten him half-senseless in the hope of getting information he did not have. A man the Grenadiers had
called 'Le Reynard.' A man who was the most devious
and duplicious intriguer the French possessed in Spain.

It could not be—not here in England, he told himself,
but it was. He knew it with sudden certainty as he
recalled Macleod's comment about always being in the
middle of the wrong army—the man had practically
told him who he was.

The walk through the trees was longer than Lallie had
thought, but she was almost at the end of the plantation
of trees when she heard footsteps, rapid and heavy,
thundering along the path towards her. A moment later
a lanky figure came flying around a bend in the path,
arms waving, coat-tails flying, running as if the hounds
of hell were on his heels.

A figure she recognised instantly, even in silhouette.
'Tom?' she said in astonishment as he slithered to an
astonished halt. 'Whatever is the matter?'

'Where's the Major?' was his breathless answer. 'I
have to speak to him, Lallie, and quick.'

'In the house,' she said, sighing. She had hoped
regular employment might have reduced Tom's taste
for the bottle. 'But you can't go in there.'

'No. I'm not foxed, Lallie, this is important,' Tom
groaned as he interpreted her tone. 'There's a Frenchie
here. I've seen him. And I've just seen him kill someone. He's a spy. He must be.'

'A spy?' If she had not known about Corton and the
letters, she would have laughed and been certain that

he was foxed. 'Are you sure? How do you know?' she found herself blurting out. 'And what do you mean, you saw him kill someone?'

'Listen. . .' Tom panted breathlessly. 'I came across him in Spain—I was doing a bit of—reconnaissance in a village, hoping to find a chicken for the pot. But I found him instead—in one of the shacks, questioning a girl and none too gently. It was behind our lines. And it was dark. He had a faded old blue uniform and I thought he was one of our Hussars at first—he didn't look like a Frenchie.

'I didn't like what he was doing to the girl—he was being a right—' Tom bit off the word. 'Sorry, but he was—and I told him so. Then he turned and stepped into the lantern light and I saw that he was one of theirs—a *cuirassier*, not a Hussar—and that he had a pistol in his hand. He just looked at me and laughed. I thought I was a dead man. I would have been if the girl hadn't grabbed his arm as he fired. The shot missed me by a whisker. And do you know what he did? Casual as you like he pistolwhipped the girl and laughed again. And said, "next time, Englishman. You are in luck today." And then he was out of the window and away before I could move. I didn't hang about there either, I can tell you. I didn't want to meet him again. But I can remember his face as if it were yesterday, and the way he laughed—I'd know him anywhere. And I saw him not ten minutes ago in the yard, dragging a man into a stable and covering him with straw. Why else would he do that if he had not killed him?'

'Go back to the stables—get help,' she said, making a sudden decision. 'I'll go and get the Major—'

The flash, the bang and Tom's look of incredulity were almost simultaneous.

She watched in utter frozen horror as he crashed to the ground like a tree that had been felled.

'Alex? You look like you've just seen a ghost!' Charles Cavendish grinned as he came up to his friend. 'Miss Ross still giving you the runaround?'

'No,' Alex said grimly. 'What would you say to some hunting, Charles?'

'Never say no to a spell at your Leicestershire place; but it's the wrong season, dear fellow—you know that,' Cavendish said, startled. 'You must be in love—not that I blame you. She's delectable, Alex.'

'I wasn't referring to foxes.' Alex sighed. 'At least not the four-legged kind. Tell me Charles, does the name 'Le Reynard' mean anything to you?'

'Far too much,' the fair-haired man frowned, serious suddenly. 'He's probably the best intelligence gatherer the French have in our area, and the most ruthless. Only a few days before I came back on leave he killed a sixteen-year-old boy because he thought he was carrying messages between us and one of the Spanish mountain bands. And it was not a quick death either.'

'It rarely is with 'Le Reynard,' Alex said harshly. 'I've seen his work far too often for my taste.'

'Yes,' Cavendish agreed. 'And he was wrong. The boy was simply going to see his sister, who had married one of the partisans. I have a number of scores I should like to settle with that particular piece of French scum.'

'What would you say if I told you I have reason to think he is England engaged in a piece of business for

Bonaparte? And not in any part of England, but outside in the garden?'

'I'd say you'd had a quart too much of champagne.' Cavendish's craggy face split into a grin, a grin which faded as he saw Alex's expression. 'My God! You are serious, aren't you?'

'Never more so,' Alex said dryly. 'So are you coming?'

'Try and stop me,' Charles Cavendish said with feeling.

'Good,' Alex said, and then, as he glanced at his friend, 'Discretion is all, Charles, so no view halloos, please?'

The two men were on the terrace when the crack of the pistol shot sent a flurry of roosting crows into the air over the copse of trees, cawing and circling in panic.

'Lallie!' The blood left Alex's face as he roared her name. He vaulted over the balustrade and was already halfway across the lawn before Charles Cavendish had moved.

'So much for discretion,' Charles Cavendish muttered as he dropped over the balustrade and followed Alex. Those in the ballroom who hadn't heard the shot, had certainly heard Alex's roar. Men were already streaming out onto the terrace, demanding to know what was going on, and there was a rising hubbub of excited female voices.

'Tom. . .' Lallie's voice was reed thin in her constricted throat as she dropped to her knees beside the still form on the gravel path. 'Tom—say something,' she said helplessly, stupidly, already knowing inside that he would never say anything again.

He was utterly still, eyes staring unseeingly upwards at the moon.

'Tom...' She put her hand on his chest, seeking a heartbeat, something which she knew was a futile gesture even before she registered the warm, sticky, wetness of his blood as it welled out of the wound in his chest.

He was dead. Someone had killed him. Shot him as coldly, as expertly as a huntsman would a horse with a broken leg. And whoever it was, was still there among the trees, watching her, perhaps raising his pistol a second time and taking aim at her. The thought surfaced suddenly in her shocked brain, immobilising her mind and body.

The man watching her frowned as he deftly reloaded his pistol. He had not seen the west countryman in the yard. He was getting careless like that fool Corton who had hired as guards two of the most disreputable and easily bribed ruffians he had ever come across...he'd had no choice but to shoot. The man had been in the way—and the hue and cry would have been raised soon enough anyway once Corton was found and it was discovered Miss Ross was missing. Not that it mattered. There would be no more mistakes. He smiled again, as he glanced at the pale slight figure, kneeling like a statue on the path.

Lallie knelt, transfixed, staring at Tom's body. It must have been the Frenchman that had killed him. But who was he? Where had he come from? She had no idea even of where the shot had come from. The killer could be anywhere in the darkness beneath the leafy trees, he could be reloading this moment, taking aim at her—

oh, God! In this dress she would show up like a lantern
in the dark. She had to think. The flash had come from
the right side of the path—no sooner had she thought
it than she flung herself to the left, rolling and scrab-
bling over the dew-wet grass into the paltry shelter of
a rhododendron bush, expecting at any moment to feel
a ball tear into her flesh. But there was nothing. Nothing
but a silence filled by the thunderous drumming of her
heart and the angry cawing of the crows overhead.

Corton, she thought, as a cloud obscured the moon
and the darkness became denser, it must be something
to do with Corton. Why else would a French spy be
here in London—in this elegant garden? Oh, dear God!
Fear rose like bile in her throat as she heard someone
move stealthily on the other side of the path. She
wanted to scream again, to shout out for Alex—but her
throat was too constricted with terror. Whoever it was,
was getting nearer. She lifted her face from where she
had pressed it flat against the earth and saw a dark
form stooping over Tom, making certain he was dead.

It was not Corton. The silhouette was wrong. But
what did it matter who it was? She had to move, had to
run now while he had his back to her. But every instinct
she possessed told her to cling to the paltry protection
of the bush. She did not want to stand up—did not
want to feel a ball drive into her flesh like it had into
Tom's—but he would have seen where she had
hidden—marked the place she had disappeared. It was
not safe here.

The man was straightening, beginning to turn
towards her. She must move. With a ragged moan she
scrambled to her feet, and threw herself down the tree-
planted slope, tripping, slipping, as she twisted this way

and that through the trees. She was close to the stables, she told herself. She could get help there—*if* she got there.

The low branches seemed to catch and snatch at her, snagging her hair, tearing her gown. She tripped over a tree root, lost one of her kid slippers and went sprawling, driving the breath from her lungs. For a moment she lay still. And then she heard him, behind her, following her steadily, quietly, moving over the ground as quietly and implacably as a ghillie stalking deer.

Sobbing for breath, she blundered to her feet and stumbled on, losing her other slipper within a step or two. And then suddenly the trees stopped and there was open ground between her and the looming block of the stable buildings. Gasping with terror, she plunged forward, her whole body shrinking in on itself as she waited for him to shoot. Why didn't he shoot? She found herself almost screaming the thought aloud as she was halfway across the open ground, every step seeming like a mile. Why did he not shoot and get it over with? And then somehow, disbelievingly, she was safe in the shadow of the buildings, running through the arch. A man standing beside a carriage and team turned as she came stumbling into the yard.

'Please, help me. . .'

The plea died on her lips as Mathias Robson turned and grinned at her. She came to a skidding halt on the cobbles. Frozen with horror, she did not cry out for help to the lofts where the stable boys lodged, nor did she hear the man who slipped into the yard behind her, made a signal to Robson with his hand, and then stooped to pick up a heavy hessian sack which had once held oats for the horses.

'Well, as I live and breathe,' sneered Mathias Robson as Lallie stared at him, her breath coming in ragged gasps. 'If that ain't luck, I don't what is—look who it is, Tyson. You've just saved us a deal of trouble, Miss Ross—there's a gentleman who's most anxious for your company. So anxious he asked us to go in to the garden and look for you. But you've saved us the trouble— hasn't she, sir?'

She heard the soft footfall behind her too late. She had not even begun to move, not even begun to scream as a heavy sack was drawn suddenly down over her head, her arms pinioned to her sides. She struggled frantically, tried to scream, but breathed in a mouthful of dust and oats which sent her into a paroxysm of coughing.

Then she was upside down, almost choking as someone picked her and pushed her into the carriage. She went sprawling in the footwell, gagging and choking. Through the muffling of the sack she heard the door shut on a shouted command.

It was dark. She could not see, could not breathe. Panicking, she clawed at the sack—and then suddenly she was free of it. It was lifted away by unseen hands and she knew she was not alone in the dark interior of the carriage. She blinked, trying to clear her vision— her eyes, like her mouth, were gritty with dust. And then, as her eyes ceased to water and she grew accustomed to the gloom of the interior of the carriage, she saw her abductor for the first time, and the pistol he held, pointed at her.

'Captain Macleod!' The scream which had been on her lips came out as a gasp of disbelief. 'You!' She stared at him, then suddenly her fear gave way to searing rage. 'You killed Tom!' She flung herself forward, grabbing for the pistol.

'I wouldna' do that, Miss Ross—' his voice was like silk, and very quiet, but his grip on her wrist was like that of a mantrap '—not if you dinna want me to hurt you a great deal. I'd also recommend that you dinna try and scream unless you want this—' he ran the cold barrel of the pistol along her jaw '—broken.'

He let go of her wrist and she jerked back from him, huddling into the furthest corner of the carriage, putting her hand to her jaw and remembering what Tom had said about the girl in Spain. He meant it. He would think nothing of crashing the heavy metal pistol into her face if she disobeyed him.

'What do you want with me?' she hissed after a moment or two in which the carriage went bumping and speeding. 'Why are you doing this? Where are you taking me?'

He laughed. A sound which sent fear slithering like a blade into her stomach. 'Did your governess niver tell ye that curiosity killed the cat, Miss Ross? Shall we just say that you are the sprat with which I mean to catch a mackerel, as I think the saying goes?'

'I do not know what you are talking about!' she said, staring at him in bewilderment. 'I do not know who you really are or what you want—except that you are a traitor!'

'*Non, mademoiselle*,' he mocked her softly, 'I cannot allow that. I am a patriot. I was born in France, my father having been forced into exile there after the clans were defeated at Culloden.'

'You are a Jacobite!'

'Ach, I think that cause is long dead, and besides,

Bonaparte pays better,' he drawled. 'And if you insist on hanging labels on me, what would you have me call you, Miss Ross—the "Major's Muslin", as they do at Horseguards? What was your price, now? Five thousand guineas, I believe?'

'How did you—?' Too late she stopped her tongue.

'There are always ways of finding things out, Miss Ross. Besides, it was easy enough to guess your part in all this after I had seen you with Haldane, then your rather obvious attempts to flatter Corton—it was sufficient to take him in, I grant you, but rather amateurish. Your attempt to pick his pocket however, was most professional, and I confess it surprised me—and worried me for a moment. I feared you might succeed. And it would have been so much more difficult to remove the plans from Haldane than Corton.'

'Would have been—you have the plans?' She stared at him in horror. Ridiculously, all she could think was that meant she would never be able to marry Alex— Wellington would be disappointed enough in him, without discovering he meant to marry her! 'How did you get—' She broke off, remembering what Tom had said about hiding a body in the straw. 'You killed Corton?'

'He was deaf to reason.' Macleod shrugged. 'And he threatened to expose me as a spy—I had little choice. But I should not waste any tears on him, Miss Ross. The man was a murderer himself and a lot of other unsavoury things beside. There were more than military secrets in Corton's pocket—there were letters from indiscreet ladies to their lovers, gambling debts— including one of yours.'

'He must have bought it from Robson,' she said

flatly. He was right—she would not weep for Corton, but murder was murder. And he had killed Tom. Tom, who for all his faults had been essentially a kind man.

'Needless to say, I will destroy all the documents except the ones that interest me. There are several people who will sleep easier in their beds tonight—or would do, if they knew.'

'And is that supposed to make amends for murder?' she asked harshly. 'Not as far as I am concerned, Captain Macleod. You have the plans—you have a head start—so what exactly do you want with me?'

He laughed softly. 'You'll find out in time, Miss Ross. Don't be so impatient—I should make yourself as comfortable as you can and rest—we have a long journey ahead of us. Oh, and no desperate attempts at escape if you please, or I might place you in Mr Robson's custody—which I am sure you would find a trifle unpleasant.'

She settled back against the squabs. A lengthy journey, he had said. Surely there would be some opportunity for her to get help—get away. She shut her eyes and concentrated as hard as she could on what she could hear outside. They were still in the fashionable district, judging by the number of carriages she could hear passing them, and the occasional burst of noise and music as they passed houses where a salon was in progress.

'No sign of her?' Cavendish asked Alex quietly an hour or so later after they had searched the garden from end to end with the assistance of some of the other men.

'Nothing except this,' Alex said grimly, holding out her kid slipper. 'I found it amongst the trees over there—and there was her scarf, of course, beside Mitchell's body. I think she must have been with him when it happened—perhaps he was trying to protect her from that French swine, I can think of no other reason why he should be killed.'

'I think I can. . .' Cavendish said tentatively. 'I've just been talking to one of the young stable lads. The older fellows had got him drunk for a laugh this evening and no one believed what he was saying. He said he was in the yard, when Tom Mitchell came tearing up to him and told him to get every man he could find because he had just seen a French spy—someone he recognised from his army days. And that he was going to find you—'

Alex swore. 'And he would have run straight into Lallie on that path—and probably told her—' He broke off and swore again. 'Reynard probably heard him, the damn fellow has been creeping about the grounds half the evening—' He broke off as one of Lady Furney's footmen came flying down the path from the stables. 'They've found another body sir, in the stables—'

'Alex,' Charles Cavendish put out an instinctive arm towards his friend as the colour left Alex's face and he gave a soft groan. Lallie couldn't be dead—she couldn't be—the thought was enough to squeeze the breath out of his lungs. He stared unseeingly at the two men.

'Alex—' Cavendish was shaking his arm '—Alex, he says its Corton, not Miss Ross.'

'Thank God!' He dragged in a breath and ran a hand through his hair. He had to pull himself together. Make himself think—and then he swore. If Corton was dead, Reynard almost certainly had the plans and would be on his way to France—or possibly Spain. He had to be stopped at all costs. The information about the defences at Torres Vedras must not get back to the French.

'Cavendish,' he snapped, 'find Houghton, tell him we have a problem and I need to see him immediately.'

Charles Cavendish, recognising his tone, did not wait to be asked twice and went off at a run.

'You,' he snapped at the footman, who was standing waiting for instructions, 'what's the fastest riding horse in Lady Furney's stable?'

'The big grey, sir, out of same sire as last year's Derby winner.'

'Saddle him for me, and bring him to the front of the house.'

'Yes, sir.' The footman fled to do his bidding.

Lallie. Where the devil was Lallie? The only explanation he could think of was that Macleod had taken her with him—if he had killed her, they would have found her body. But why would Macleod take Lallie as a hostage? He had the plans. All he had to do was get to the coast and find a boat to take him to France—and that was not difficult for a man of Macleod's talents.

'Alex?' He started at his sister's voice. 'I have to speak to you.'

'Izzy?' He turned, frowning as he saw how white her face was in the light of the lantern she held. 'What are you doing here? What is wrong?'

'I have to speak to you, alone,' she said in a low tone. 'Quickly—I've been looking over half the town for you.'

'I will not be a moment, Cavendish,' he sighed. 'Izzy,

if you are here to lecture, let me tell you it is not the moment—'

'I am not.' His sister groaned. 'I came to find you because of this.'

She handed him a small package which rattled. 'A repulsive man brought it to the house, insisted on giving it into my hands only—and then demanded that I take it to you at once and mention it to no one if I valued Miss Ross's life.'

'What—?' He ripped open the packet with shaking hands. Inside were Lallie's pearls and a folded slip of paper. 'Keep that lantern still,' he told his sister as he unfolded it. There were some directions, the name of a house. A curt instruction to come alone and tell no one if he did not want Lallie to die.

'So that's it,' he spoke his thought aloud. Macleod was not content with the plans—he wanted him as well—possibly his death. And he could not really blame him—these last three years he had ruined a great many of Le Reynard's efforts to deceive Wellington into making a rash move with his carefully husbanded army.

'What is it?' Isabelle asked, frowning.

'The answer,' he said heavily. 'Now, I want you to do something very important for me. Get Charles to one side and tell him to go to the Ship Inn at Poole as soon as he is able. I will contact him there. Tell him lives depend on discretion and to bring every side arm he can lay his hands on—and that he must say nothing to anyone of where I am. Understand?'

'No, but I will do it.' Isabelle sighed.

'Thank you.' He gave her a swift hug.

'I suppose that means you're about to go and try and get yourself killed again!' his sister said fiercely as he released her. 'And what about the child? What's to happen to her if neither you nor her sister comes back?'

'Then you'd take care of her, wouldn't you, Izzy— for my sake?'

'Of course I should. I'll go and fetch her and her nurse in the morning, they can stay with us until it is all settled.' Isabelle sighed again.

'Izzy, you're the best sister a man could wish for,' her brother said, planting a light kiss on her cheek before turning away and setting off at a run.

CHAPTER THIRTEEN

'WAKE up, Miss Ross, we have arrived.' Lallie opened her eyes slowly and yawned and stretched. Macleod had not lied when he said they had a lengthy journey ahead of them—it was hours and many changes of horses since they had left the noise of the capital behind them. She had not slept at all, but she had long since lost all sense of the direction of their travel. They had passed through one or two sizeable towns—the last at around dawn when she had been able to hear the noise of wagons and market traders beginning to call out their wares. But she had no idea which—the carriage flaps had been kept firmly closed.

'Here we are, sir.' Robson threw open the carriage door and she blinked at the brightness of the morning sunshine. 'I trust you enjoyed the journey.' He leered at Lallie with his bleary eyes.

'Keep your thoughts and eyes to yourself if you wish to be paid,' Macleod retorted coldly. 'I do not tolerate insolence of any kind.'

'Beg pardon, sir. I meant no offence.' Robson backed away.

Macleod got out of the carriage and offered Lallie a hand which she pointedly ignored, scrambling out by herself onto an orange brick path already warm from the sun beneath her stockinged feet.

She stared in astonishment. For some reason she had expected anything but the view in front her. Beside the

path, was an overgrown profusion of wild and culti-
vated flowers. There was a low grey stone wall, a
stretch of spongy turf sprinkled with pink thrift which
seemed to end in mid-air—and beyond that sea and
sky. A glittering, millpond of a blue sea, beneath an
already cloudless azure sky.

She turned slowly and found that behind her was a
house of weathered silvery-grey stone with a blue slate
roof. It was long and low with small mullioned windows
and looked as if it had grown out of the bright,
overgrown garden that surrounded it rather than the
other way about. She stared at the borders of flowers
near the house, the sun was already far enough up in
the sky for there to be several blue butterflies fluttering
over a sage bush, and drowsy bumble bees humming
over the lavender. It was so utterly charming, so
peaceful, that she found it difficult to hold on to the
idea that she was in danger—until she let her gaze
come back to Macleod and Robson. And then she
realised with a sinking heart that she could not see any
other habitation, except for what she took to be a farm,
far away on the other side of the great cliff-lined sweep
of the bay. The track along which they had come here
seemed to wind back into endless undulating heath-
land. You would be able to see anyone coming for
miles from any direction, she realised—or leaving.

'Picturesque, don't you think?' Macleod smiled at
her and she knew that he had guessed what was going
through her mind.

'Very. Where are we?' she said as casually as she was
able.

'Very close to the edge of a very high cliff,' Macleod
said with deliberate emphasis, glancing towards the

wall and the little stretch of turf that seemed to hang in the sky. 'Any more questions, Miss Ross?'

'No.' She swallowed, her mouth dry.

'Shall we go in? You—' he gestured to Tyson and Robson '—the stables are at the back—see to the horses.'

The low door was studded with iron, and looked as ancient as the rest of the house, but swung open easily enough on well-oiled hinges as Macleod lifted its iron latch and pushed it and went in, putting out a hand to pull her after him.

She followed and shook off his hand as the door swung shut behind them.

It was cooler inside; the grey slate flags were cold beneath her feet. But the walls were freshly limed, the dark oak furniture well polished, the rag rug in front of the huge stone fireplace, bright and clean.

Somewhere else in the house, was the sound of a slamming door, then the sound of footsteps.

'Sarah!' Macleod called out as he stepped past Lallie.

The speed of the footsteps increased, a curtain which covered an arch in the wall at the far end of the room was flung aside and a sultry looking young woman stepped into the room. She was short, and darkly pretty in a sulky sort of way. Her cotton gown was of a waisted and full-skirted style which Lallie could only just remember from her early childhood. A maid— housekeeper even, Lallie wondered as she stared at her. Though the style of her gown was old fashioned, the fabric looked new and expensive enough, and there was lace edging her pristine white apron. Perhaps, she thought, with a leap of hope, perhaps help was not so far away as she thought.

'Well, you took yer time,' the girl said, flashing Macleod a look of appraisal with her dark, black-lashed eyes. 'It must be a year since you were last here. I was beginning to think you'd forgotten me,' she added in her slow west-country drawl, putting a hand up lazily to tuck back a strand of black hair from her face.

'Ach, I'd niver do that, Sarah.' Macleod grinned at her.

Lallie's hope of assistance died as she saw the glance the two exchanged. Macleod and Sarah were obviously more than old acquaintances.

'Who's this, then?' Sarah's dark strong brows rose disdainfully as she treated Lallie to a long stare that encompassed everything from her uncombed hair, her torn gown, to her bare and dirty feet. 'Sommat the cat dragged in by the look of it.'

'Now, now—Sarah, put your claws in.' Macleod laughed. 'Miss Ross has suffered a most upsetting few hours. The least you could do is offer her a bath, clean clothes and refreshment.'

'Whatever you says, *sir*.' The emphasis on the last word was definitely insolent. 'I'll want paying, though, for whatever I give her—and some more money for the extra food. Not that she looks as if she eats much,' she said, treating Lallie to another disparaging stare while smoothing a hand over the gathered cloth on her hips to draw attention to her own luxuriant curves.

'Sarah!' There was a note of warning in Macleod's voice. 'Do as I say. Take her upstairs will you? I have some business to attend to and do not wish to be disturbed. You have pens and ink?'

'In the box, by the winder,' Sarah said brusquely.

'Is Peter here?' Macleod asked as he went over to lift the lid of the plain writing box by the window.

'He's down in the village. Said he'd be back by evening tide,' Sarah replied.

'Good. I will have a packet for him to take to France. It must go tonight. And so I am afraid, must I. I must get back to Spain with all speed.'

'Not so soon, surely.' Sarah's face expressed disappointment. 'Ye promised me ye'd stay a while longer this time.'

'I can't.' Macleod sighed. 'But I will be back, Sarah, I promise you that.'

'Oh, yes! But when? Another year or ten?' Sarah tossed her dark head and turned to Lallie. 'Come on then, Miss Beanpole, let's see what we can do with you.'

'Thank you,' Lallie said grittily and followed her out through the curtained arch.

Sarah flounced up a flight of narrow twisting stairs in a flurry of white petticoats, leaving Lallie to follow in her wake.

'In 'ere,' Sarah said, ushering Lallie into a bedchamber which contained a narrow wooden bed with a white coverlet, a small table, a china basin and jug and a wooden chest, stained with salt water.

'You'll find what you need in that chest—not that any of it'll fit you, you're too tall.' Sarah pointed to a coffer. 'You'll not hold his interest long, you're not his type. He likes his women small and dark, like me.'

'Then I wish you joy of him.' Lallie sighed wearily. She was too tired and miserable at this moment to attempt explanations or to dissipate the girl's hostility.

'I have no desire for anything at this moment but some hot water with which to wash.'

'You'll have to wait a bit. I've got other things to do than boil up water for you,' Sarah said, taking up the jug. 'We ain't all lucky enough to have servants, you know.' With that she flounced out of the room, slamming the door shut behind her.

Lallie sighed and sat down upon the bed. She was so tired—too tired to think. She did not understand why Macleod had brought her with him. He had the plans. All he had to do was get on his boat to France—or Spain. Why had he brought her to this place? She lifted her feet onto the bed and lay back against the pillows. If Macleod got the plans to France, Alex would have failed—she couldn't let that happen. She couldn't—she had to think of something—she shut her eyes. But all that would come into her head were jumbled images. Images of Alex's face as he smiled at her, Emily— Oh God, what would happen to Emily if Macleod killed her? She had to get away for Emily's sake. . .had to get the plans back. . .had to see Alex, at least once more, she prayed. At least let her see him once more and be able to tell him how sorry she was for misjudging him.

'You'd better wake up, 'cos I'm not fetching you any more hot water.' Sarah's voice, followed by the crash of a jug being put down and then the slam of a door, woke her out of her doze.

She got off the bed stiffly, wondering how long she had been sleeping. Glancing out of the window, she saw that the sun was now well down in the west. It must be late afternoon, she thought, as she began to strip off her tattered gown.

She washed as thoroughly as she could, combed her hair out with her fingers since Sarah had not thought to provide a comb and then dressed in what she found in the chest.

Sarah was right, she thought wryly as she glimpsed her reflection in a rather mottled glass in a carved wooden frame which hung upon the wall. The old fashioned gown of green sprigged cotton with its laced low-waisted front and split skirt was far too short, as was the crimson petticoat she had found to wear beneath it. Her ankles and bare feet were clearly visible. With her hair hanging loose about her shoulders for want of any pins or combs, she looked like a beggar maid.

'Well, ain't going to be going to a ball in that, are yer?' Sarah said maliciously as she opened the door without knocking and looked her over. 'There's food on the table in the small parlour. Help yerself.'

'Wait, please,' Lallie said, making her tone as placating as she could manage. 'I must talk to you. Do you know who Captain Macleod is?'

'He's a Frenchie.' Sarah shrugged. 'I know that. I'm not daft. I've helped him signal to his boat some nights. And that's how I get the money to keep this place up— taking messages for him.'

'And you do not think that is wrong?' Lallie stared at her. 'We are at war with the French.'

Sarah laughed. 'You might be. I don't see the sense of it. Our lads fighting and dying in all them foreign places—its not as if there's any danger of them invading us any more. What does it matter if the odd Frenchie goes back and forth and pays generously for doing so?'

'You don't understand,' Lallie groaned. 'He is a

murderer, he has information that might lose us the Peninsula.'

'Good riddance to it, is what I say.' Sarah shrugged. 'My Jem went there three year back and I've never had a word since. Mind you, if he's dead it's his own fault. I told him he was a bloody fool—we made a fair living here with the wrecks and the contrabrand. He didn't have to take the shilling. We all warned him about going off to foreign parts. Look what happened to Sam Brickle's grandfather, I said to him. Went off to the war in Bristol and no one ever saw him again.'

'Bristol,' Lallie said bemusedly. 'What war in Bristol?'

'The King's war.' Sarah looked at her as if she were a particularly slow child. 'Don't tell me you never heard about it!'

Lallie exhaled slowly. Evidently so little happened in this corner of England that Sarah's acquaintances still regarded the Civil War of a hundred and sixty or so years ago as an event of major importance in their lives.

'Is Bristol far from here?' she asked, tentatively thinking that at least she might get some idea as to where she was.

Sarah gave what was becoming a familiar shrug. 'No use asking me, I've never bin further east than Dorchester and never wanted to.'

'Dorchester? So this is the Dorset coast?' Lallie asked.

''Course it is, where else would it be?' Sarah gave her another disparaging look.

Lallie sighed. Somehow she did not think she was ever going to convince Sarah of her patriotic duty or

the vital importance of a few miles of defences along
the Portuguese border with Spain. Her only hope was
to get away, get help. There was a barracks at
Dorchester—a garrison—one of the young men who
had danced with her at Lady Furney's had mentioned
being posted there.

'How do you get to Dorchester?' she asked quietly.
'Do you walk from here?'

'Walk—no.' Sarah shook her head. 'The carter
comes past and I get a ride with him. I don't know how
far it is. All I know is it takes all afternoon to get there
at a trot with an empty wagon—and a day to get back
when it's laden.'

'This carter, what time does he go past?'

'About noon on the first Thursday of every month.'

'Every month. . .' Lallie's brief moment of hope died
abruptly. The carter would not be passing for days. She
had no choice now but to try and appeal to Sarah's
better nature.

'Sarah, please—is there no way I can get away from
here? Captain Macleod is holding me prisoner here
against my will.'

'Holding you prisoner?' For a moment Sarah looked
startled. 'You're not one of his informants, then, like
that stuck-up fellow he brought here before? And
you're not his fancy woman?'

'No,' Lallie said impatiently. 'He kidnapped me—'

'Well, you'd better behave then,' Sarah said, her
countenance lightening considerably. 'He's not a man
to cross.' With that she flounced off down the stairs
again, calling over her shoulder that the soup would be
cold if Lallie did not hurry up and go down.

Lallie entered the small panelled parlour tentatively.

Macleod was already sitting at an oak table, black and shiny with age, on which were loaves of coarse bread, a leg of ham, a great wedge of cheese, a pot of butter, and a small steaming cauldron of what smelt like a fish soup. Somewhat to her surprise, she realised suddenly that she was ravenous after so many hours without food.

Macleod looked up. He smiled as his hazel eyes studied her dispassionately. 'No need to look so dismal, Miss Ross. I am sure the Major will find you as beguiling as a shepherdess as he does in the latest mode. Sit down, eat—I should hate him to think I was neglecting you.'

She sat down upon a chair, her legs suddenly weak. 'Do you mean Major Haldane is coming here?'

He did not answer her for a moment as he cut off a slice of ham with a knife and flipped it deftly onto a pewter plate and pushed it towards her.

'I hope so, Miss Ross, for your sake,' he went on calmly as he sliced off a piece of bread and proffered it to her.

'You told him where we are?' she said in disbelief. 'But are you not afraid he will bring half a regiment with him?'

'No. But you should be, because if he does I shall have no choice but to kill you, Miss Ross. You see, I am a man of my word. If Major Haldane wishes to see you alive, he knows he must come alone and unarmed.'

She took the bread mechanically. Alex knew where she was. Relief washed through her, only to be followed by a new piercing fear. Why had Macleod told Alex where they were? To lure him into a trap. The answer was like a blade in her heart. She thought of the emptiness of the landscape surrounding the house, of how easy it would be for Macleod simply to shoot him as he had Tom. And the fact that Robson and Tyson would also be armed. But surely he would not come alone? Not when Macleod had the plans. Surely he would not put her before his duty to recover them? But he would, she knew with sudden certainty. Because he was Alex. Because he loved her.

She swallowed, her mouth and throat dry. 'Do you—do you mean to kill him?'

'It is very tempting,' he said as he picked up a wooden tankard. He took a long draught of cider and then put it down. 'Major Haldane has caused me a great deal of trouble these last three years. You see, he is not only remarkably brave in his pursuit of information, as are all of the exploring officers, but he is intelligent enough to draw the correct conclusions from what he sees. Believe me, I know, I captured one of his despatches once, and it read like our orders of the day. That makes him a very valuable man to Wellington—a very dangerous one to us.'

'So you intend to murder him in cold blood,' she said contemptuously. 'You could not manage it with an entire army in Spain—so you mean to do it here—and me as well, I presume, since I shall have served my purpose in bringing him here.'

He smiled. 'There are always choices, Miss Ross, the decision will be Haldane's. You are not eating—I trust you have not lost your appetite.'

'No,' she said savagely, picking up her bread. She was angry now as well as afraid.

They both continued eating in silence, he with every

appearance of enjoyment, she having to force herself to swallow.

'I anticipate it will be a few more hours before Major Haldane arrives,' he said as she put down her tankard of barely touched cider with a bang upon the table. 'I have some business to attend to. You may do as you please, so long as you do not go out of the garden. Your old acquaintances are on guard, so don't be foolish, Miss Ross.'

She did not answer him but walked out into the room she had first entered. On a small table near the window was a neat packet of papers, sealed with a direction written upon them that she decided must be in some sort of code for it made no sense. She did not dare do more than glance at it and walk quickly on and out into the garden, her heart racing. Those were the plans, she was sure of it—he must feel very safe here, she thought, to leave them lying about so carelessly. She walked around the house and glanced in at the window. He was sat at the table now, his head bent over a small black notebook as he scribbled something on another piece of paper.

'Enjoying the sunshine,' Robson sneered from behind her. 'I'd make the most of it, Miss Ross, might be the last you get.'

'Shut up and get back on guard at the gate!' Macleod threw open the small window and leant out. 'And tell Tyson to watch the back—if I know Haldane, he will not come walking in the front door.'

'Alistair. . .' Sarah's wheedling tone floated after Lallie from the open window as she walked on around the garden. 'Why don't you come and have a rest for a bit. . .?'

For the next hour or so, Lallie wandered restlessly about the garden, glancing at the landward horizon from time to time, at others looking for anything—a garden tool, a stick, even—that she might be able to conceal and use as a weapon. She walked back past the open window. Macleod had gone. The bulky packet of plans was still there, piled neatly with another smaller packet.

She turned away as she heard footsteps in the lane. Surely Alex would not be such a fool as to simply walk up the lane. No. It wasn't Alex. She heard Robson challenge the man, and then grunt permission to come into the garden.

It was a seaman, so burned from the sun and wind that he looked like a Spaniard. It must be Peter, she guessed.

'Where's this packet he was on about?' he said, gesturing back to Robson. 'I need to get on if I'm to get the tide.'

Like Sarah, he had assumed she was in league with Macleod. She could not just let him take the plans, she thought, not when so much hung on it. She had to try something, anything. And then as Sarah's laughter and the sound of a creaking bed issued from the window above their heads, she knew she had a chance, albeit a slight one.

'Captain Macleod is a little busy at the moment. Won't you go into the parlour and take some refreshment while I call him?'

'All right, but be quick about it, will you?' he said and walked on into the house.

She waited until she was sure he was safely in the parlour and then reached through the window, her fingers straining. Then she had the two packets. On an afterthought she reached again and took the notebook as well. Now what? she wondered. Hide them? They would search. Destroy them by burning them—but that might take too long...and she might be discovered in the act. She had to get rid of them quickly. The solution came suddenly as she glanced at the glittering, shining expanse of sea which filled the horizon.

Stuffing the notebook into the bosom of her gown, the two packets into the waistband of her petticoat, she moved quietly away from the window and back onto the brick path near the low wall.

Robson was there, sat leaning against the gatepost, watching the lane—no, she exhaled with relief as she saw the tankard beside him and heard him snore. He was asleep.

Her heart in her mouth, she listened intently. From above her head came more muffled laughter and scufflings from Sarah's attic room. That only left Tyson—where was Tyson? The answer came in the footsteps pacing to and fro across the stable yard. The house would block his view of her. She tiptoed to the border, knelt with her back to the house and picked a handful of blooms. If Macleod did happen to look out of the window, she hoped she would appear innocent enough. Then in the shelter of the overgrown plants, she slid out the packets, broke their seals, and crumpled each sheet about the largest stones she could find. It seemed to take forever, and the drumming of her heart drowned out all else, even the rhythmic slap of the waves below as they hit the shore.

At last it was done. With shaking hands she scooped them into her petticoat, lifting it from the hem to make a pocket. Then she stood up, climbed over the low grey stone wall and went as close to the edge of the cliff as she dared. The cliff was sheer, hanging out at an angle that made it impossible to see its base. The drop made her feel dizzy and sick. She had to force her hands to relax enough to release the hem of her petticoat. The stones dropped out and rolled into space. There was a moment of silence, and then the splashing and clatter as they hit the shore below.

The tide was out, she realised in despair. She had hoped it would be in and the papers would be washed safely out to sea or sink without trace. She should have risked burning them.

'What the—?' Charles Cavendish almost swore aloud as he pressed himself against the base of the cliff as the shower of rocks rained down from above.

'We're never going to be able to climb this, Alex, the damn thing will be down on our heads in a minute.'

But Haldane put a finger to his lips and crept forward, using the shelter of the larger rocks to prevent being seen from above. Reaching into a shallow rock pool he picked up one of the strange looking stones. He unwrapped it—and stared in disbelief. Then, still taking the utmost care, he moved from rock to rock, picking up the others.

'Charles,' he said in a low voice as he came back to the cliff face, clutching the crumpled papers, 'I can scarce believe it, but these are the plans.'

'What? Why go to all that trouble to get them and then throw them over a cliff?' Charles frowned.

'Lallie.' Alex groaned. 'It has to be Lallie—somehow

she has got hold of them and has hit on this way of getting rid of them.'

'Monsieur Le Reynard is not going to be happy about that,' Charles said grimly.

'No,' Alex agreed, his face taut with anxiety. 'We have to get up there quickly—'

He glanced up at the towering cliff overhanging them. So near and yet so far. It would be impossible to climb—or would it? Towards the left the cliff was still almost sheer, but it did not overhang like the part immediately above them.

'I'm going to try and get up there,' he said, pointing to the cliff face. 'It's the one direction from which Macleod will not expect me. You stay here—the frigate should arrive soon. When it does, get the storming party up there as fast as you can.'

At the same moment, Lallie breathed a sigh of relief as Peter went striding off down the lane, a hastily sealed packet of papers in his pocket, addressed as much like the original as she could remember.

It was over an hour later when Alex finally reached the top of the cliff. His chest felt like there were hot knifes in it; his hands and knees were torn and bleeding where he had dragged himself up over the ragged rocks. But he dare not rest for more than a minute. Taking his pistols, which had been strung about his neck, he loaded them in the lee of the low stone wall which ran down the length of the property on the seaward side.

Away to his left he could hear a man moving in the yard, then heard him speak to another. Neither voice was Macleod's, so that meant he had at least three men to deal with. He lifted his head a little and looked between two of the capstones and swore softly as he recognised Robson and Tyson. How the devil had they got mixed up in this? he wondered briefly. He should have shot those two while he had the chance, he thought grimly. But it should not be too difficult to get rid of them. He picked up a stone and threw it down the cliff. It bounced and rattled. Then he did it again.

'There's someone on the cliff,' Robson growled.

'Don't be stupid. Nobody could get up that.'

'Go and have look.'

'All right.' Tyson came lumbering up to the wall. Alex rose from the ground like a wraith, caught his jacket and jerked him off his feet, then fell backwards, using his weight to bring the other man down, and then his feet into the stomach to push the man into a soaring arc. Tyson fell into space, too winded even to scream.

'Tyson—' Robson's exclamation died as a knife thudded into his chest and he crumpled to the ground.

After waiting to see that no alarm had been raised, Alex slipped over the wall and ran softly to the side of the house. He never enjoyed killing, but he passed Robson's body without a second glance. There was no room for mercy when you were dealing with a man like Le Reynard, no second chances. You had to be as ruthless as he was, or you would die. That was a lesson he had learnt all too well in Spain.

Lallie started as she heard the muffled thud from the stable yard. It could not be long now before Macleod discovered the papers were missing. Perhaps he had already. She had barely had the thought before she heard the door of the house being thrown back upon its hinges and Macleod came striding towards her, eyes blazing and white faced with rage.

'Where are the papers?' he demanded as he caught her arm and dragged her up from where she had been sitting upon the wall staring out to sea.

'The papers—' she stammered. 'The ones on the table—I gave them to Peter—I thought that was what you wanted.'

'Do you take me for a fool? Where are they?' Macleod repeated, his eyes as cold as glass as he caught her arm and twisted it savagely.

She screamed and dropped the flowers she had gathered on the path.

'You are hurting me,' she sobbed.

'I will do more than that!' he hissed. 'You and I are going for a little walk beside the cliff—'

'No!' She twisted and writhed as he picked her up and threw her over his shoulder, stepped over the wall, strode to the edge of the cliff and dropped her face-down. She screamed as she began to fall, arms flailing towards the beach far below.

Her fall was arrested abruptly, brutally, as Macleod caught her legs and dragged her back so that she lay, half-hanging over the sheer cliff, staring down in helpless terror at the black rocks and white-fringed waves below.

If he let go, she would fall, fall like a stone onto the jagged black rocks so far below. She wanted to shut her eyes. But she couldn't—she could not stop looking.

'The papers, Miss Ross, where are they?'

'I don't know—I don't know—' She was gibbering, crying with fear.

He let her slide another inch forward over the dizzying drop.

'Where are they?'

She did not know what to say. If she told him, he might let go of her—he might if she did not tell him. Oh, God! She had to think—but she was too afraid, too afraid of those jagged black rocks smashing into her flesh.

'Tell me,' Macleod hissed. 'You have three seconds, Miss Ross—one, two—'

'I've got them,' said a voice that was so cold and level that it was like ice along her spine. 'Care to bargain for them, Macleod?'

Alex. She thought she was hallucinating out of terror, until she heard Macleod give a soft startled laugh. 'Haldane, I was not expecting you for several hours yet. Put the pistol down or I will let go of her.'

'I will put the pistol down when Miss Ross is safely away from the edge and not before.'

'Very well.'

She gasped with relief as she was dragged back from the edge and then on to her feet, her arm twisted cruelly behind her as Macleod turned her to face the house, using her as his shield.

'Alex!' She blurted out his name in sheer relief as she saw him. Tall, implacable, his eyes like ice under a winter sky as he stared at Macleod, the pistol still in his hand pointed unwaveringly at the Scot's head, which was inches from her own.

'It will be all right, Lallie,' he said coolly, never taking his eyes off Macleod. 'Just keep still.'

'The pistol, Haldane.' There was an edge in Macleod's voice, an edge of fear. 'You know you will not use it. You could so easily miss and even if you don't, if I fall. . .we both fall.'

'Not until you let her her go, Macleod,' he said, still with the same icy calm. 'I want to see her riding out of this place—then you may have your life and mine, if that is your price?'

'No!' Lallie moaned. But neither man seemed to hear her—they were too intent upon each other.

'I don't think so.' Macleod laughed as he produced a knife from his pocket and put the point to Lallie's throat, just below her ear. 'When Miss Ross leaves here, we will be travelling together. I am looking forward to showing her the delights of Spain. Such a beautiful if savage country, is it not, Major Haldane? I cannot promise her safety, of course, not until the war between our nations is over and the last English transport sails from Lisbon. And I fear that is going to be a very long time, unless Lord Wellington is foolish, or unfortunate, enough to engage our army in any strength.'

'So that is it!' Alex gave a jagged laugh. 'You think I would betray my country in return for Miss Ross's safety?'

Macleod smiled. 'Every man has his price, Major. I knew yours would not be money. Now, if you value her life, don't do anything foolish. I have men I can call—'

'No, you do not. Not any longer,' Alex said succinctly, hoping that he was right in his assumption that Robson and Tyson had been Macleod's only assistants.

'Well, in that case I suppose we had better begin our journey, Miss Ross.' The Scot laughed, but rather less steadily as he began to edge backwards along the cliff tow path taking Lallie with him.

Alex watched helplessly for a moment or two. The naval frigate had only just sailed over the horizon. He did not dare shoot, not while Lallie was so close to Macleod. If he did not do something, Macleod could get away—and take Lallie with him as a hostage or kill her if she proved too much of a hindrance.

Lallie's gaze was fixed on him, her eyes huge and dark in her terrified face.

He stared back at her. If only he could get a clear shot! As if reading his mind, she chose that moment to stumble and throw herself flat on the turf almost pulling Macleod with her.

There was no time to think. He fired. Macleod reeled, fell sideways and rolled, throwing out his arms, searching for an anchor as he slid over the cliff.

Time stood still as Alex watched in horror as Macleod's frantically searching fingers found Lallie's petticoat before she could even begin to move away from the cliff edge.

Lallie screamed as she found herself sliding backwards, pulled by Macleod's weight as he hung over the void.

Alex dropped his pistol and dived in the same second. He caught her fingers, then her wrists, in a grip of iron, halting her with only her head and shoulders still above the cliff.

'Let go, Macleod! Let go!' he roared as the combined weight of Lallie and Macleod began to drag him slowly and inexorably forward. 'Kick him, Lallie!'

'I can't,' she sobbed. Her arms were being pulled out of their sockets, by her weight and that of Macleod, still dangling from her petticoat, which was being slowly dragged down her body. The pain was excruciating.

'You've got to hold on to me, help me,' he groaned as her fingers, which had been curled around his wrists slackened.

'I can't,' she said again, despairingly, as she felt her wrists begin to slip through his fingers. And then, without warning, the strings of her petticoat gave and Macleod fell away with a gurgling scream, and she could curl her nails into Alex's wrists, and get some purchase against the rock with her bare feet. Then he was hauling her up, by her arms, her shoulders, until the upper half of her body was back on the cliff top, and he could drag her to safety.

She lay sobbing for breath on the wonderful, beautiful, solid turf, with Alex's arms locked about her. For a minute or so they simply lay panting for breath, not speaking, not moving, just clinging to each other.

'I'm sorry, I'm sorry,' he said raggedly as his breathing slowed and he held her so tightly she thought her ribs would crack. 'I had to kill him, he'd read the plans I couldn't let him go back to Spain with you. And I knew he was going to kill you sooner or later, whatever I said—whatever I promised.'

He was shaking, she realised, shaking as much as she was, his face chalky.

'I know, it's all right, I understand,' she said helplessly. 'I know you had no choice.'

'I nearly killed you.' He groaned against her hair. 'If I had lost you—'

'You didn't.' She clung to him, kissed his grimy, unshaven cheek. 'I am here, safe.'

'Yes.' He exhaled a ragged breath and became the soldier again, and leant sideways to pick up his pistol.

'I've dealt with Robson and Tyson—are there any other men here?' he asked as he reloaded.

'No. There is a girl called Sarah, Macleod's mistress. I think she is still in bed.'

'Does she know what the plans were of? Did she see them?'

Lallie shook her head. 'Even if she had, I think she would have made nothing of them.'

'Thank God.' He exhaled again. 'I have had enough of killing for one day and I draw the line at women.'

'I should think so too,' said a laconic voice from behind them.

They turned to see Charles Cavendish standing behind them, his pistols at the ready.

'How the devil did you get up here so quickly?' Alex said in astonishment.

Cavendish grinned. 'Found a smuggler's tunnel leading from the cave up through the rock. 'Now, where is Macleod?'

'What did you say about the cavalry?' Alex said, his voice suddenly full of laughter as his eyes met Lallie's gaze.

'Better late than never.' Suddenly she was laughing too—or was she crying? She wasn't sure. All she knew was that the nightmare was over. She was safe and so was he. And he loved her—and nothing else mattered.

CHAPTER FOURTEEN

'Are the plans really so important that you would have killed Sarah if she had seen them?' she asked that evening as they lay in each other's arms in a deep feather bed in a Dorchester inn.

'If I could not ensure her silence any other way,' he said after a moment. 'I should not have wanted to, but if secrecy is maintained until they are needed, the lines at Torres Vedras will save thousands of British lives, preserve our army and possibly, just possibly give us the chance to drive the French out of Spain and prevent this Austrian alliance of Bonaparte's from allowing him to dominate all Europe.'

'I wish you had told me all this in the beginning,' she sighed. 'If you had asked me, I should have been happy to help for nothing.'

'I know. I behaved like a fool.' He sighed as he pushed back his dark hair from his face. 'My only excuse is that I could not bring myself to risk having you hate me again. Not when I had just got you back again. And then when you accepted the General's offer of money—and it seemed that was all you cared for—I was so confused I could not think straight. And the idea of any man but me touching you, let alone Corton—that was enough to make me want to kill you, Corton and the General!'

'I only said it at first because I wanted to hurt you,' she admitted ashamedly. 'And then afterwards when you were so cold, I thought it was the only chance Emily and I had of avoiding poverty again.'

'I know—I did finally realise that—' he smiled at her wryly '—with a little help from my great aunt. I'm sorry. Do you forgive me?'

'Only if you forgive me?' She smiled at him.

'I'll forgive you anything and everything,' he said lazily as he began to stroke the curve of her waist and hip, 'except that nasty little barb about "necessity"— that really did send me into the boughs. Until that moment I never doubted that you had given yourself to me for any reason but love.'

'You were right.' She sighed languorously and wriggled closer to him. 'Do you think I should have let even you make love to me merely because of "necessity"?' she asked with a faint smile. 'There have been other occasions during these last five years when such offers have been made to me, Alex. I refused them all, even when we had not so much as a loaf of bread to eat.'

'By the likes of Robson, I suppose,' he said, his eyes darkening as he looked at her.

'They were not all like Robson,' she said with a flicker of a smile. 'When we first came to London, my father still had a little money left and we still pretended to respectability. I used to go to church on a Sunday where I met a curate. He asked me to marry him—he was a kindly man who could see which way my father was headed and wanted to help me. But I refused because I did not love him, and he deserved better than that.'

'A curate!' He gave a ragged laugh. 'I never thought of you wed to a curate. Sometimes I used to dream about you—it would be so vivid, so real that I would wake full of ridiculous plans to get the next ship home to come and find you. And then in the cold light of dawn I made myself remember that I was still betrothed to Cressida and that you were probably already married to Hetherington or some other stolid industrialist approved by your father. And then I would begin to daydream that somehow I would be free of Cressida, and that you had married a soldier and I would come home and find you a widow and free to marry whom you chose.'

'Did you really use to think of me so often?' Her mouth curved in a half-smile as she glanced at his stern profile.

'Yes—all the time. But in my arrogance the one thing that never occurred to me was that you might have stopped loving me—it was quite a shock to me when I came after you that day you had been to Isabelle's. You were so cold, so cynical—and then even after I thought we had finally put the past behind us, you were adamant about not marrying me.'

'Alex—' she put her fingers to his lips '—I have never stopped loving you. Oh, I tried. I told myself I hated you. And then I read that you had been killed in the gazette—and then it was as if all the point went out of my life. All the hope. If it had not been for Emily, I think I should have wanted to die myself.'.

'Then say you will marry me.' He sighed as he nuzzled at her throat. 'It won't be as difficult as you think—what does it matter if one or two fools decide to cut us, if we have each other?'

'And your career?' she said thickly as a lump rose in her throat. 'Alex, I heard what General Houghton said in the garden about what marrying me would do to your career, your prospects. He is right. You know he is right.'

'And supposing I do not care if he is right, so long as I have you?'

'Please—don't let us talk about it now,' she pleaded. 'I don't want to waste the time we have in argument. You forget I know how important the army is to you— when I first met you, you told me that you were determined to be the youngest general in the British Army.'

'Did I really?' He laughed. 'I'd forgotten what a conceited idiot I was then. Let me tell you something, after five years of war, Lallie, I'd be happy never to see the Army again. Do you know what I want most, once the French are beaten?'

'Tell me,' she said as she traced the scar that ran from the base of his throat to the bottom of his ribcage with a fingertip.

'To buy a small estate and live quietly in the country with my neighbours, and my wife and family and never have to go near Almack's or the like again. That is the one luxury all younger sons have—they are not expected to maintain the family's standing.'

She stared at him. If that really was what he wanted, then perhaps, perhaps it might just be possible for her to marry him. Perhaps the difference in their standing would not to destroy their love as it had that between her mother and father.

'So. . .' he smiled at her, reading her all too well as he always had done '. . .now will you marry me?'

'I will think about it,' she said, her eyes suddenly luminous with a mixture of joy and hope. 'At least now Corton is dead he will not be able to tell everyone of my past. Why did he hate you so much?' she asked, frowning suddenly.

'A great many reasons,' he said wryly. 'We were at the same school, he was a bully and I thrashed him for it, and again when he raped a housemaid at a country house party of a mutual acquaintance. Then, later, I exposed him as a cheat at cards, something he never forgave me for, particularly as he seemed to think that incident was responsible for putting off an heiress he had hoped to marry. He was wrong, as it happens, her father had already got Corton's measure and had forbidden the match. But after that Corton seemed to blame me for each and every misfortune which befell him, whether it was being blackballed by a club or disappointed by a woman—'

'In the Row?' she said softly. 'Why did you challenge him? Was it because of that boy he killed?'

'No,' he said as he drew her closer against him. 'It was because of the way he looked at you—I wanted to kill him for that.'

'But you thought I was a demi-rep then—'

'I might have thought it, but what I felt was something entirely different. Do you know that when I saw you on the stairs at Isabelle's, I thought for a moment that I had been hit by a thunderbolt—and then I remembered that was exactly how I felt the first time I set eyes on you. As if my heart had stopped beating, the world stopped turning—'

'I wish you had told me that when you brought me my bonnet. That was exactly how I felt upon seeing you again. We've both been such fools.' She sighed. 'Do you think we are always going to get ourselves into such tangles, Alex?'

'Probably.' He smiled at her. 'Love and passion are not exactly conducive to clear thinking. And I expect us to suffer from both conditions for the rest of our lives since you are going to marry me, aren't you?'

'I said I will think about it.' She smiled back at him, knowing suddenly that her answer would be yes and feeling as if someone had removed a lead weight from her shoulders.

'You can have a week, not an hour more,' he said and kissed her.

'It's Lord Carteret, Miss Ross,' the maid announced as Lallie lifted her head enquiringly from Alex's shoulder as they sat upon the sofa in the drawing-room of Rosemount House several days later. 'He says that he is sorry to call at such an hour, but he must speak with the Major.'

'Robert—here at this time of night?' Alex frowned and put down his glass of brandy. 'Tell him to come in.'

Lallie took her feet hastily off the sofa, and got up to try and smooth some of the creases out of her gown. She had never met Lord Carteret, but expected him to share his wife's disapproval of her liaison with Alex.

She was still trying to push a loose pin back into her hair when Robert Carteret came in, dressed in a travelling coat, his face grave as he apologised to her for his intrusion.

She stammered out that it did not matter at all and she would leave them to talk.

'No, Miss Ross,' he said in an unexpectedly gentle tone, 'I think you had better stay—I have some bad news for Alex.'

'Robert—what is it?' Alex said frowning. 'Is Izzy all right, the children?'

'They are quite well. But I am afraid both your brother James, and your father are dead. The messenger came to us a half hour ago from Fairhill, he tried your town house but could get no answer.' He cleared his throat and looked a little embarrassed. 'Isabelle suggested we try here.'

'Dead? Both of them?' Alex stared at him. 'How?'

'They were in a curricle. James was foxed, apparently, and driving too fast—the curricle came off the bridge over the ravine. James's neck was broken and your father, they think, was kicked in the head by one of the horses.'

'The stupid, drunken fools!' Alex said fiercely. 'The fools! I must have told James a hundred times about that turn before the bridge—and why the devil didn't the old man stop him?'

'Probably because, in his eyes, James could do no wrong, I suppose,' Lord Carteret said, looking even more uncomfortable.

'They were both fools!'

'Alex—they are dead,' Lallie said softly as she put a hand on his arm, knowing his anger was against the fate that had taken away his brother and father, not them.

'Yes.' He seemed to fold suddenly and sat down heavily upon the sofa, reached out for his brandy and drained it.

'Lord Carteret, can I get you something, some brandy?' she asked, thinking that Isabelle's husband looked in need of a drink as well.

'No, thank you.' He shook his fair head. 'I am taking

my wife to Fairhill to be with her mother,' he said. 'I just thought Alex should know he is now the Earl of Fairhill and I am afraid the inheritor of a great number of debts. I will do all I can to help you save the estate, Alex,' he said awkwardly, 'but it will take every penny you have, all I can spare and you will still need more.'

Alex gave no sign of having heard him, but was staring down at the carpeted floor. Lallie sat down suddenly on a chair opposite Alex. Her thoughts should have been of sorrow for him, his family, but all she felt was a black, black rage and despair at the fate which had caused this particular accident now. A younger son might get away with a scandalous match which brought him no advantage, but Alex could no longer afford such self-indulgence. He was the head of his family, responsible for their standing, their security. How could he marry her and see his mother be turned out of her home, his family lands sold, when marriage to an heiress would save them?

It was not fair, she thought, as misery welled up in her like a black wave...it just was not fair. Another two weeks and they would have been married. It would have been too late for either of them to do the right thing.

Alex lifted his head suddenly and she saw the same despair in his eyes as he looked at her.

'You should go with your sister,' she said, dragging her gaze from his, 'I will get your cloak.'

'Yes—but wait a moment.' He got abruptly to his feet. 'You do not mind my travelling with you, Robert?'

'Of course not, I'll just go and tell Izzy that we will be out in a minute or so,' Lord Carteret said, making a hasty retreat as he glanced from Alex's stricken face to Lallie's chalky complexion.

The door had barely closed behind him, before Lallie found herself in Alex's arms.

'I am not going to lose you as well, do you understand that?' he said fiercely as he held her to him. 'I should set fire to Fairhill before I give you up! My brother's stupidity forced me to leave you once before—he is not going to do it from the grave!'

'You do not have to give me up,' she said thickly. 'I know I said before that if you married I should not stay, but I will if that is what you want...'

'I want you for my wife!' he rasped. 'That is what I want!'

'I know,' she said thickly. 'But this is not the time to talk about it, Alex. Your family will need you.'

'And I need *you*,' he groaned as he held her close and inhaled the scent of her hair. 'Promise me you will be here when I return, Lallie, promise.'

'Of course I will be here,' She said gently, knowing that she was going to break that promise even as she made it. To leave was the only thing to do for them both. Despite what she had said a few minutes ago, she knew she could never bear to share him with a wife, and that while she remained in his life, he would not marry the heiress who would allow him to keep his family estate.

'I don't want to go!' Emily's face crumpled as they left Rosemount House the following morning. 'I don't want to!'

And neither do I, Lallie thought, her own eyes filling with tears as she glanced up at the elegant façade of the house. But they had to go. There was no choice, not if Alex were to keep Fairhill.

'It will be all right,' she did her best to reassure Emily as they walked down the steps and climbed into a hired carriage. 'We have money now, the General paid me for helping him. We will be able to have our own little house.'

Emily's only response was to throw herself flat upon the squabs and sob inconsolably.

Watching her helplessly, Lallie felt like doing the same. But she forced herself to swallow the lump in her throat. This gnawing, aching misery would ease. She had lived without him before, she told herself, she could do so again. People did not die of broken hearts, no matter how much it hurt at the time.

Two weeks later, she stood shivering in the chill of dawn watching dockhands and sailors load supplies onto the frigate that bobbed up and down upon its moorings.

It was due to sail within the hour. He must be coming soon, she thought as she glanced along the dock. And then, above the creaking of timbers and flap and rustle of canvas sails in the light breeze, she heard the sound of hooves and the rattle of a carriage approaching over the cobbles.

She shrank back into the shadow of a pile of kegs that smelt strongly of brandy and pulled her hood further forward about her face. She should not have come, but she had to see him once more—just once more. And then perhaps the pain inside her would start to ease.

Her heart began to pound as the carriage with the Fairhill arms on its door halted opposite the frigate.

And then as the door opened and he got out, her heart seemed to stop completely. Dear God, she should not have come...to see him and not be able to touch him, to speak to him, was agony.

She stared helplessly. He looked impossibly handsome in a new blue and silver uniform, with a high-collared cloak swirling from his shoulders to the top of his boots as he moved with the lithe, fluid grace that caught at her insides.

She watched him supervise the loading of his boxes, with crisp military efficiency, watched him smile and lift a hand in response to a greeting from a naval officer upon the bridge. She had done the right thing, she told herself fiercely, she had—he would be happier without her. And then, suddenly, unexpectedly, he turned and she glimpsed his face.

It was haggard, so bleak and empty that she wanted to run to him and put her arms around him. She had taken a step forward when a second carriage came up at speed, almost running her down.

She stepped back as the carriage door was flung open.

'Alex!' Lady Carteret scrambled out of the carriage, closely followed by Lady Cressida Penwyrth. 'We could not let you go with coming to say farewell.'

Lallie slumped back against the kegs as she watched him greet the two woman, forcing a smile. And then the three of them climbed the gangplank onto the ship.

Cressida Penwyrth? Had Rutherstone released her from her betrothal so the former arrangement could be honoured? Was that who Alex had chosen to save

Fairhill for him? Or had the choice been made for him? Whichever it was, she could hardly bear it. But nevertheless she stayed, watching, straining for a glimpse of him, long after Lady Carteret and Lady Cressida had said their farewells and left the ship, long after it had sailed from the quay. It was only when it was quite out of sight that she turned away and began to walk back to her own hired carriage at the other end of the dock.

The sound of another rapidly approaching carriage behind made her step hastily aside.

'Stop!' said an imperious female voice. 'Miss Ross!' She looked up, the hood falling back from her ashen face.

'Lady Ashton?'

'I thought it was you,' said the older woman grimly as she regarded her with cold blue eyes. 'Had to get the final knife thrust in, did you? Wasn't that note you left for him enough?'

'Don't—please.' To her horror, Lallie felt tears begin to slide down her face. 'He did not see me, I kept out of the way.'

'Oh, get in,' said Lady Ashton exasperatedly, throwing open the door of the gig. 'I think it is high time you and I had another little talk, Miss Ross.'

'Sit down, girl,' Lady Ashton instructed as she practically propelled Lallie into the morning-room of her town house. 'You look like a ghost. You—' she turned in a sweep of lilac silk to address the rather flustered maid who had been surprised in the midst of dusting '—fetch me a bottle of the best brandy—quickly!'

The maid fled and came scurrying back with the brandy and glasses in barely a minute and then retreated at speed. For a few seconds there was a silence as Lallie watched Lady Ashton pour what looked like a pint of brandy into each of two glasses.

'Go on—take it,' Lady Ashton said, holding out a glass to her. 'It won't bite.'

Lallie took the glass and watched with something akin to disbelief as the Countess of Ashton sat down opposite her, kicked off her shoes with the aid of the fender, untied the ribbons on her cartwheel of a hat and tossed it carelessly onto the sofa and then took a large draught of brandy. Lallie had to press her lips together to stop herself from gaping. It was not how her mother had told her that Countesses of impeccable lineage and advanced years behaved.

'Drink!' commanded the Countess as Lallie sat transfixed, the glass in her hand. 'You'll feel much better, I promise you.'

Lallie obeyed and drained a quarter of her glass. What did it matter? What did anything matter when she would never see Alex again?

'Well, Miss Ross,' Lady Ashton said as she met Lallie's stare, 'I gather on learning of his inherited debts you have decided you will not marry my great nephew after all. Isn't he rich enough for you now?'

'No. You have it all the wrong way about,' Lallie said miserably.

'Really? That was the impression your note gave,' Lady Ashton said tartly.

'Yes, I know, I thought it would be best. . .I thought it would stop him coming after me. . .'

'And did you also think it might just have broken his heart as well as your own?' Lady Ashton said considerably more gently.

'He will get over me. It would break his heart more to lose Fairhill, which he will unless he marries an heiress.'

'If you think that, then you cannot love him as he loves you!' Lady Ashton said dismissively. 'And to think I thought you genuinely loved him—still, at least I need not feel guilty about my interference five years ago—'

'I do love him! That is why I will not marry him!' Lallie said despairingly as she took another swallow of her brandy. 'And what do you mean, interference?'

'It was the night of his betrothal party to Cressida Penwyrth. I'd never seen Alex more miserable or more foxed. He was all for telling the family to go to the devil and riding post haste for Scotland to whip you off to Gretna—at that time not having met you, I was inclined to think you an adventuress, so I locked him in my cellar, until he had sobered up. I cannot help wishing now that I had not—marriage to a wealthy heiress, even if the background were trade, would have been rather easier to pass off than marriage to a woman who is perceived by half of his acquaintances to be a demi-rep.'

'I am not a remi-dep!' Lallie said after taking a much larger mouthful of brandy than she had intended. There was something wrong with that sentence, she thought blurredly. But she could not decide quite what.

'You hardly have to tell me that, since Alex wished to marry you!' Lady Ashton snorted, reaching for the brandy bottle and topping up her own glass and Lallie's. 'And if he does marry you, you would not have to tell his acquaintances that either. They would know he would never choose anyone of the sort.'

'I can't marry him,' Lallie began, forming her words with extra care. 'I wish I could—no—' she protested as the Countess put more spirit into her glass '—I've never drunk spirits before and I think it is going to my head.'

'Nonsense,' said Lady Ashton firmly. 'Best thing for you when you're miserable. You girls are all so prissy nowadays, so concerned about what other people think. When I was young, men appreciated women with some spirit, not some pallid miss who is so concerned with convention that she gives up at the first hurdle.'

'That's not fair!' Lallie said passionately. 'And it's hardly a case of the wirst furdle! There are all kinds of im —im—'

'Impediments?' Lady Ashton sighed. 'You are both of age, both single. There is no one who has the right to prevent you from marrying. So what is stopping you, Miss Ross? You say it is not his sudden lack of a fortune. Are you so afraid of what vulgarians like Lady Jersey will say? Or don't you love him enough to put up with the occasional social slight from people whom you would not wish to know anyway?'

'I do love him. More than anything—' Lallie groaned '—but he needs to marry an heiress to save Fairhill from being sold. And you don't understand about unequal matches—I do. My mother and father were happy at first—but then as every one of her old acquaintances cut her, she came to resent him for it until they ended up hating one another—'

'Miss Ross, what I have learnt from mutual acquaintances is that your mother was a selfish, spoilt and snobbish young woman who thought she could have everything she wanted and never have to give anything up. Alex is none of those things, and nor, I believe, are you. If you love him, for heaven's sake marry him and make him happy instead of as miserable as he is at the moment.'

'You really do not think I will be ruining everything for him?' She looked at the older woman. 'He said he does not care about his career or Fairhill, but Charles Cavendish told me that Wellington thinks he is one of his most brilliant young officers.'

'And so he should,' said the Countess. 'And I hardly think that marrying you, Miss Ross, is going to change Arthur Wellesley's opinion. Believe it or not, he can see beyond the end of his aristocratic nose—as can most of Alex's true friends.'

'And his family?'

'His family will be falling over themselves to promote the match,' the Countess informed her with a smile. 'Because the moment you are wed, Miss Ross, I shall settle all the outstanding debts against Fairhill.'

'What?' Lallie stared at her, thinking that she must be far more drunk than she had thought. She knew from what Lord Carteret had said that the debts were huge.

'You heard me,' said Lady Ashton. 'I happen to agree with you that Alex would never be entirely happy if he lost Fairhill. It was hard enough for him being the younger son, when he always loved the place far more than his brother ever did. I also do not think he will ever be happy without you.'

'Why? Why would you do that for me? For Alex?'

'Because I have no children of my own and Alex has always been the one of my relations whom I loved best.' Lady Ashton sighed. 'And because I was at the dockside this morning and I saw your face and his and remembered how I felt at your age when I was forced to give up the man I loved because my familiy required me to marry for money.'

'You were at the dock? I—I did not see you,' Lallie said apologetically.

'No,' Lady Ashton said wryly, 'both of you were so sunk in misery you would not have noticed Napoleon invading. Now then, Miss Ross, you had better get back to Rosemount House and pack your boxes, Alex told me you left everything he bought you there.'

'Pack my boxes?' Lallie stared at her.

'There is a boat sailing for Lisbon on the evening tide, which should get you to Portugal a day or two after Alex. Charles Cavendish will be on it and I am sure he will act as your escort—and you had best take your maid as chaperon, of course.'

'Portugal?' Lallie's lips parted. 'You mean go after him?'

'Of course I mean go after him,' Lady Ashton replied. 'The mood he went off in, he is quite like to go and get himself killed—or worse, wed to some Spanish chit. Besides, if you get wed out there, all the talk will have died down by the time you come back. Now off you go, and don't worry about that sister of yours, I will move into Rosemount while you are away. After all, she is also supposed to be my ward, I believe.'

For a moment Lallie sat frozen. She could marry Alex. She could! What did it matter if people did cut them, so long as they had each other and he had his beloved Fairhill? Then as sheer soaring happiness engulfed her, she got up and kissed the surprised Lady Ashton upon her powdery cheek.

'Thank you, I will never forget this—'

'Nor will Isabelle,' Lady Ashton said with a sudden wicked cackle. 'I can't wait to see her face! But don't worry, she will get over it, she has Alex's best interests at heart—so you will have something in common.'

Lallie stirred beneath her blankets as the sun rose. Hard Portuguese earth was not conducive to sleep, neither was sleeping in your clothes. But that was something Charles Cavendish insisted upon, pointing out that they were in the midst of a war and were liable to attack at any time, not only by the French but also any of the lawless partisan bands which roamed the Spanish and Portuguese hills. She threw back her blankets, stretched and got up. A few minutes later, after a hasty toilette at the nearby stream, she was back at the campsite, and feeding the fire so that the water for their morning coffee would boil quickly.

She was pleased to see that Charles Cavendish was already up and tending to the horses. It was proving hard enough to catch up with Alex without wasting a single minute.

Storms at sea had meant that she and Charles had arrived in Lisbon three days after Alex had left the city. Then another day had been lost, finding an English family who were prepared to take Jenny on while she recovered from a totally debilitating seasickness. Since leaving Lisbon, they had been riding night and day, resting only when desperate for sleep or when the midday heat became too much to endure. But no matter how fast they travelled, Alex always seemed to have left a village or army encampment a day or so before they arrived.

The journey across endless dusty plains and the climbs up steep stony mountains and hills were beginning to seem eternal. And she was starting to feel as if it were going to go on for ever, starting to be afraid that she would never catch up with Alex, or that even if she did, he would have changed his mind about wanting to marry her. Perhaps he already had, she thought gloomily, remembering Cressida's presence at the dock as she sat down upon a flat rock near the fire. Supposing, now he was an Earl, he had decided that Lady Cressida was a much more suitable match than the disreputable Miss Ross?

'Cheer up!' Charles Cavendish's voice startled her out of her gloomy reverie. 'It might never happen.'

No, it might not, she thought, as she forced herself to smile back at him. Sitting here, in a dusty and crumpled habit in the midst of the Portuguese wilderness, she found it difficult to believe that any man, let alone an Earl, would wish to marry her.

'You're getting good at this.' Charles grinned at her as she roused herself out of her gloom and carefully poured the streaming coffee into two beakers she had wedged between stones to stop them over turning. 'Haldane—Lord Fairhill, I mean—he's not going to want to let you go home.'

'You really think he will be pleased to see me?'

'Certain of it,' Charles said confidently. 'I've never seen Alex as happy as when he was with you that night you gave me dinner at Rosemount House—or as angry and miserable as when you vanished,' he added wryly.

'Do you think he will still be angry?' she asked anxiously.

Charles did not reply for a moment, then he laughed.

'Probably, but it's going to be with me for bringing you this near the front lines, not with you.'

'I wish I was as sure of that as you,' Lallie sighed and sipped her coffee.

'By Jupiter! Just look at that! I had no idea it was here!' Charles exclaimed excitedly the following morning as they came over a mountain ridge. 'Now I can see why Macleod was going to such lengths to try and find out what Wellington was about at Torres Vedras.'

'It's like a giant fortress,' Lallie said in astonishment as she looked right and left along the line of hills. 'Look there are trenches, stockades, guns absolutely everywhere.'

'Yes.' The breath whistled through Charles's teeth as he raised his telescope and studied the fortifications. 'Whatever you say about Wellington, there is one thing for sure, he does nothing by halves. This place is a killing ground, there's not a hollow that hasn't been filled, not a bush left to give the French a scrap of cover. We could hold this place for a hundred years. If I were Masséna, I should not care to attack this place if my life depended upon it. Here, take a look.'

Lallie took the telescope and looked for a minute or so, and then she put it down with a shiver. As she looked at the silent, waiting, deadly guns overlooking the bare, shelterless ground she found herself thinking suddenly of what might lie ahead once they came nearer to the Spanish border where the war was being fought in deadly earnest.

'Perhaps it would be better if you stayed behind these lines,' Charles said, his thoughts obviously going in the same direction as her own. 'I'm sure that engineering officer we met would ask his wife if you could stay with them while I look for Alex—'

'No.' She shook her head emphatically. 'I have to see him and explain, and tell him that he need not worry about Fairhill. If he were—if something were to happen before that.'

'It's all right, you don't have to say any more,' Charles said kindly. 'Come on, then, let's keep going before someone decides not to let us through.'

Please let him be here, Lallie prayed a week later as she rode alongside Charles Cavendish into an army encampment on the banks of the Coa river near the fortress of Almeida. Please. . .

But he was not, Charles soon ascertained. Lord Fairhill was out on reconnaissance.

'He'll be back tomorrow, I'm sure of it,' Charles said that evening as they shared a campfire with some officers of the Rifle brigade. 'I am sure of it. Now try and stop worrying and get some sleep.'

Tomorrow. She could not actually believe that she would finally get to see him the next day. She lay awake for hours, staring up at the clear night sky. Not merely because the ground was hard beneath her blankets, she had grown used to that in the last few weeks, but because she was so afraid that he might not forgive her, might have changed his mind about marrying her.

Which was why she was wide awake just before dawn when a rider came into the camp at a gallop, shouting urgent, angry instructions. And then everything seemed to explode into chaos. There were men shouting, horses whinnying, bugle calls and above and through it all the crackle of muskets and rifles and the boom of cannons.

She had already struggled out of her blankets and into her riding boots when Charles Cavendish appeared beside her, dragging her grey forward by its bridle. 'Mount up and follow the others,' he said breathlessly. 'Ney has just caught us on the wrong damned side of the river. We've got to get to the bridge before he does or we'll be cut off from the rest of the army. Come on!'

She scrambled onto her grey. She was too bemused, too afraid to ask questions as they shot off at a gallop with several other Hussars. Dimly she was aware of shots, whistling and cracking around them. Instinct rather than thought made her cling to her horse's mane and keep her head low as they careered down a track which was nothing but one hairpin bend after another.

'Blast Craufurd!' she heard a Hussar alongside her say to another. 'He should never have stayed this side for so long—we've already lost one company of Rifles—'

'The rest will hold 'em off,' his companion said with determined optimism. 'We're more likely to break our necks on this track than get shot by the French!'

As she rode neck and neck with Charles, Lallie could not but help agree with him, especially when an artillery team and gun went slewing sideways in front of them, causing their own mounts to swerve dangerously near the crumbling edge.

They were within sight of the bridge when her horse fell without warning, so suddenly that Charles was yards ahead before he realised she was no longer with him.

'Miss Ross!' she heard him shout even as she kicked

free of her stirrups and flung herself away from her somersaulting horse.

And then she was rolling on the stony track, was almost trampled by the Hussar on her left, cursed at by another as his horse leapt over her. She curled into a ball, arms over her head as what seemed like another hundred horses thundered past at a gallop. And then she heard the rumble of a gun, felt the hooves of its team shaking the earth she lay on. She could not stay here. She had to move or be crushed by the gun carriage and team.

She scrabbled to her feet. There was nowhere to go. Only vertical crumbling mountainside on one side, a sheer drop upon the other. Desperately, she pressed herself against the sheer rock wall, tried to find handholds, footholds, anything to get off the narrow track and out of the way of the team.

'Get out of the way!' a rider flying ahead of the team roared.

'I'm trying!' she shouted back.

'Lallie!' Alex brought his horse to a rearing halt. For a half-second he stared at her in utter disbelief. And then with an oath he reached for her, dragged her up in front of him and kicked his horse on again as the gun team threatened to overrun them.

Alex. She had found him at last. She shut her eyes as his arms closed about her waist and he said something incomprehensible. The total terror she had felt moments before had vanished. It was ridiculous to feel this soaring, overwhelming sense of relief. Ridiculous to feel safe in the midst of a nightmare retreat with bullets flying all about when you were galloping on a doubly laden horse down a track that no one in their right senses would have taken at anything other than a cautious walk. But she did feel safe. Or perhaps it was just that she did not care if she died now, so long as he was with her, holding her. I love you, she wanted to say, but knew she dare not. This was not the moment for distractions, and his whole attention was upon keeping his horse upon its feet.

'Alex! Miss Ross! Thank God, you have her safe!' Charles Cavendish greeted them with breathless relief after they had galloped over the bridge into the comparative safety of the reformed rearguard.

'You knew! You knew she was here!' Alex rasped breathlessly as he got down from his sweat-soaked horse.

'I brought her here,' Charles said somewhat sheepishly as Alex regarded him with a murderous gaze.

'You did what? Do you know how close she was to being killed?' Alex roared as he lifted Lallie down, his hands like a vice upon her waist as she swayed a little on her distinctly shaky legs and thought that she could do with one of Lady Ashton's measures of brandy. He stared down at her for a moment and then abruptly let go of her.

'I did not know that Almeida had fallen or that Craufurd had left himself so exposed until I got here,' Charles began warily.

'Well, you bl—'

'It was my fault,' Lallie put in hastily as she found her voice. 'I made him bring me, I wanted to see you—'

'Well, that makes a change!' he snarled as his gaze snapped down to her white face. 'Why did you want to

see me? I thought you just about covered everything
there was to say in that letter you left for me!'

'Why—' She found herself stammering in the face of
his blazing anger. All thought of telling him about
Fairhill, or of telling him that she would marry him if
he wanted, went out of her head.

'I. . .I forgot to give you this.' She reached into her
habit jacket and took out the little notebook she had
taken from Macleod. 'I forgot about it, what with your
father dying and everything. . . I thought it might be
useful,' she added lamely as he made no move to take
it. 'It was Macleod's.'

'Macleod's?' He snatched the book abruptly from
her fingers, flicked through it, his face suddenly intent.
And then his gaze flashed back to her face.

'Useful? Do you know what this is? It's the key to
Masséna's cyphers!'

'Oh—' Her exclamation was cut short as he took her
quite suddenly into his arms, gave her a rib cracking
hug and kissed her parted lips.

Then he almost pushed her into Charles Cavendish's
arms. 'Take care of her, Charles, put her on the first
boat back to England—I have to get this to Wellesley.'

'Alex—wait,' she began, outraged. 'Listen to me—'

'Sorry—can't,' he replied as he swung into the
saddle. 'I'll see you in England.' Then without so much
as a backward glance, he rode off.

Lallie watched him in speechless rage. He was not
going to do that to her! She had not suffered sea
sickness, being shot at, and endless, bone-jarring, dusty
miles on non-existent roads to be packed off back to
England before he had even had the grace to
listen to her.

'Charles!' She wheeled, her eyes blazing in her face like silver fire. 'Find me a horse.'

Four days later, she rode into the encamped main body of Wellington's army. There was row after row of tents, campfires, soldiers and ragged-looking women everywhere.

'You stay here,' Charles said. 'I'll go and see if the quartermaster can find you a tent, and if Alex is here.'

Lallie got off her horse and leant against it. She was exhausted and covered in dust from head to foot. What would she not give for a bath or even a stream—

'You! Madam!' She turned to see herself being regarded coolly by a slight, upright figure in a well tailored but very plain coat, who sat easily upon a large chestnut horse. 'There are no women allowed in this part of the camp. The married quarters are over there.'

Lallie glared back up at him, her grey eyes glittering in her dust-smeared face. She was in no mood for more male arrogance. 'I am not moving until Major Cavendish returns—and neither am I married, though I intend to be, if I ever catch up with Major Haldane— Lord Fairhill!'

Cool grey eyes, not so different from her own, looked at her with a degree more interest.

'Fairhill? You are not Miss Ross?'

'Yes.'

The rather stern face broke into a sudden grin. 'Then I owe you my thanks. I understand that, if it were not for you, a certain set of plans might have reached France, and that we might not have gained some extremely useful knowledge of French codes.'

'How do you know about that. . .?' she began.

The grey eyes twinkled and he gave a bark of laughter which made his horse twitch its ears and start.

'Perhaps you will allow me to introduce myself, Miss Ross—Wellesley, Arthur Wellesley at your service. 'Fairhill's out on reconnaissance, so perhaps you will allow me to offer you some hospitality in his absence?' He bowed in his saddle. 'It seems the least I can do in return for your assistance.'

'Yes. Thank you, my lord,' she said, recovering from her astonishment and cursing herself for not recognising a face she had seen caricatured often enough in the broadsheets.

Late that afternoon Alex sighed as he swung down from his sweating horse and handed it to a trooper. He was hot, tired and thirsty.

He strode up to his tent and came to a sudden halt a few yards from the door. Someone had hung a muslin scarf from the pole where it was fluttering like a pennant, a scarf that seemed oddly familiar. It could not be, he thought as his heart began to race. She would not have forgiven him for his behaviour at the Coa bridge, would she. . .? If she had any sense she'd be heading back to England post-haste. . .or persuading some calm, good-tempered fellow like Cavendish to marry her.

He threw aside the tent flap and stared into the interior. All was as it usually was except that someone had put flowers in his water glass. He stood still for a moment, leaning against the tent pole and staring into the empty interior, feeling utterly weary.

'Better late than never,' said a soft voice from behind him, bringing him wheeling around, his weariness instantly forgotten as he stared at the young woman who was as bedaubed in dust as he was. 'I was beginning to be afraid that I'd lost you again.'

'No such luck, I am afraid.' He smiled at her, and then caught his breath as her face lit in the way it always had for him.

Lallie. Passionate, reckless, stubborn and beautiful, Lallie. His love. His wife to be—perhaps—if she would still have him?

'Lallie?' Even as his hands reached out to catch hers, he still could not quite believe she was really there. 'What—what the devil are you doing here?'

'Here?' Her grey eyes sparked as they met his blue gaze. 'Well, Lord Wellington said I might have your tent, he said he was sure you would not mind sleeping outside.'

'Did he? How thoughtful of him,' he said drily. 'I think what I meant to ask you is why you are here in Portugal? And don't tell me it was to bring me that notebook.'

'Because I love you,' she said simply. 'Because Lady Ashton has paid off your father's debts and I can marry you with a clear conscience. That's if you still want me?'

'Want you?' His dark brows lifted. 'There is only one answer to that!'

He tasted of dust and wine, and smelt of horse, but as he kissed her, she did not care in the least.

'You have not changed your mind then?' she said mischievously much, much later as they sat side by side at a campfire where Charles and the other officers had tactfully left them alone. 'I saw Cressida at the dock and I—'

'You were at the dock! Why didn't you come and see me?' He groaned and hugged her. 'Listen, my lovely fool. Rutherstone was commanding the frigate. Cressida was there to see him off. . .'

'Oh.' She smiled. 'I am glad of that, as Lord Wellington has offered to give me away, since I have no father to perform the office.'

'Wellesley never misses an opportunity, in war—or with pretty women.' He laughed. 'And I think he has a very soft spot for you, I have never seen him laugh so much as when we got that intelligence report from Paris.'

'Paris?' She looked at him blankly.

'The false packet of papers you sent with Peter— apparently they reached Bonaparte himself and he read your very rude message.'

'Oh.' She blushed. 'I just wrote down a rhyme the children in Petticoat Lane used to chant about him.'

'And signed it "The Major's Muslin", I gather.' He laughed.

'Macleod told me that was how I was referred to by someone at Horseguards.'

'They won't call you that any more,' he said softly, 'not when they find out Wellington has given you away and that our marriage has his approval.'

'I don't care if they do,' she said, and meant it. 'I should still rather be your muslin than anyone else's wife.'

'Prove it?' he invited her softly as he picked her up in his arms and carried her to his tent. And she did.

Historical Romance™

Coming next month

THE KNIGHT, THE KNAVE AND THE LADY
Juliet Landon

NORTH YORKSHIRE, 1350S

Marietta Wardle *never* wanted to get married—but her
stance proved no hindrance to the desires of Lord Alain of
Thorsgeld! He wanted her and had no scruples about
compromising her into marriage. Their nights were
ecstatic, and Thorsgeld Castle provided her with plenty of
work. Marietta began to love her role, and her husband,
until she realised that she was playing second best to his
dead wife—a position that would lead her into danger…

A HIGHLY IRREGULAR FOOTMAN
Sarah Westleigh

KENT/LONDON 1803

Jack Hamilton was the new footman at Stonar Hall, and
housekeeper Thalia Marsh could sense that he was
trouble! He was so charming, smooth and friendly, spoke
a little too well and liked to take charge—even though she
was his superior! He was surely no footman and Thalia
was determined to discover his true identity even if this
risked the exposure of *her* darkest secrets. But Thalia soon
succumbed to his charms—and fell in love! But *who* had
Thalia fallen in love with—the footman
…or someone else?

FREE!

FOUR FREE
specially selected
Historical Romance™ novels
PLUS a Mystery Gift
when you return this card...

Return this coupon and we'll send you 4 Historical Romance novels and a mystery gift absolutely FREE! We'll even pay the postage and packing for you.

We're making you this offer to introduce you to the benefits of the Reader Service™– FREE home delivery of brand-new Historical Romance novels, at least a month before they are available in the shops, FREE gifts and a monthly Newsletter packed with information.

Accepting these FREE books and gift places you under no obligation to buy, you may cancel at any time, even after receiving just your free shipment. Simply complete the coupon below and send it to:

MILLS & BOON READER SERVICE, FREEPOST, CROYDON, SURREY, CR9 3WZ.

No stamp needed

Yes, please send me 4 free Historical Romance novels and a mystery gift. I understand that unless you hear from me, I will receive 4 superb new titles every month for just £2.99* each, postage and packing free. I am under no obligation to purchase any books and I may cancel or suspend my subscription at any time, but the free books and gift will be mine to keep in any case. (I am over 18 years of age)

H7XE

Ms/Mrs/Miss/Mr _____

Address _____

_____

_____ Postcode _____